# The CHOSEN®

BOOK ONE I HAVE CALLED YOU BY NAME

REVISED AND EXPANDED EDITION

JERRY B. JENKINS

FOCUS ON THE FAMILY.

BroadStreet PUBLISHING

I Have Called You by Name


A Focus on the Family book published by BroadStreet Publishing.



Editor: Larry Weeden
Cover design: Michael Harrigan
Cover photo: Michael Harrigan/Wirestock/stock.adobe.com



978-1-64607-108-1 (revised edition hardcover)
978-1-64607-087-9 (revised edition trade paperback)

Library of Congress Cataloging-in-Publication Data can be found at www.loc.gov.

Printed in China

25 24 23 22 21 5 4 3 2 1

Any author who has written and sold as many books as Jerry Jenkins might be forgiven a tendency to lean on familiar structure while producing yet another manuscript. Fortunately, Jenkins is not just "any author." While the broad storyline of Jesus choosing his disciples will be familiar to some, it is the author's deft handling of the historical language and customs of the time that give his newest release a vibrancy rarely felt by readers of any novel. *The Chosen: I Have Called You by Name* has been crafted with wise and insightful context. This is the book Jerry Jenkins was born to write.

—**Andy Andrews**, *New York Times* bestselling author of *The Traveler's Gift, The Noticer,* and *Just Jones*

The only thing better than the film is the book, and the only thing better than the book is the film. Jerry B. Jenkins has taken the brilliant project of Dallas Jenkins—this look into the lives of those Jesus *chose* to be his followers, his friends, and his "family"—and gone a step (or more) deeper. Readers will be drawn as quickly into the pages as viewers were into the theatrical moments of *The Chosen* film project. I cannot say enough about both.

—**Eva Marie Everson**, president, Word Weavers International, and bestselling author

The movie series brought me to tears, but Jerry's book showed me the Jesus I wanted to know. *The Chosen: I Have Called You by Name* draws the reader into the humanity of Jesus. This story captures authentic insight into his personality. His love, humor, wisdom, and compassion are revealed for every person he encountered. Through Jesus' interaction with the real-life characters, I too experienced the Savior who calls the lost, poor, needy, and forsaken into an authentic relationship.

—**DiAnn Mills**, Christy Award winner and director, Blue Ridge Mountain Christian Writers Conference

Jerry Jenkins is a master storyteller who has captured the action, drama, and emotion of *The Chosen* video series in written form. Far more than a mere synopsis of season 1, Jerry has shaped and developed the first eight episodes into a fast-paced novel. If you enjoyed the videos, you will savor the story again as Jerry brings each character to life. And if you haven't watched the video series, this novel will make you want to start … just as soon as you've finished reading the book, of course!

—**Dr. Charlie Dyer**, professor-at-large of Bible, host of *The Land and the Book* radio program

Writing with accuracy and immediacy, Jerry Jenkins immerses us in the greatest story ever told in a fresh and powerful way. Jenkins is a master of taking profound scenes and themes from the Bible and weaving them into captivating journeys, whether they are centered on the time of Jesus or the end times. *The Chosen: I Have Called You by Name* expands on the amazing TV series and will move readers through its unique retelling of the gospel story.

—**Travis Thrasher**, bestselling author and publishing industry veteran

To a girl who cut her teeth on Bible stories, it's no easy task to transform all-too-familiar characters into an experience that is fresh and alive. That is precisely what Jerry Jenkins has done with his newest novel, *The Chosen: I Have Called You by Name*. From the first chapter, I was enamored. And by the second and third, I started to see the Jesus I've long loved with new eyes and a more open heart. This book offers the reader more than mere diversion. It offers the possibility of true transformation.

—**Michele Cushatt**, author of *Relentless: The Unshakeable Presence of a God Who Never Leaves*

What better way to bring the gospel to life than to explore the impact Jesus had upon those with whom he came into contact. And what better encouragement for those of us today who hunger for his life-changing presence. I heartily recommend both the video and the book for any who long to experience his transforming love more deeply.

—**Bill Myers**, author of the bestselling novel *Eli*

The story of Jesus has been told and re-told, but with this beautiful novelization, Jerry Jenkins brings unique and compelling perspectives to the biblical accounts of Jesus and his followers, echoing those in the acclaimed *The Chosen* video series created by Dallas Jenkins. As someone who always thinks the book was better than the movie, I was delighted to discover a book and film series that are equally enthralling and even life-changing.

—**Deborah Raney**, author of *A Nest of Sparrows* and *A Vow to Cherish*

To Sister Pam,
who radiates the love of God

Based on *The Chosen,* a multi-season TV show
created and directed by Dallas Jenkins
and written by Ryan M. Swanson, Dallas Jenkins,
and Tyler Thompson.

"There's little doubt *The Chosen* will become one of
the most well-known and celebrated pieces
of Christian media in history."
*MOVIEGUIDE® Magazine*

# NOTE

The Chosen was created by lovers of and believers in the Bible and Jesus Christ. Our deepest desire is that you delve into the New Testament Gospels yourself and discover Jesus.

“Fear not,
for I have redeemed you;
I have called you by name,
you are mine.”
Isaiah 43:1

# PART 1
# The Shepherd

When Augustus Caesar became emperor of Rome, Judea was made a Roman province.

For 400 years the prophets of Israel had been silent. Priests read the Scriptures aloud in synagogues while Roman officers patrolled the streets, heavily taxing the Hebrews.

The prophecies whispered of a coming Messiah who would save God's people.

## Chapter 1

# OBSESSION

*Kedron, Israel*

Short but well-muscled, with a cascade of curls bouncing on his forehead, Shimon knows he looks younger than his twenty years. Yet he'll be responsible for his three younger sisters once he's bequeathed his father's land and sheep. Which could happen today if it's why his parents have summoned him when he should be in the pasture.

His father has been sickly for nearly two years and unable to join him in the fields. Shimon misses his father's help and mentoring, but he has been forced to learn much. Officials from Kedron had visited his parents the day before. While Shimon wished he had been included, he assumes he will be informed of the details today.

They meet in his parents' bedchamber, where his father lies. "I have failed," the old man begins.

"Don't say that," Shimon says. "You have done all you could."

"Let him speak," his mother says. "He's trying to apologize."

"But he has nothing to apologize for! I know he would be out there with me if not for—"

His father raises a hand. "We have lost everything. I have nothing to leave you."

"But—"

"Let me speak!" his father rasps. "I feel terrible, but I have failed you all."

"What are you saying?"

"You need not return to the fields. The new owners are already here."

Shimon reels. "But the sheep, my sisters, our fut—"

"It's my fault," his father says. "I'm sorry! There's no more to say."

Stunned, yet eager to console his father, Shimon wants to thank him for all he has taught him, how he's fed the boy's obsession with the Scriptures, the prophecies, the promised Messiah. What will he do now? And what will become of all that study?

"You'll have to leave and find work," his mother says. "We're left with this home but no land, no livestock. And still five mouths to feed."

"I'll do whatever I have to, of course," Shimon says. "But where will I go? What should I do?"

His father rises onto an elbow. "You've always wanted to go to Bethlehem. Their herds supply the Jerusalem temple with sacrifices. Sheepherders there must always need help."

Bethlehem! Just more than twenty miles east but named in the prophecies! Shimon can only imagine visiting the synagogue there. But would he ever have time? He'd need to become a hireling if he hoped to keep his parents and sisters alive.

Shimon's entire future has changed in an instant, yet the prospect of relocating to Bethlehem has already softened the blow.

• • •

*One week later*

Desperate to keep up, Shimon yanks the tether on a white lamb and forces himself along on the rough-hewn crutch he's fashioned from a tree branch. Ahead, the three older shepherds he serves—each leading his own lamb toward Bethlehem—pause and turn to needle him. Aaron, ebony skin stark against his white cotton tunic, mimics Shimon's limp, pretending his own walking stick is a crutch.

"C'mon!" Yoram, the eldest, shouts, his white-rimmed head gleaming in the relentless sun. "Let's go!"

Shimon's eagerness to prove he cares as much about their sheep as his bosses do had resulted in his injury. He'd led a flock into a limestone cave during a storm, and when one escaped, he chased after it, plunging into a ravine and badly rolling his left ankle. He would have welcomed a little sympathy—or gratitude—but he got only disdain. And no help, save for a gruff suggestion from dark-bearded Natan to "wrap it tight." Natan is the only one who even looks at the young man when he speaks.

Shimon hopes to catch the three men when they stop at the well on the way into the city, so he pushes himself. He winces with every stride, sweat pouring from his grimy face.

From a short distance, Shimon sees the other shepherds reaching the well. Five women bearing clay pots and leathern buckets busy themselves there until the shepherds approach. It strikes Shimon that the women make no attempt to hide their aversion, four of them immediately backing away, holding their noses.

"Lovely day today, isn't it?" Natan says loudly to one, nodding and smiling, but she covers her face and hurries off. "Come back!" he calls after her.

By the time Shimon reaches the well, the other shepherds

have filled their goatskin water sacs and begin to move on. The only remaining woman leaves as Shimon arrives. He fills his sac and hurries off, trying not to let the others get too far ahead. Passing the sign pointing to Bethlehem, he's reminded of the Scriptures he so cherishes, his father having raised him to study the Torah. Though Aaron and the others mock his passion, Shimon has memorized lengthy passages, especially about his new home. As he forces himself along, the lamb bleating, Shimon rehearses aloud:

"'But you, O Bethlehem Ephrathah, who are too little to be among the clans of Judah, from you shall come forth for me one who is to be ruler in Israel, whose coming forth is from of old, from ancient days.'

"Therefore he shall give them up until the time when she who is in labor has given birth; then the rest of his brothers shall return to the people of Israel.

"And he shall stand and shepherd his flock in the strength of the Lord, in the majesty of the name of the Lord his God. And they shall dwell secure, for now he shall be great to the ends of the earth.

"And he shall be their peace."

*Could it be? The Messiah could come from right here?* It seems too much to hope for, and yet Shimon believes the prophets with his whole heart. He imagines the Chosen One defending the Jews and setting things right between them and the Romans.

Chapter 2

# A SIGN

On the final stretch of the more than 100 mile walk from Nazareth to Bethlehem, Joseph realizes that his hope that this arduous journey would be some sort of respite from his work was a fantasy. How he would love to be back on the job right now, sweating in the sun because he and his mates were building something—something that would last! But now he smells of another kind of sweat as he leads his powerful but ratty-looking donkey slowly along, his pregnant fiancée delicately balanced on its back. He can't help believing this compulsory registration and taxation has come at the worst possible time.

Mary is due any day, and he silently prays it is not *this* very day. What will he do? What *can* he do in the middle of the desert on this dusty road? Sure, strangers pass from both directions, but who will stop to help a couple whose very garb makes it clear they are Nazarenes? They'd more likely be spit upon than helped in the hour of their greatest need. Fortunately, the last person to have blessed them with a sip of his own water had been a shepherd, nearly as much an outcast as they are.

Joseph is desperate to get to Bethlehem, as much to find a well as to find a place for Mary to rest. She barely complains, but he knows she must be miserable.

There is, he must confess, a bit of relief from all they've already endured. His betrothed is the godliest woman he has ever known, even having privately learned to read so she could study the Torah, though only males are allowed in Hebrew school. So when she began to show—long before their wedding had even been scheduled—he was as shocked and disappointed, yes, in her, as anyone in Nazareth. Knowing her as he did, he could in no way make it make sense. And while many naturally blamed him for her predicament, he refused to protect his own reputation by breaking the marriage contract as any offended fiancé would have been justified to do.

But then had come the messenger from heaven, who appeared to him in a dream and assured him the baby Mary carried was the son of God. Filled with wonder and still finding it hard to believe, he traded stories with Mary, only to discover that their heavenly messengers had urged them both to fear not. That, they agreed, was one thing to be told and quite another to practice.

Right now, Joseph is afraid. He assures Mary he will look up Samuel, a distant relative, as soon as they arrive in Bethlehem. He has to confess it's been a long time since he's seen him. "I don't know if he's living in the same home."

"I hope so," Mary says. "You've said so much about him."

Joseph sighs. "We will see. We won't have any time to look for him if he's moved, of course."

"We'll see," she says, fingering the water sac as if hoping something, anything, will appear in it.

"Not even a drop?" Joseph says.

She shakes her head.

He sighs as the donkey stalls. Joseph clicks his tongue and jerks the beast on.

"Um, Joseph?"

"Yes."

"Can you stop please? I'd like to walk for a bit."

"No, Mary! Why would you want to walk?" He worries about her and the baby, of course, but mainly he wants to get to Bethlehem—for his own sake as well as hers. She's strong, he knows. She went to visit her cousin Elizabeth by herself, walking 100 miles uphill the other direction from Nazareth, while three and a half months pregnant! She traversed a route known for bandits and other dangers, then stayed with Elizabeth for three months, returning alone more than six months into her pregnancy.

That temporarily saved her from ridicule in her hometown, ridicule that Joseph was not spared. His coworkers mocked and jeered, and some—painfully—just silently looked upon him with obvious disgust, having considered him a devout Jew. All he could do was rest in the promise of God.

But this trek is different. Mary cannot seem to stifle her cries of discomfort and pain, so Joseph teeters between rushing and slowing. They must find shelter, but he must also be so careful with his beloved and her child. He hopes to discourage her from dismounting the donkey. "It's dangerous."

"I'm getting a bit uncomfortable …"

*How is she able to sound so sweet, so precious, despite her agony?*

"… Elizabeth actually told me it's good to walk and move when I feel up to it."

He sighs again, looking into the distance and then behind them. "We won't have any water until I get you to town. You need your rest." He stops the donkey. "Let me get you more comfortable, eh?" He tucks his walking stick under his arm and tries to straighten the blanket beneath her.

"Joseph," she says, "you don't need to be the only one walking. Plus we're far enough away from Nazareth that I don't have to hide my condition anymore."

"Mary, this blanket is stuck! There is no way that you are comfortable."

"Joseph. I'd like to walk with you. Please."

What is he to do? Deep inside he wants to do whatever she wants him to. But he feels the weight of it. "I am responsible for you, Mary. For you and …" He lays a hand gently on her belly.

"You protect us …"

"Yes!"

"I'll let you help me down."

This amuses him, and he points at her. "All right, you can walk for a few minutes, huh? But please, not too far!" He moves back to the head of the donkey to urge it on. "You need to save your strength."

"I actually need you to help me down," she says.

"Aah, yes, sorry." He heads back and supports her as she reaches for him. "Slowly, slowly. Watch the baby."

She whimpers as he lowers her to the ground.

"You okay?"

"Yes, yes. Ooh, this feels better."

"Mm," he says, not so sure he should have allowed this but grateful she seems to enjoy it.

"Thank you."

He doesn't know how to respond.

"Thank you for protecting me," she adds. "I don't know that I've said that yet."

How can she say that? She's been thanking him for days

since they left home. “We have a little ways to go yet. Let’s see how the night goes and—”

“I’m not talking about that. I’m talking about—before.”

“Oh. Ah …”

“I’ve been meaning to say something this whole journey. And I just … I didn’t, and I should have.”

Again, Joseph doesn’t know what to say. She’s so much better at such conversations. “Mm.”

“I should have months ago.”

“You don’t have to,” he says, eyes straight ahead as they mosey on, she a step behind. Where is she going with this? He very nearly put her away privately before God visited him.

“Yes, yes, I do. You could have gotten all the bride price back from my father.”

*The bride price!* “It was never about the money.”

“I know it wasn’t, and I know it’s not polite to talk about. But no one would have blamed you.”

“For what?”

“For divorcing me. Publicly.”

“Mary, I—”

“You could be betrothed to someone whom you don’t have to hide. And people wouldn’t be gossiping about you. And you could go be registered without having to drag me on this donkey all day for five days.”

Now he’s totally at a loss. He would never dream of such a thing, not after …

He feels her hand on his arm. “Joseph?”

He stops and turns to face her.

“You are a brave man, and you are godly. And I should have said thank you.”

He stares at her. How he loves this woman! He points to the sky with his stick. “God told me to.”

"I know He did. But you had a choice."

*A choice? When God speaks?* "Ah, ha! I don't believe that I did. But I'm glad either way. I wouldn't change a single thing that has happened, since that dream, hm?"

She smiles at him. "Neither would I."

They walk on again. "Oh, this all seems impossible, huh?" he says.

"Yes, yes. But remember what the messenger said to me?"

"Hm?"

"'Nothing is impossible with God.'"

"My messenger didn't say that. That would have been nice, huh?"

She sighs and smiles but looks weary. He draws her close. "Are you feeling better?"

"A bit, yes."

"Okay. Up, up."

She grunts as she mounts the donkey.

"We need to move quicker," Joseph says. "You need water, and I planned to get settled for the part where your messenger and my messenger said the same thing. 'And she will give birth to a son …'"

They speak together. "'And you shall call his name Jesus.'"

"Yes," he says. "That part."

• • •

Children frolic in the crowded Bethlehem marketplace as men loudly haggle. Merchants are buying, filling their pens with animals they will sell to pilgrims for sacrifice at the temple in Jerusalem, fewer than six miles away. Shimon and his superiors have culled only the best from their herds, eager to garner the highest prices.

The merchants cajole shepherds and farmers to cut their

prices, while the shepherds and farmers laud the quality of their livestock and produce. Yoram gestures passionately as he wrangles with a merchant near where a child runs his hands through a freshly shorn hide of wool. Aaron bends at a stall to sniff fresh spices. As Shimon gingerly shoulders his way through the crowd, bleats and baas rise from all over, assaulting him with the stench of dung.

A Pharisee emerges from the local synagogue to judge the potential sacrifices, and Shimon sees his opportunity. The holy man holds Natan's black lamb, turning it this way and that as Natan entreats, "Perfect! Nothing, no blemish, nothing. Nothing wrong. See?"

"Spotless!" the Pharisee says. "This one's good."

Now Shimon's turn, he lifts his white lamb to the Pharisee and speaks over its plaintive cry. "Teacher, I have a question about the Messiah. I've studied Torah every day and—"

The Pharisee sighs, not looking up from his inspection. "A *shepherd* wants to learn ..."

"Yes!" Shimon says, smiling, then turns serious again. "Do you believe the Messiah will set us free from the occupation?"

"Yes," the Pharisee says flatly, clearly bored. "He will make a great military leader."

"Are you sure?" Shimon says, rushing to continue, "because last Shabbat the priest read from prophet Ezekiel, and he did not say—"

"How dare you!" the Pharisee says.

Aaron rushes over. "I'm sorry, Teacher. He is obsessed—"

"You brought this animal?"

Shimon and Aaron nod.

"I said 'spotless'!" the Pharisee says.

"Spotless, yes!" Aaron says.

The Pharisee turns the animal so they can see a wound on

its flank. "These are for righteous men, for the *perfect* sacrifice." He sets the animal down. "I can't send this to Jerusalem!"

Aaron grabs its rope and begins to lead it away, bowing. "Very sorry. Very sorry. Very sorry."

The Pharisee wags a finger in Shimon's face as Yoram and Natan approach. "You wonder why the Messiah hasn't come? It's because of people like you, keeping him away with your stains! If you come back here without a *perfect* lamb, I will banish you all from the marketplace."

As the Pharisee spits on the ground in front of the shepherds, Shimon hesitates as if he wants to apologize. But Natan whispers, "Now, come. Come."

Shimon moves to follow, but Yoram steps before him. "We warned you about this! Are you deaf as well as lame?"

"I'm sorry!"

"We are not slowing down for you! You take this runt back up the hill. And try to keep up or find your own way back."

Shimon stares at the ground, and as the others leave, Natan stops and cups the young man's cheek.

Humiliated but not wanting to return to the flocks alone, Shimon tries to make his way through the crowd to catch the three. But his ankle and the lamb slow him, and his crutch slips in the mud. He falls hard on his right elbow and gashes his forearm. From his knees he scans the crowd for the others, but they have disappeared.

Shimon struggles to his feet and hears a sonorous voice. He finds he is just outside the small synagogue, so praying no one will notice him, he slips through a curtained side door to find an elegantly appointed sanctuary.

At the bimah, the priest reads from a scroll: "The people who walked in darkness have seen a great light; those who dwelt in a land of deep darkness, on them has light shone.

"You have multiplied the nation; you have increased its joy; they rejoice before you as with joy at the harvest, as they are glad when they divide the spoil."

At the back of the synagogue, a man glares at Shimon in the doorway with his lamb. The man rises and hurries to him, scowling at the sight of Shimon's elbow, which—to Shimon's horror—drips blood onto the threshold. He shoves Shimon. "You need to go!"

"Can I not just listen?"

"No! This is a holy place!"

"Please!"

"Go! Get out!" He pushes Shimon back through the curtain and wipes the floor as the priest continues to speak. Shimon listens from outside.

"For the yoke of his burden, and the staff for his shoulder, the rod of his oppressor, you have broken as on the day of Midian. For every boot of the tramping warrior in battle tumult and every garment rolled in blood will be burned as fuel for the fire."

Shimon hobbles back into the bustle of the marketplace, thrilled with what he has heard about the Messiah but crestfallen at having been banished. He merely wants to learn, to understand, to worship. He averts his eyes from the Pharisee who had berated him and avoids a Roman guard.

As Shimon makes his way through the crowd, a bedraggled, sharp-featured wayfarer approaches—his dirty face streaked with sweat. He leads a donkey bearing a pregnant young woman. "Excuse me, friend," the man says. "Could you point me to a well in this town? My wife hasn't had a drink in hours."

Shimon nods. "Yes. The other end of the square."

"Thank you, brother."

As the man pulls the donkey away, Shimon gets a better look at the woman, great with child and clearly suffering. He must act. "Wait, wait. Here." Shimon hands the man his own water sac.

"Oh, thank you for your kindness," the man says, handing it to the woman. She drinks greedily.

They appear to have been on the road for days. "How far have you come?" Shimon says.

"From Galilee. Nazareth."

Shimon looks around and whispers, "Don't say that too loud here. You know they say nothing good can come from—"

"I know what they say about Nazareth," the man says, smiling. He seems so kind, despite how exhausted he looks.

"Don't worry. I won't tell anyone. Your secret's safe with me."

"Thank you for your kindness," the Nazarene says, and his wife smiles shyly.

Shimon reaches to shake the man's hand and introduces himself.

But before the man can respond, the Pharisee approaches, shouting, "Out of my way!"

"We have to go," the man says, and his wife hands back the water sac as they move on.

As Shimon leads his lamb out of the market, he can still faintly hear the priest: "Strengthen the weak hands, and make firm the feeble knees. Say to those who have an anxious heart, 'Be strong; fear not! Behold, your God will come with vengeance, with the recompense of God. He will come and save you.'"

• • •

Joseph was bone weary and could only imagine how Mary was feeling as they finally trudged through the small gate into the tiny, but somehow bustling, village of Bethlehem. He had no idea how many of the house and lineage of David would be required to sojourn here from all over the land. Now, the water from the shepherd has slightly refreshed Mary, but does it still make sense to try to find his distant relative, whom he has not, of course, had opportunity to inform of his and Mary's unique situation?

Distracted by the crowds, he desperately tries to keep everything in his mind at once. Mary is tired, still thirsty, in pain, and due. He has no idea where to turn. He looks this way and that, up one street and down another alley. "I believe Samuel's house is through here," he says, trying to sound surer than he feels. It's been so long. "I'm not sure how he'll respond to your, uh, condition, but he will have water, and it will be nice to see him."

She appears relieved to hear that, but the more Joseph stares, scanning the market and all the intersecting streets, the less sure he is—of anything. "Actually, I don't know if this is it. It looks so different. Maybe because there are so many people. I think if we, um—" But he doesn't like Mary's look. She appears ready to topple off the donkey, pressing her fist against her glistening face, eyes shut.

She gazes at him. "Yes?"

"We don't have time to look for Samuel," he decides.

"No," she says, "no, it will be fine. I know you wanted to find him."

"I need to get you to the inn, Mary. You need your rest. Maybe I can find a well so you can drink more fully, and I'll take you straight to the inn, eh?"

She nods, looking relieved. "Thank you."

He carefully guides the donkey, with its precious cargo, through the square. "Aah, so many people …"

• • •

The sun hangs low on the horizon as Shimon begins the long trek back to the hill and the rest of the sheep, hoping his employers can forgive him. His emotions have risen and fallen so quickly in such a short time. He'd been eager to sell what he thought was a perfect lamb. Then he'd hoped to sit—or at least stand—under a formal synagogue reading of the Scriptures. His disappointment had been briefly assuaged when he was able to aid the bedraggled traveling couple, only to see the gentle husband quickly retreat from the anger of the Pharisee.

• • •

Mary sits atop the donkey, her body telling her the time is near. She watches as Joseph finally reaches the front of the line at the entrance to the inn, where he had long ago arranged their lodging. It does not appear to be going well between him and the innkeeper, an elderly man with a full white beard. The man seems earnest, trying to explain something, and Joseph is clearly exercised. He's waving a rolled document he has kept deep in a pocket throughout the entire journey.

"So this is what, bull droppings?" he says. "How can you send confirmation and now—"

The man appears to be apologizing, but Joseph is having none of it. "You're lying to me now!" he shouts, and when he glances Mary's way, she pretends to focus elsewhere so he won't know she's witnessing his outburst. When she peeks back, the two men are in earnest conversation.

Pain digs at her abdomen, and she presses a palm against it, raising her gaze to the darkening sky. "Oh, God," she breathes quietly, "You are my God. Earnestly I seek You. My soul thirsts for You. My flesh faints for You, as in a dry and weary land where there is no water."

Her abdomen clenches, and she winces, stifling a cry. As Joseph approaches, looking defeated, she desperately composes herself.

"Mary ..." It's as if he can't speak.

She forces a smile in spite of herself. *Please don't let it be bad news.* But she fears the worst. "Well, what did he say?"

"You won't believe it. He said they are completely full. With the census, the whole town is overrun." As he shakes the water sac in vain, he adds, "I think it's because he knows we aren't exactly, you know, that I can't just give him more money like the others can. I was furious, but I kept my calm as I promised."

"Of course."

"I told him about our situation, but that didn't make a difference either."

Mary struggles not to panic. The last thing she wants is to give birth right here, not only in public, but also in the busiest area of Bethlehem. She looks up eagerly as Joseph continues.

"Finally, his wife said that if we wanted, we could try—camping in the stable. They promised us water and blankets to help, even lamb's cloths for the baby. They promised they would be clean. But I can go look for Samuel. If he's living in the same home, then he will have room."

Mary decides this has all been her doing. "I'm sorry I slowed us down. I should have stayed on the don—"

"Oh, Mary, it's not your fault."

"Joseph," she says gravely, grasping his hand. "We can't keep looking."

He looks alarmed. "Have the pangs started?"

She nods. "He's coming."

His eyes go wide. "I'm sorry, he said there was nothing."

"I know. I know."

"All right," he says. "All right. We will make it work, hm?"

"Yes, yes, we will make it work."

Joseph has for months been puzzling over all that has happened between him and young Mary. One day he marvels at the invasion of his dream and the message from the angel, and the next he wonders if it could really be true. He has of course studied the Torah from his youth and knows of such visitations from God. But as far as he knows, it has been hundreds of years since anyone has experienced such a thing.

Naturally he knew and trusted and believed Mary's account of her own angel's message, and when he allows himself to dwell on it, it makes some irrational sense. He has seen in his beloved what God sees in her—a woman of true and pure character. Would he have thought in a million years that she would be chosen to carry and deliver the very son of God? Such a thing had never crossed his mind. He and every Jew before him awaited the promised Messiah, and that the man was to be born of a virgin was a great mystery that even many learned rabbis interpreted in different ways. Who is Joseph that he should be betrothed to the very woman God chose for such a task?

If any of this makes any sense, the choice of Mary does. But surely God knew who her fiancé would be. Joseph has never before even considered that the Creator could make a mistake. Yet why a carpenter, a builder, a man with a short temper? He tries to be devout, certainly, and he loves God. But he also knows who he is—and who he isn't.

Against his better judgment, Joseph timidly leads Mary inside to tell the innkeeper they will take him up on his offer. "The baby is coming, and we have no choice."

The man loads Joseph with the promised supplies—a basin of water and blankets—and his wife hands Mary strips of cloth she says are used to wrap lambs to keep them unblemished as they're transported to the temple for sacrifice. Busy with other guests filling the place, they point Joseph and Mary to the stable, crowded with animals.

Once there, Joseph can tell Mary has the same reaction he does to the squalor and the stench. Large, curious eyes of cows, sheep, goats, and donkeys peer passively at them in the low flickering of a few meager lamps. Tentative bleats and moos greet them as Joseph carefully leads Mary around heaps of dung.

"There's enough wood here," he says, struck by how ashen she looks. "I can put something together for you."

"There's no time. They're coming faster now."

"All right. We can do this. Try to find a spot to sit on this blanket, and I'll put *something* together for you. And I'll clean up, huh?"

• • •

It will be dark by the time young herder hireling Shimon arrives back at the sheepfold, and hunger gnaws at him. But despite what he's endured, he has been buoyed by the priest's reading, and as he leads the blemished lamb, he reminds himself of the rest of the passage from the prophet Isaiah. He recites:

"Then the eyes of the blind shall be opened, and the ears of the deaf unstopped; then shall the lame man leap like a deer, and the tongue of the mute sing for joy. For waters break forth in the wilderness, and streams in the desert; the burning sand shall become a pool, and the thirsty ground springs of water; in the haunt of jackals, where they lie down, the grass shall become reeds and rushes."

• • •

In the pitch darkness, Shimon reaches the hill where the sheep lie for the night. Yoram, Natan, and Aaron sit around a small fire, enjoying their evening meal. They laugh, plainly recounting the marketplace encounter. Aaron says, "Yes, well, next time I will wipe my hands with his robe. He will faint!"

Natan gestures with a crust of bread. "A Pharisee is so cheap, when he writes his will, he names himself as the heir!"

"And he still doesn't get much!" Aaron says.

Yoram turns as Shimon steps into the light of the campfire. Pots of flame hang from the tent, giving light as well. "Huh! Finally! He's back!"

"Hello, Shimon," Natan says.

"Stay with the sheep!" Yoram calls out.

"He is useless," Aaron says. "Why do you keep him around?"

"He's a good boy." Yoram shrugs. "He'll want some dinner."

"Aaron made dinner tonight," Natan says. "So, nothing is cooked!"

As Yoram laughs, Aaron says, "The food is fine. It's my grandmother's recipe, so leave it alone!"

"That is why your grandfather left," Yoram says, and Natan howls.

Shimon wearily returns the lamb to its mother and watches as they settle in the grass. When he starts up toward the others again, he finds his ankle has grown only worse, and he can barely move. The older three are still recounting the day.

"I wish that woman wouldn't have left the well," Natan says.

Aaron nods, eyes distant. "She was very beautiful."

"Very pretty, very pretty," Yoram says.

Shimon leans on his crutch, his stomach growling. "Can I have my dinner now?"

"Not with us." Aaron shakes his head. "Take your plate over there." He points back toward the flocks.

"After what happened this morning," Yoram says, "you sleep with the sheep tonight."

"And pay attention this time," Aaron tells him.

Yoram points at Shimon. "Watch out for wolves."

Natan shakes a morsel of food in his palm. "Watch out for the Pharisee—he might come after you."

Shimon grabs a torch and holds it in the fire till it bursts into flame.

"A Roman took another sheep yesterday," Aaron tells the others.

Grateful not to have to try to speak over the lump in his throat, Shimon shuffles off with his plate. Natan calls out. "Shimon! They're talking about the Romans again."

"He cooked it right in front of me!" Aaron says. "They take whatever they want!"

Yoram shakes his head. "Let's talk about something else."

Shimon trudges down a grassy embankment toward a brook, panting now, each step taking more out of him. He has never felt so lonely. He sets his plate on a rock and wades into the marshy shallows, pokes his torch into the mud, and slowly bends to dip his gouged arm into the stream, gingerly rinsing it. Above him, the other three have fallen silent, and all he hears are the pokes of their sticks into the fire.

• • •

"He needs a place to sleep," Mary says.

"What?" Joseph says.

"When he gets here, he needs a place to lie down. You make my bed. I'll make his."

"Already a mother, eh?"

Joseph finds not a square foot on the floor not covered with dung. He finds a shovel and quickly begins to clear a spot where he can spread hay and a blanket. Meanwhile, Mary—clearly hurrying in her distress—wipes a small feed trough with water and layers it with straw. Working largely with one hand—the other on her stomach—she folds and spreads a blanket in the manger. A goat sticks his nose over a wood railing, and she reaches to push it away. She winces and groans.

Mary presses the back of her hand against her forehead. "My soul magnifies the Lord," she whispers. "And my spirit rejoices in God my savior, for He has looked on the humble estate of His servant."

Joseph stops shoveling and straightens. "What is that?" he says.

"What?"

"What are you saying?"

"Oh, nothing ..."

"Is it a song of David? We could use one right about now."

"No, sorry, it's—just something to myself."

He gets back to working quickly. "A poem you created?"

"Yes, but—"

"When?"

"Several months ago."

"I would love to hear it."

She looks self-conscious and shakes her head.

• • •

Shimon sets his crutch aside and slides down to sit next to his plate. Weary, he continues to fight tears. His wound makes him feel unclean, and he is too exhausted to eat. With his torch illuminating the water, he is surprised to find it murky. In the daylight, the stream had been clear.

Abruptly the air stills, and sheep and birds and insects fall silent. When the wind kicks up again, the sheep are on their feet. Branches sway, leaves flutter, and Shimon's torch blows out. He steals a glance up the hill where Yoram, Natan, and Aaron struggle to their feet, pulling their garments about them in the wind. Their fire and their hanging pots blow out, and the three disappear from sight—until the sky fills with light brighter than the noonday sun. The men fall to their knees, Yoram burying his face in the dirt, Natan and Aaron staring wide-eyed, mouths agape.

An angel appears in their midst, and what Shimon can describe only as the very glory of God shines all around. He cannot move. The angel says, "Fear not, for behold, I bring you good news of great joy that will be for all the people. For unto you is born this day in the city of David a Savior, who is Christ the Lord."

*Dreaming*, Shimon tells himself. *I'm dreaming. This cannot be! This day? In my lifetime!*

The angel continues, "And this will be a sign for you: you will find a baby wrapped in swaddling cloths and lying in a manger."

Suddenly, there is with the angel a multitude of the heavenly host, praising God and saying, "Glory to God in the highest, and on earth peace among those with whom he is pleased!"

• • •

Joseph peers outside to the horizon. "Mary, are you seeing this?" He steps past her to gaze at the sky in the distance, radiating with light and color. "Mary? Mary!"

She gasps, and he turns to find her looking terrified, liquid gushing to her feet. "Joseph, it's time!"

Barely able to breathe, he rushes to her. "Come! I've got you. Come, sit."

"Shouldn't we call for help? You've never done this before! Maybe the wife could come and help?"

"No, there isn't time. We've got this." He reaches to lay her down.

"No, no, no! I don't want you to see me like this!"

As he settles her onto the blanket, she cries out.

"Mary, look at me."

"No, no, no, I can wait!" she says, looking past him. "Go get someone."

"Don't look over there, Mary. Look at me." With all that is within him, he wants to be for her all that she needs. Plainly terrified, she meets his eyes. "We are not alone," he tells her.

"I am so scared."

"Hey, remember what your messenger said—the first thing your messenger said. It was the same thing my messenger said to me, remember?"

She nods. "'Don't be afraid.'"

"Don't be afraid!"

She appears to force a smile. "I love you."

He presses his forehead against hers. "I love you."

"Thank you for taking care of me," she sobs. "God gave you to me."

"'He has been our help,'" Joseph says, "'and in the shadow of His wings, we will sing for joy.' A song of David."

"Yes."

"Can I hear yours now?"

She laughs through it all. "Not now." She groans.

"I know, I know. It is time, yes?"

"Yes."

He folds a cloth and submerges it into the basin of water, dabbing her face as she groans. "It's okay. I've got you."

And in the steamy night, sweat pouring down both their faces as she screams, Joseph delivers the son of God. Mary's tears stream as he cuts and ties the cord and hands her the baby. As she wipes down the boy with a cloth, Joseph pulls a leather pouch from his tunic and pours salt into the water, immersing his fingers and helping clean the baby. The salt will toughen the baby's velvety skin, but it also symbolically affirms that the child is Joseph's legitimate son. The woodworker has already endured embarrassment and disdain to claim the babe as his own. He will never waver.

Mary wraps the infant in the swaddling cloths and rocks him, gazing in wonder at Joseph.

"Are you better?" he says. "Is this comfortable?" He knows better, of course. How comfortable can it be?

But she smiles wearily at him. "Yes, thank you."

"Are you still in pain?"

"Yes, but, uh, the blanket underneath is helping."

They look at each other and shake their heads, and Joseph feels such relief wash over him that all he can do is lean back and laugh. "Oh, I don't know how you did that! I feel like my heart is going to explode!"

"Oh, don't make me laugh," Mary says. "It hurts to laugh."

• • •

As quickly as they had come, the angels are gone. Shimon labors to his feet and hears his compatriots laughing like children. He knows they, like he, will light out for Bethlehem again as fast as they can go.

Shimon digs his crutch into the ground and propels himself from the brook to the hillside and begins to run. He seems to forget his damaged ankle, running as he had when he was whole. And the faster he goes, the more of his ragged bandage falls away until his left foot is bare. Soon he sheds the crutch and feels as if he's flying toward the city.

What must the others be thinking? He has annoyed them for days, regaling them with his fascination with the ancient prophecies and his questioning of the Pharisees. But even more, what must they make of their inability to catch him? Shimon has slowed them for so long.

Can it be true? What did the angel mean, "lying in a manger"? The *Messiah*? The king?

Shimon turns to see Yoram, Natan, and Aaron racing, yet falling farther behind. Like him, they had been paralyzed with fear, and now they whoop and holler and laugh. If Shimon is only imagining all this, they are part of his fantasy. Has he wanted this, longed for this for so many years that he has invented it in his mind? The prophets have not spoken for hundreds of years, and now angels appear with this news?

Shimon feels no pain, no fatigue, not even shortness of breath as he runs all the way across the fields to the road and past the well, verses of Scripture coming to him from endless hours of reading, studying, memorizing. *Therefore the Lord himself will give you a sign. Behold, the virgin shall conceive and bear a son.*

But in a *manger*? Where? How far?

Shimon slows and stops within sight of a small barn, animals milling inside and out. Surely this cannot be the place.

And yet it is lit from within, while everything around it lies in darkness.

Chapter 3

# PEOPLE MUST KNOW

Beaming, Mary says, "He's so small."

"Smaller than I expected," Joseph says.

"I don't know what I expected," Mary says. "But it wasn't any of this."

"No. From the beginning of it all …" He pauses, just taking it all in, his fiancée cradling his Lord. "So, your messenger said that he would be called holy, the son of God. The prophecy mentions Immanuel. Are we going to stick with the name Jesus?"

"Hmm, I think we should."

"Probably best, huh?"

She nods. "He needs to sleep."

"You both do. Let me put him in the manger. It's a better bed than the one I made for you."

• • •

Through the stable door, Shimon sees a man inside lift a

squalling baby. The man is the wayfarer, the kind, exhausted one to whom Shimon gave water in the marketplace! Shimon stands transfixed as the man, face shining, holds the baby in swaddling cloths, just as the angel said.

This is happening! Actually happening! The woman who had drunk from his supply had been carrying the Messiah!

Yoram blows past Shimon, bumping him aside. Aaron and Natan are right behind Yoram. Shimon has been the first to arrive, but now he will be the last inside. Yoram pushes open the door, and as the four shepherds burst in, the man hands the baby back to its mother and faces them, hands up, terror on his face. His wife looks drained, hair matted from sweat, but also relieved.

Yoram gushes the story of the angel's announcement and the heavenly host. When the man sees Shimon behind the others, his face softens, and he welcomes them all. His wife greets them with a smile as the shepherds slowly kneel before the new family.

The man again takes the baby, now sleeping, and holds him toward the shepherds. Yoram reaches for him, but the man locks eyes with Shimon and hands him the infant. The others look on, eyes wide with wonder.

Shimon is speechless. The babe is like a feather compared to a lamb. Could he really be holding the Christ, the Lord? It is too much to take in. His eyes fill.

"So beautiful!" Yoram says.

Time seems to stand still. Gazing at the baby, Shimon is vaguely aware that his compatriots are conversing with the parents, who introduce themselves as Joseph and Mary from Nazareth. The shepherds offer help, suggesting they might find them more appropriate lodging. But the wayfarer and his wife demur, insisting they are fine.

Shimon would hold the Christ child for hours if they'd let him. Who will believe this? He'll not even be able to convince his own family! He wants to tell the whole world.

Still kneeling, the others look at him as if to hint that he should share the privilege, but he's not about to unless the parents insist.

At long last, Aaron says, "We must tell someone."

Natan rises. "We must tell *everyone*!"

"Yes, everyone!" Yoram says.

"Yes, yes, thank you!" Shimon says.

They run out, leaving Shimon tenderly cradling the child. This tiny, precious bundle will liberate Israel from her oppressors. Shimon whispers to Joseph, "We've waited for this for so long! So long!"

Shimon hands the baby back, and the child begins to fuss again. Joseph hands him to Mary, who notices the wound on Shimon's arm. "You are hurt," she says.

"Oh, I'll be fine."

Mary unwraps a piece of swaddling cloth from the baby and hands it to Joseph, who gives it to Shimon. He holds one end in his teeth and quickly wraps the wound.

"What will you name him?" Shimon says.

Mary glances at Joseph and says, "Jesus."

"We'll name him Jesus," Joseph says.

"I must go," Shimon says. "People must know. People must know."

Joseph nods. "People must know."

• • •

Shimon sprints for the marketplace, more scriptures echoing in his mind. *For to us a child is born, to us a son is given; and the government shall be upon his shoulder, and his name shall be called Wonderful Counselor, Mighty God, Everlasting Father, Prince of Peace.*

*Of the increase of his government and of peace there will be no end, on the throne of David and over his kingdom, to establish it and to uphold it with justice and with righteousness from this time forth and forevermore.*

By the time Shimon reaches the market, Yoram and Natan and Aaron have caused such a ruckus that townspeople appear in their doorways. The shepherds grab everyone in sight—Romans, religious leaders, anyone—and spout their story of the angel, the heavenly host, finding the baby, the Messiah. "The baby, the Christ child, lies in a manger!" Aaron cries out.

"In a barn!" Natan says. "Angels told us where we'd find him. And we did!"

The shepherds cannot contain themselves, not even waiting for responses. One even accosts the man who had thrown Shimon from the synagogue, but he wrenches away, clearly convinced these men are mad. "The Messiah, I tell you!" Yoram shouts.

Shimon moves into the middle of the square just as Natan turns from someone. He bursts into a grin and embraces Shimon, pulling him close. "You were right!" he says. "You were right all along!"

As Natan pulls away to tell others, Shimon finds himself face-to-face with the Pharisee he had encountered that very morning. "You!" the leader says, pointing in his face. "I told you not to come back here! So where is it? Have you found a spotless lamb for sacrifice?"

Shimon stops, eyes bright, as the truth washes over his countenance. And he slowly begins to smile.

# PART 2

# I Have Called You by Name

When you pass through the waters, I will be with you;
And through the rivers,
they will not overflow you.

When you walk through the fire, you will not be scorched,
Nor will the flame burn you.
For I am the Lord your God,
The Holy One of Israel,
your Savior. …

I, even I, am the one who
wipes out your transgressions
for My own sake,
And I will not remember
your sins.
Isaiah 43:2-3, 25 (nasb)

Chapter 4

# POSSESSED

*Two years later*

*Bedouin camp*

Just outside the small, torchlit city of Magdala, nestled between rolling hills, Anouk, a burly, swarthy man, sits outside his family's tent in the wee hours of the morning. Humming softly, he tends a small fire.

His humming turns to coughing, however, and the more he tries to squelch it for the sake of his sleeping family, the worse it becomes. His five-year-old daughter, Mary, appears at the tent flap, barefoot and carrying a crude doll he has fashioned for her. "Abba?"

Anouk starts, ruing that he has awakened her and desperate to keep from her that his cough is even worse and more foreboding than it sounds. "You should be sleeping, little one."

"I can't sleep," she says, her tone wounding him.

He reaches for her. "Sit down. Sit down." Anouk draws her

into his lap, hoping she is not suffering as she often has. "Is your head hurting you again?"

"No."

"Are you thinking of the big new star? Hey, look, it's right there! See?" He points.

"No."

"Why can't you sleep?"

"I'm scared."

"Of what?"

"I don't know."

• • •

It's true. Little Mary doesn't know. She loves the cool of the night, when the temperature dips under a hundred degrees and she doesn't soak her clothes with sweat. But she's a fearful child, afraid of lions, wolves, jackals, cheetahs, even the striped hyenas. She has never encountered any of these up close, but she has heard them, seen them from a distance, and knows they're out there.

Mary also feels threatened by what she does not know. Something inside her gives her headaches, keeps her from sleeping. But that's not it tonight. She's worried about her father's cough.

• • •

Anouk pulls Mary closer and holds her tight. Such a wee one to be so troubled. Perhaps he and the other men in the camp should be more mindful of who's within earshot when they discuss the menace of the wild animals nearby. "Hey. What do we do when we are scared?"

"We say the words."

He nods. "Adonai's words. From the prophet …"

"Isaiah," she says.

"From the prophet Isaiah." He nods. "Thus says the Lord who created you, O Jacob, and He who formed you, O Israel: 'Fear not.'" Anouk pats her hand. "Come now, Mary, I want to hear you say it. I want to hear your pretty voice. Come …"

"Fear not, for I have redeemed you; I have called you by name, you are mine."

"'You are mine.' That's right." And he gently kisses her cheek.

• • •

*City of Capernaum, twenty-eight years later*

A woman in her early thirties bolts upright in bed and takes in her surroundings as the harsh morning sunlight invades. She gasps as if emerging from deep water. Her eyes dart, and she rises to peek into a reflective plate on the wall. Her painted face is smeared under a thick layer of sweat.

Has she only dreamed of her father comforting her so many years before? She touches her cheek where he had kissed her and only then sees blood across her palm. Her nails are broken on both hands.

*What's happened to me?* She examines her torn robe, also soaked with blood, and from outside a man yells, "Help! Somebody help me!" She peeks through the curtain to the bazaar, stall upon stall, crowds of every ethnicity bargaining in foreign tongues.

The man smashes through, knocking over goods, pointing back to her place. "She tried to kill me! Somebody—somebody—some—!"

The market grinds to a halt as everyone stares. Everywhere he turns, people recoil from the crazy man. A mother ushers her child away. Customers and merchants curse him.

A massive Roman guard seizes him by the shoulder, then pulls back with blood on his hand. "You filthy dog!"

The man grabs the guard and stares him square in the eyes. "Demons! They live inside her."

In confusion and shame, the woman turns back to her filthy chamber at Rivka's inn, recalling nothing of what happened. She's been accused of this before, though she's never been a woman of the night. She knows why some mistake her for one, because such are common in the Red Quarter. And people tell of her spells. No longer little Mary of the desert camp near Magdala, she has for years hidden behind the name Lilith.

She's always had a way with other women's hair. But she feels soiled, damaged, impossible to hire. She cobbles a meager living begging and scrounging, and she trades dressing Rivka's exotic African hair for this shabby place among the local denizens. Whatever she has done to the man—or the demons have tried to do through her—she does not doubt him for a second.

Chapter 5

# TEACHER OF TEACHERS

In the faint pre-dawn light, slaves lead a lavishly appointed carriage along a rutted path from Judea to Capernaum. Inside, Nicodemus prays silently as his maturely beautiful wife, Zohara, sits across from him. The eighteen ostentatious garments adorning him, and his trimmed, gold dust-flecked beard identify him as a leading Pharisee of the Jerusalem Sanhedrin. Of late, he has grown weary of all the trappings of his station. In fact, that's what he is praying about, silently seeking forgiveness for having reveled in the adulation of younger clerics and deference from the public.

He must confess that this very trip, his annual sojourn to teach at the synagogue and rabbinical school in Capernaum, had proved a stumbling block to his humility in the past. And he doesn't want that to be the case this time. He knows his lessors here will fawn over him and treat him and Zohara to lavish accommodations. Nicodemus does not want to appear above it all or dismissive of it, either one, such treatment being appropriate to his office. But he longs to be as devout as the younger version of himself, years before when he was elected by the great assemblage itself to join the Sanhedrin. Too many of his colleagues let their spiritual disciplines wane once they reach that pinnacle, letting their positions and reputations substitute for a real relationship with the divine. *Lord, spare me that conceit*, he prays silently.

"Stop!" a slave shouts before appearing at Nicodemus' window. "Forgive me, Rabbi—"

Zohara scolds the slave for not recognizing that Nicodemus is in prayer, but when the slave turns his attention to her, he quickly averts his eyes as if he's caught her bathing. She immediately covers her head.

"But, woman—ahead!"

Five Roman legionnaires on horseback approach at full gallop, the lead equine bearing a youngish man in an immaculate tunic and imperial helmet that contrast sharply with the attire of his fellow soldiers. The slaves stand with heads bowed as he dismounts, and the other four legionnaires appear to keep a watchful eye.

"Why have you stopped us?" Nicodemus asks the young officer.

"It's not enough to say hello?"

"I'm on official business," the Pharisee says.

"Only Roman business is official business," the young man says, clearly pleased with himself. "My name is Quintus. I'm the praetor of Capernaum."

"I am—"

"You're the great Nicodemus. Word travels fast."

"Are you arresting me?"

Quintus laughs. “No, my friend. I’m a magistrate, not a military man. I serve the will of the people. And Pilate.”

“And I serve only God.”

“Yes, yes. So do your enemies, the Sadducees. The Essenes. The Zealots. Rogue preachers in the wilderness raving about a coming messiah. They’re all vying for the people’s affection.”

Nicodemus has heard enough. “What do you want, Quintus?”

“I believe taxes are going unpaid. If you help me, I will help the Pharisees continue to—thrive.”

“How can I? The people are already drowning in tax.”

“Tell me, Nicodemus, what can be under the water and yet never drown?”

What kind of a question is this? Nicodemus furrows his brow. “Fish?”

Chapter 6

# TAXMAN

*Capernaum, northern district*

The exquisite home bathes in early morning light, its huge living room decorated in expensive, high style with floor-to-ceiling windows looking out over the city. The floors sparkle, and a plush deerskin mat lies before a marble fireplace. The room is impeccable, yet oddly impersonal.

A slight man in his late twenties with sharp eyes, smooth skin, and full lips stands expressionless before a huge wardrobe stocked with rows of immaculately pressed linens. He painstakingly riffles through the choices several times and finally selects one before wrapping himself in it. He knows exactly which garment he will select, but he also feels compelled to perform this seemingly endless routine every day.

No one else he knows suffers from this. Teased unmercifully as a child for being strange, he has somehow channeled his love of order and precision, of things adding up and lining up, into something that has served him well. While he holds a position his fellow Jews revile, he's far outdistanced them in income.

Though even his family has disowned him, this house, in what is known as the publicanus community, serves as his reward. Here he feels safe, able to be himself, no one watching or judging his every mood.

Since long before he was ten years old, he's been preternaturally able to focus on one thing at a time, keeping his eccentricities at bay through various rituals. He eats the last grape from a porcelain plate, applies frankincense to his wrists, and then repeats the same process as he did with the linens to select sandals from among several expensive pairs. Finally, he takes a cloth napkin from a stack and heads out.

As he approaches a large, monolithic door, a servant hands him a leather shoulder bag containing his ledger and tablet, among other essentials—he's prepared for anything. And despite the servant's endlessly promising to secure the palatial home upon his departure, he slips outside, closing the heavy door and locking it himself with a brass key—three times, just to be sure.

He moves quickly down kinked, narrow alleys behind the luxurious homes of others of his wealth and station. He avoids the normal passageways where he'd be recognized, jeered, spit upon, perhaps assaulted. Keeping to the alleys where people dump trash and raw sewage, and where flies buzz, he covers his nose and mouth with the napkin. He's looking for his ride to the market where his tax booth is situated. He gives a citizen a tax break in exchange for the privilege of hiding under a tarpaulin in the bed of his delivery cart. While it's not ideal, in this way, Matthew escapes the ridicule he would endure if he walked the entire way.

Moving around a commoner, he deftly sidesteps a pack of rats but steps directly into a pile of dung. He doubles over and gags. While extricating his sodden sandal, he hears from the end of the alley, "Matthew! Psst, psst!" His ride to work.

"Keep your voice down!"

"Pardon me, Mr. Public Anus," the grubby deliveryman says. "It's me that don't wanna be seen with you, remember?"

"It's public-AH-nus," Matthew says.

"I like it the other way, taxman."

Matthew slips out of his soiled sandals and slides a new pair from his tote, tossing the others aside in the street.

"Hey, hey, hey!" the driver cries out. "That's a month's salary for all my sons combined right here! You just toss them out?"

"These are my property. I do with them as I wish. I pay you to drive. You sift through trash on your own time."

"Driving you is a bit of both now, isn't it?" the man says, laughing. He pulls back the tarp, revealing a filthy wood floor. As Matthew climbs in, the driver adds, "But if any citizen asks about my cargo, I must tell the truth—it's the biggest pile of dung in all Capernaum!"

Matthew scowls and covers himself.

Chapter 7

# THE RED QUARTER

Rabbinical students dressed in white eagerly surround Nicodemus, the Hebrew school's revered guest from the Sanhedrin in Jerusalem and today's featured speaker. Behind them, in black, stand their teachers, including a longtime protégé of Nicodemus' and chief rabbi of the school, Shmuel. With an ease and confidence befitting his position, Nicodemus begins: "Now, honestly, I always look forward to my annual visit to Capernaum. And your magnificent Sea of Galilee. It is truly the envy of the kingdom."

The students and faculty applaud, appearing spellbound.

"Even my children were enamored of it. All day they would swim, frolic in the sand, and watch the people. Finally, one day I said, 'You love it here so much, why is it you never go to the sea when we visit your grandparents back home?' My son said, 'But, Father, there's never anyone there. It's dead!'"

As his adoring audience laughs, Nicodemus leans in and

shifts his tone. "And your sea boasts the most exquisite fish! How unfortunate that those who do the actual fishing are unholy, foul-mouthed, given to gambling in secret dens, and even fishing on Shabbat." He pauses. "Can we eat the catch and not be stained by the sins of the catcher?

"Make no mistake—it is a sin to eat fish caught on Shabbat. What goes into the body of a man defiles him. Why are our Jewish brethren taking their boats to sea on Shabbat?"

He has stunned his young charges to silence.

"I assure you, the Messiah will not come until this wickedness is purged from our midst." Nicodemus searches their faces, but most look away. "Your actions are being watched, studied. God has entrusted you to be exemplary in every way. Now, if your status is too great a burden, you do not deserve to bear the name of Israel."

It has always fascinated the Pharisee that he's able to speak while pondering other things at the same time. His mind seems to spin away at the thought of the coming of Messiah. For years Nicodemus has wondered why his Sanhedrin cohorts talk less and less of this most sacred—and to his mind, thrilling—of all the prophecies. Should they not watch and wait for the Messiah? Perhaps the years of silence from heaven have dulled his colleagues' anticipation. All they've done is to heighten his own.

• • •

As Nicodemus finishes his address, Shmuel and his student Yusef rush ahead to an ornate chamber, the next stop for the guest of honor. Two slaves are busy polishing the gold and leather, plus the brass of a magnificent table that lies before what looks more like a throne than a mere chair.

"I want to see my reflection in it plain as day," Shmuel tells the slaves. "This teacher has traveled all the way from Judea. He is a member of the Great Sanhedrin in Jerusalem, and I won't have him seated at a dull table."

As his student pours a goblet of wine, Shmuel says, "Yusef, straighten your tallit."

The young man quickly adjusts his prayer shawl, then peeks out at commotion in the hallway. "Here he comes!"

Shmuel tells the slaves, "Away! Go! Get the others!" As they scurry off, he straightens his robe and slips out to welcome Nicodemus, who's surrounded by several students and faculty. Shmuel bows and beams. "Teacher! You have moved us all!"

Nicodemus greets him flatly. "Shmuel."

Shmuel melts and points to the Torah room with another bow. "Will you do us the honor, Rabbi?"

"If it's where you keep the white sardines—"

Shmuel looks stricken, turning to Yusef. "Well, I—we—certainly could get—"

"It was a joke, Shmuel," Nicodemus says, and Shmuel smiles like a condemned prisoner pardoned.

Nicodemus' servant steps through the curtain and holds it aside as he enters. The slaves have been replaced by more students, stiffly lined up as if awaiting inspection. "A fine Torah room is the heartbeat of a worthy synagogue, Shmuel," Nicodemus says.

"Thank you, Teacher of Israel. You do us a great honor."

The servant slides back the seat of honor, and Nicodemus sits. "The honor is mine. Not only for your bright students, but also for the soul of this city. You heard my address?"

"Of course," Shmuel says. "Your words will resonate for generations."

"You were luminous," Yusef says.

"In my remarks, I asked, for rhetorical purposes, why are Jews taking boats to sea on Shabbat? That question was meant for you, Rabbi Shmuel. The reports are becoming too frequent to ignore."

Ashen faced, Shmuel nods. "Of course, Rabbi. We—*I* will control it better. The Romans believe we do not work on the Sabbath, thus they do not patrol. Greed has overcome the fishermen, I'm afr—"

"Or they are just trying to feed their families," Yusef says.

Shmuel fixes Yusef with an acid look as if he had blasphemed, but they're interrupted when another Pharisee appears at the door. "Begging your pardon, Rabbi. A centurion is here. He demands to speak with you."

"Please tell him we have an honored guest," Shmuel says, "and cannot be interrupted!"

A Roman guard shoves past the Pharisee. "Can't wait," he says.

Shmuel looks to heaven. "Messiah, come quickly."

The guard removes his helmet and looks around, whistling. "Impressive. Looks like we're not the only ones taxing the people."

"What do you want, Commander?" Nicodemus says.

"I'm no commander. But at least you know your place."

"This is Nicodemus," Shmuel says. "Teacher of teachers! Show some respect!"

"Aah! Just the man I want to see. I'm here about a Hebrew woman in the Red Quarter. Let's just say she's been causing a disturbance."

"You have an entire Roman legion at your disposal!" Shmuel says.

"Thank you for the reminder, Jew. But she needs a holy man."

"We are men of God," Nicodemus says. "It is not our custom to frequent the Red Quarter."

"Perhaps I wasn't clear, teacher of teachers. You'll accompany me to the Red Quarter or we'll burn it down with our fire of fires."

Chapter 8

# THE TAX BOOTH

Matthew's driver halts. "Psst. This is your stop."

Matthew lifts the tarp, and his face falls. "Wait, we're on the far side of the market!"

"Get out!"

"No."

"No?"

"This is the job! You drive so I don't walk through the market!"

"It's too crowded! Out!"

"I'll pay you double."

"Money won't buy the stink off my family and me if I'm seen with you. Out!"

Matthew stands and brushes off his robes. "This is very unprofessional."

"Fire me," the man says and scurries away with his cart.

Matthew hurries through the heart of the market, head down, counting his steps.

"Tax collector!" someone calls out.

"Oh, there he is!"

"I see it!"

Someone spits. "Traitor!"

"You should be ashamed!"

Matthew feels all eyes on him, but he doesn't break stride. He nearly falls as someone yanks his robe—a blind beggar, and he's hanging on.

"Please," Matthew says, repulsed. Somewhere, deep inside, he feels for the man. But the beggar is filthy, vile, smelly—and he's actually touching Matthew.

"Are you the Messiah? Are you the Messiah?"

"No! I am not." In that instant, Matthew wishes he were the Messiah, not that he even believes such a prophecy anymore. He was rushed ahead so quickly in Hebrew school because of his acumen with numbers that he remembers little of the Scriptures he memorized before age eight.

"Please, tell me when he comes! Please!"

Matthew pulls away and quickly rounds a corner, emitting a sigh of relief. A line about twelve deep leads to his collection booth. A motley assortment, they stare at him warily, dark circles under their eyes. Some hold the hands of barefoot children. In tattered clothes, they exude poverty and oppression. For years he has steeled himself against empathizing with such rabble—which would not serve his task. He's paid to exact shekels from these people, not try to help them. He's grateful his secure booth will separate him from them.

Matthew stalls, feeling conspicuous, waiting for his Roman guard to show up and unlock his government-owned cage. When he finally arrives, Matthew says, "You are late, Gaius."

Gaius, bald, sharp-featured, and tautly muscled, grins, plainly relishing the idea of Matthew standing out here, alone and exposed.

"Could you feel it?" Gaius says.

"Feel what?"

"The market. It's on fire today. Everybody's on edge. All it would take is one person to snap and you're—"

"Just do your job."

"You'd better hope I do," Gaius says with a chuckle. He produces a key and unlocks the booth, letting Matthew in before locking it again for the taxman's own safety.

• • •

*The Red Quarter*

Meanwhile, another Roman guard leads Nicodemus, Shmuel, and Yusef down a cramped alley behind a two-story brick inn that appears to have seen better days. The guard smirks at Nicodemus' obvious revulsion. The Pharisee leader has only heard of this district, and he has to admit his imagination barely scratched the surface of its tawdry reality.

Peddlers hawk their wares in garbage-strewn streets that make him wish he'd lost his sense of smell. Ghastly prostitutes—women and young men—beckon passersby from the shadows. Another guard vigorously tries to scrub from a wall a sign that reads: "MESSIAH WILL DESTROY THE ROMANS."

*Wouldn't that be nice?* Nicodemus thinks. *If only he were here now to spare me this.*

The Roman stops outside an inn. "Upstairs." He points. "Rivka's joint."

The Pharisee grimaces at even the thought of having to enter such a hellish dive.

The guard says, "Don't worry, Rabbi. We took out the other lowlifes to protect your delicate sensibilities."

Nicodemus jumps at the sound of an inhuman shriek from an upstairs window. "No! No!"

"What *is* that?" Shmuel says, clearly horrified.

Nicodemus' mind races. If that isn't the sound of demonic possession, he doesn't know what is. He witnessed an exorcism years before, and while he had been taught the particulars, he had hoped that was as close as he would ever get to such a spectacle.

*How can I possibly combat such evil?*

But everyone seems to look to him alone.

"I need materials, Shmuel! Sulfur, nettles—uh, hyssop, wormwood. Go!"

"Yes, Teacher," Shmuel says, and he and Yusef disappear.

"Well," the guard says, "do your job."

Nicodemus fortifies himself and faces the man. It's all he can do to keep from shouting. "Listen. I agreed to Quintus' *request*—not a *demand*, because he should not demand anything of me—to stop Shabbat fishing, which was already our law, and by doing so was not in violation of my practice. And I will try to help this woman, even though it falls outside my purview. But do not think of me as a tool to fix Roman problems.

"I will *not* continue to use my position of religious influence to benefit those who look down on my people, whether it's you or even someone like Quintus! So, I *will* perform this task, but I want it noted for your superiors: This is an exception!"

The guard stares blankly. "Can we go up now?"

"Yes!" Nicodemus says, having mustered every ounce of false bravado he can conjure.

## Chapter 9

# THE FIGHTING FISHERMAN

*Outskirts of Capernaum*

A robust young man lies writhing in the dust as two dozen others surround him, cheering and jeering as their money changes hands. Over him stands a taller man. "Stay down, Simon!" says the man. "Suck dirt if you know what's good for you!"

Trying to shake the stars from his eyes, Simon rolls to one side to peek at his brother, Andrew, watching with the rest. The two have been inseparable since early childhood, their late father, Jonah, taking them fishing before they were even big enough to be able to help him. They learned the man's trade by watching his every move and have made their livings on the Sea of Galilee ever since.

They can communicate wordlessly, as so many close siblings learn to do. Andrew surreptitiously points to Simon's opponent, advancing. With tremendous effort, Simon rises to one knee, just in time to be decked again, flopping with a thud.

His assailant grunts and shakes out his obviously painful fist. Half the onlookers cheer as more money passes back and forth.

"Too much, Jehoshaphat," Simon manages. "You're too powerful."

"That's right!" Jehoshaphat roars. "Like I tell you every time I see you." He turns to the crowd. "Like I tell my *sister*!"

They howl with laughter.

Simon turns to his brother again. "Seriously, I can only take, maybe, two—"

Andrew shakes his head.

"One?"

His brother nods.

"One more punch! One more and I'm done."

The crowd erupts. Someone shouts, "He says he's had it!"

Others scream, "No!" and more bets switch to Jehoshaphat, who turns his back to Simon to encourage the crowd.

Deftly, Simon leaps to his feet. "Jeho—?"

The man turns, and before he can even raise his hands, Simon lands a hard right to his face. Then a left. "What was it you were saying? Something about your sister?" He follows with two shots to Jehoshaphat's midsection. "You think if you keep hitting me hard enough, I won't be married to Eden anymore?" He drives a left hand into Jehoshaphat's lower back, and the man goes down. "That's why they call me 'wine hands,' because of what I do to your liver."

As his brother-in-law tries to rise, Simon squats and whispers in his ear. "I don't wanna do this, Jehoshaphat. Can we please stop fighting every week? I know you've never trusted me, but I love your sister more than anything."

On his hands and knees, gasping, Jehoshaphat says, "I will stop fighting you."

"You will?"

"But my brother won't."

"Your brother?" Simon turns just in time to take from his other brother-in-law a left to his nose that ends the fight. As he lands on his back, he sees Andrew handing over their money.

• • •

Half an hour later, Simon and Andrew are on the shore of the Sea of Galilee, their boat anchored nearby. Simon paces, face to the sky, pressing a rag to his bleeding nose. Andrew sits in the sand, looking dejected.

"Where's it written down, Andrew? Huh? Answer me that."

Andrew shakes his head and mutters, "I'm so foolish."

"How's a double knockout a push if it's two on one? That's a made-up rule right there."

"Made up or in stone, who cares? We lost, and I know better."

"No, no," Simon says. He sits next to Andrew. "It's my fault. I talked you into it."

They silently listen to the gentle lapping of the waves.

Andrew finally says, "Wine hands?"

Simon shrugs. "It sounded more clever in my head." He changes the subject. "Tax day's coming."

"Mm-hm."

"Two sunrises away. Shabbat and then—"

"I realize, Simon. Thank you. We could lose the boat."

"What are you going to do?" Simon says.

"Don't know. Matthew will demand blood from a stone."

Simon stands suddenly. He makes for the boat.

"Where are you going?" Andrew says.

"Going to work."

"Work? It's Shabbat in an hour."

"The Pharisees make allowances for that if lives are at stake," Simon says, untying the boat.

"No one's life is at stake!"

"No, no, not this moment, but it's coming." He gives Andrew a look. "What, you gonna tell your bug-eating friend about it?" His brother has become enamored of a crazy preacher in the wilderness who rants about the coming Messiah. The man is a laughingstock, dressed in animal skins and subsisting on locusts and honey.

Andrew sighs and throws up his hands. He moves to help Simon with the boat, but Simon stops him. "Just me. I'm not dragging you into this."

"What about Eden?"

"She's staying at her ima's tonight."

"You're crazy, you know that?" Andrew says.

"Nah, just desperate."

Chapter 10

# UNHOLY ENCOUNTER

"How long has she been like this?" Nicodemus asks Rivka, whose ebony face bears the signs of a life lived hard.

Clearly annoyed by all the attention from the Romans and now the Pharisee, she says, "Like what?"

Nicodemus can barely contain his rage. "I'm trying to help her, Rivka."

"All you're gonna do is mess this place up. Then what? You gonna stop by and help clean, Rabbi?"

"The demons that torment her soul will turn your place to dust! Even if you care nothing for her soul, at least—"

"Lilith never hurt anyone who didn't hurt her first—mostly." Rivka looks sad. "She has these spells. We let her be, and then she's sweet as an angel again." Rivka turns at more animal-like screeches from upstairs. Then a crash. "Curse it all, Lil!" Rivka softens and turns back to Nicodemus. "You can put an end to this?"

The Pharisee would love to assure her that he can, but in truth he isn't sure and would rather be anywhere else. But this is on him now.

Centurions use a battering ram to blow the door open, then quickly retreat to allow Nicodemus through. He approaches slowly, swinging a thurible, wafting the smoke of incense. Shmuel and Yusef stop at the doorway, intently peering inside.

Nicodemus ventures in, feeling swallowed by a room lit only by shafts of sunlight. It lies in ruin, walls stained, bed flipped, everything breakable scattered in pieces. How did exorcism become part of his duties? Usually, wearing such finery, he is welcomed, deferred to, revered, adored. Now it's as if he's entered hell.

He knows the possessed, Lilith, is here somewhere. He can feel it. He rattles the thurible chain and tries to muster a tone of authority, but his voice comes out monotone, barely masking his dread. "I adjure you by the holy angels Michael, Gabriel, Rafael, Uriel, and Raziel! I adjure you, cursed dragon and diabolical legions, come out!"

The woman gasps, and he sees movement under a pile of bedding. Lilith in a fetal position, frail yet menacing, is thrashing, sweating, long hair matted.

It's all Nicodemus can do to continue. "I adjure you, spawn of Beelzebub, Abaddon, and Sheol! By the utterance of all the watchers and the holy ones—"

Lilith's wails come raspy and low.

Nicodemus cries out, "—in the name of Adonai, God of the heavens, cease to deceive this human creature!" He inches closer, the smoke is in her face now. "I command you, in covenant with Abraham and the names of Jacob, Isaac, Moses, the all-powerful El Shaddai—"

Lilith squirms, moaning and groaning.

Urgent, emboldened, he finishes with a shout, "Fly from this innocent soul!"

Lilith bellows, otherworldly and inhuman, and spasms, finally lying still.

Nicodemus inches closer, reaching, until she turns to face him with a cold, knowing stare. Her condescending eyes never leave his. She appears amused, as if toying with him. A strange exotic beauty remains in her tortured face, but her voice sounds like several men speaking at once.

"We are not afraid of you."

Nicodemus freezes.

"You have no power here, Teacher."

Nicodemus feels the truth of that to his very soul. He has nothing else to offer and hurries to the doorway. "We're finished here," he says and lurches past Shmuel and Yusef, their stares of horror at the possessed woman becoming pitiful looks of surprise and disappointment.

Chapter 11

# STOIC

Early Shabbat morning, after a long night of fishing illegally, a bone-weary Simon trudges through his working-class ghetto on the east edge of Capernaum. Feeling conspicuous carrying his wood bucket, he nods sheepishly to neighbors in their going-to-synagogue clothes. He should have thought through the timing of his return.

Finally home, he slips in as quietly as possible and washes his feet, wondering if Eden is still at her Ima's house. No such luck. She appears as if from nowhere, her face contorted.

"Simon!"

"Oh!" he says brightly. "Hello, love."

She stands with arms crossed. "Don't you 'hello, love' me. Why did you fight Jehoshaphat?"

"What?"

"My own brother!"

"He attacked *me*! Again!"

"He needs to know the husband of his sister is strong. But Andrew had no right to jump Abrahim from behind!"

What in the world is she talking about? Abrahim was the one who ended the fight! "Where are you getting this?"

Eden bursts out laughing. "My brothers. They are fantastic storytellers, no?"

"Tellers of fantastic stories. Yes, they are."

"They went into such great detail. You must have really given them a pounding."

"Yeah, well, I was doing okay. Till Abe came out of nowhere. Cost me and Andrew a lot of money."

"Oh no! They shouldn't cheat you like that when you are also cheating!"

"All right, all right," Simon says, sitting on a low table. "Pardon me for saying so, love, but your family—"

"Don't!"

"What?"

"Don't you say that my family is troubled in the mind, Simon."

"Okay," he says, smiling.

"We are colorful," she says, moving toward him. "And fun." She takes his face in her hands. "You are stoic and purposeful." She sits in his lap.

"You think I'm stoic?"

"Well, compared to me. Together, we're perfection."

Simon can't argue with that. He kisses her. "Stoic, huh? Never heard that before. I like it. You and me. Fire and water."

"Mm-hm," she says. "I like it."

"So how was Ima's Shabbat dinner?"

"It was lovely. How was fishing?"

"What?" *She knows?*

"Last night's catch? Good news?"

"Oh, yeah," he says. "Pulled something in. Could be big."

"Good! Let's go to synagogue. And please go change—you still smell."

Simon's mind is elsewhere. What he'd pulled in could be big all right.

Chapter 12

# THE WOODEN DOLL

*The Red Quarter*

Lilith lies dead asleep in an alley near Rivka's.

In her dream, she's a child again in Magdala, snug in her father's lap.

"What do we do when we are scared?" he says.

"We say the words."

"Adonai's words. 'Thus says the Lord who created you, O Jacob, and He who formed you, O Israel: "Fear not …"'"

She could stay here forever in his warm embrace. Cherished. Safe.

But she wakes with a start, disheartened to her core. How has it come to this? She's covered head to toe in filth and blood, yet passersby cast not even a glance. They know who she is. Think they know *what* she is. She struggles to sit up, her back against a wall. Has she had another of her spells? How can she face another day like this?

She pushes herself erect and waits for the dizziness to pass. She totters slowly among the crowd, drawing attention only when she comes too near a merchant's stall. "Get away!" he shouts.

She finally reaches Rivka's and begins the slow ascent to her room. She stops before her damaged door, sobs caught in her throat. This is her life. Where else can she go? Lilith pushes the door open. She has no memory of what caused this chaos. She makes her way to the basin below the reflective plate on the wall, but she can barely stand to look at herself. She dips a cloth into the water and dabs at her face. It will take much more than that.

Lilith rubs and rubs at her cheeks until blood and grime give way and expose her olive skin. From down the hall, someone's cough abruptly transports her again to her childhood and her father's troubling hack. She stands in his bedchamber, clutching the doll he has made her, her mother behind her, hands on her shoulders.

Anouk stops coughing. Little Mary whispers, "Abba?" as someone pulls her father's blanket over his face.

Lilith bursts into tears and turns to find what's left of the doll now. She drops to her knees to retrieve it—the wood worn smooth over time—and slides off its head to reveal a tiny bit of rolled parchment inside. Weeping, she quickly unrolls it and haltingly reads the words aloud: "Thus says the Lord who created you, O Jacob, and He who formed you, O Israel: 'Fear not …'"

*Fear not? So says the Lord who created me? The same one who took my father! And my mother!*

Yet another memory invades Lilith. Her father had been sick and weak for so long that upon his death, Mary—as she had been known then—and her mother lost their land. Though she later learned it was fewer than seven miles, to a little girl it seemed an endless trudge from the plains of Magdala to the fishing village of Capernaum. Mary carried only her doll, and much as she yearned for her mother to carry her, the woman was laden with a bundle of their clothes, household items, and a few meager personal belongings.

Most terrifying to Mary, her mother was unwell. She had apparently worn herself thin and frail by assuming her husband's duties as well as her own. The trek to Capernaum left her hobbling for days, even as she sought lodging and work in the fishing village. All she could find was housekeeping work in the wealthy district, where she and Mary were assigned a tiny servants' hovel and paid a few mites and food left over from the master's meals.

By the time Mary became a teenager, her mother was decrepit far beyond her years and unable to work. Mary took over her duties so they wouldn't lose their accommodations, but the master paid her even less, though she had come of age. Now a beautiful young woman, she became aware that men looked at her differently than they ever had before.

One day while shopping in the marketplace for her master, Mary endured a Roman soldier leering at her. Shaken, she hurried away. The next time she was in the market, however, she could not escape his advances. Even now, years later, she's tormented by the memory of his yanking her into a small room off the alley and having his way with her. His red garment and plume flash through her mind.

She dared not tell even her mother what had happened before the woman died a few months later. Mary found reasons to avoid the marketplace, which resulted in her being fired. True or not, she felt as if all eyes were on her and that everyone knew she had been violated. Any dream she had ever had to one day marry and have a family vanished. Forcing herself to search for work and a place to live, she eventually found her way to the Red Quarter and Rivka's inn.

Desperate to start over, she introduced herself to the African proprietress as Lilith and offered to take any job in exchange for shelter.

"You know what most of the women living here do for money, don't you, Lilith?" Rivka had said.

"I can only imagine."

"No, you can't. And much as my clientele might love thinking you were an option, I would not do that to you. You're not much more than a child. And the fire in your eyes scares me."

Her eyes scared her, too, so much that "Lilith" no longer looked at her own reflection if she could help it. And she couldn't tell Rivka of her spells either, when something or someone inside her made her shriek and spasm.

"I'm no one to fear," Lilith had told Rivka.

"I hope not. Who does your hair?"

"I do it myself."

"Could you do that for me?"

"I could try."

"Many other women here need the same service," Rivka said. "That might be worth a small room, even some food—not much."

Lilith proved as good with other women's hair as she was with her own, but she soon became aware that the public—men—lumped her with the others in their minds. She seemed to spend most of her time avoiding and evading them. All the while she wished she were working in one of the hairdressing establishments outside the Red Quarter, rather than in a dingy chamber not far from her own paltry room.

Fortunately, Lilith had endeared herself to Rivka and many of the other women in the inn before they witnessed her first spell. Every so often she felt overtaken—with what, she could not say. It started with a vague feeling of angst, and then of darkness, and she often blacked out, only to be told later that she'd screamed and thrashed about, sometimes growling, speaking with a man's voice, sometimes more than one at a time.

• • •

Lilith breaks into sobs anew, desperate to rid her mind of the images of her past. But it's no use. How could the God who formed her, created her, and admonished her not to fear, allow all that had happened to her? Desperate, she tries reading the parchment again. "Fear not, for I have redeemed—redeemed—"

The words offer no relief. Lilith feels anything but redeemed. She screams, ripping the parchment to pieces. Exhausted, she can stand the room no longer. Wiping herself down, she changes into an only-slightly-less-soiled covering, tucks the wooden doll in a bag, and ventures out. At an inconspicuous door on a dead-end street, she quietly raps a code. When the door opens a crack, she whispers a password and slips in.

This dimly lit secret tavern/apothecary, known to the regulars—mostly working men—as The Hammer, was named for Judas "The Hammer" Maccabeus, a legendary zealot who led a famous revolt.

Patrons hunch over their drinks and games of dice and knucklebones at tables crowded across the main floor. Casks of potables, jars of potions, and goblets of herbs dominate one wall.

Solomon, the African eunuch behind the bar, rushes to her, and she can tell by the look on his face that he's stunned at her appearance. "Lili! You're alive!" He embraces her. "We heard there was trouble. Come, sit."

"I can't stay long."

"I know. Please sit." He points to a bubbling caldron. "Fresh off the boat from Cypress."

It smells strong. Lilith says, "No, I don't have the strength."

"Come now. You know what they say—a mote of prevention ..." He pours a drink for her and mixes in herbs.

"There is no preventing this, Sol, and there is no cure."

"C'mon, Lili—"

"It's getting worse. Yesterday, they brought in a holy man, someone important—maybe even from Jerusalem. I remember only bits and pieces and flashes."

"A Pharisee?"

"He's a leader of the Pharisees. And he ran away in terror."

"One religious big shot's just as full of it as the next."

"No, I am in hell!" Lilith shouts, causing others to fall silent and look. She shrinks.

"I'm sorry," Sol says quietly, placing the cup before her. "Please—just try."

Lilith tilts her head in gratitude but ignores the drink. She remembers. "I brought you something." She hands him the doll from her bag.

"You didn't have to."

"It's for your nephew. Or one of your nephews."

"Thank you. Looks like it was loved for a very long time."

"It used to hold something valuable. I don't need it anymore."

"You're beginning to scare me," he says.

"You and everyone else." She sips from the cup and grimaces. "Oh, that's terrible!" Sol laughs and she smiles, but her chuckle immediately turns to a sob as she thanks him. He studies her as a tear rolls down her cheek. Dare she tell him she's come to the end of herself? She cannot go on like this. "There's something I need to do," she manages.

Someone hollers, "Eunuch!"

Before leaving to attend to his customer, Sol tells Lilith, "Listen to me—you drink that up. And the next one, and then the next one. And then you stay here till you feel better or till hell comes. And if it does, we face it together."

Lilith smiles her thanks and gives him a long, fond look—a goodbye. "Not if you were my worst enemy."

"Eunuch, we're thirsty here!"

"Okay!"

As Sol moves away, Lilith drains her drink and hurries out.

Chapter 13

# ONLY GOD HIMSELF

*Capernaum guesthouse, late afternoon*

Nicodemus sits preoccupied, plagued by his failure in the Red Quarter.

Zohara opens the wardrobe. "We'll be late to dinner."

He sighs, hand pressed to his forehead. "I know."

"You did everything you could for her. Now put it out of your mind." She makes it sound so easy.

"I can never forget what I saw."

Zohara approaches with a vestal garment and drapes it around him. "Tonight, you are an honored guest. Leaders will expect you to perform and to have your wits about you."

"Why?" he demands. "Why must I perform? First I perform for Quintus—"

"You taught God's Law—"

"—then for the soldiers! Then for the slum dwellers! And

this! What sort of performance is this? When did Shabbat become theater?"

Zohara returns to the wardrobe. "You are the Teacher of Israel." She points at him. "You do not have questions, you have answers. You have authority. You bring clarity, not confusion."

Nicodemus softens and gazes at the only person in the world he allows to speak to him this way. Scolding, but loving. "Come," he says. She stops and squints at him. "Come here." She slowly approaches again, and he gestures toward the wall. "Tell me. What do you see in the mirror?"

She looks, plainly just to humor him. "It is a cheap glass. I can barely make out anything at all."

He's lost in thought. "Sometimes I wonder if what we can know of Adonai and the Law is just as blurred. What if we're not seeing the whole picture? What if it's more beautiful and—and more strange—than we can ever imagine?"

Her face clouds over as she seems to study him. "That is the most ridiculous thing I ever heard. It might even be blasphemy."

She's wounded him. "It's just a thought," he says.

"And you will never utter that thought in public."

Now she has gone too far. Indignant, he says, "A man is free to question in his heart, Zohara."

"So, leave it in your heart!" Her eyes plead. "This is a serious engagement. They expect an erudite teacher, not a doubting, blaspheming fool."

Nicodemus busies himself, slipping on a ring. Finally, he mutters, "Others saw what happened in the Red District."

"What did they see? You rose to your rank on merit. You have dedicated your life's work to serving God—not to becoming Him."

That's true, he knows. But he can't avoid the larger truth. "I failed," he whispers.

"Stop it! It was a mistake to be there in the first place. From now on, stick to the academy. Leave exorcism to the exorcists."

Such wisdom! That's why he married her so long ago. "You're right. I should never have been there."

"You spoke the words; the demon did not respond."

"*Demons*. Many. Only God Himself could have drawn them out."

She's at the door, ready to go. "Nico!"

"I'm coming." And to himself, "Only God Himself!"

## Chapter 14

# DEFENSE

*The next morning*

Stood up by his driver, Matthew reluctantly sets out for his tax booth alone, exposed.

Meanwhile, Andrew tucks a small change purse into his tunic and heads for the same place.

Not far away, Simon peeks in on his slumbering wife before venturing out to accompany Andrew.

• • •

Back at the Hebrew school, Nicodemus can tell the students—and the faculty—see him in a new light. No longer leaning forward, eager for his wisdom, they seem to eye him warily. But there's a reason he bears the title and rank he does. He is nothing if not thorough and prepared, and he faces the controversy head-on.

Without preamble he says, "Your first thought might be that I should never have set foot in the Red District at all. And I would say you are probably correct. Often, we make decisions in haste in our desire to correct the lost soul. But—how to explain what happened when I was there? Brothers, when we follow God's Law to the letter, God is alive through us. Would you agree, pupil?"

"Yes, Rabbi."

"And He lives through you, and you, and you," he says, pointing, "*if* you follow His Law. Now, imagine—if you can—one who heeds only wickedness for a lifetime." He pauses to let them consider the unthinkable. "Demons root in wicked souls—as pigs in filth. A possession like this was fatal. And souls such as hers, sadly, are beyond all human aid."

Nicodemus affects an air of regret and pity, and he can tell he's won back both students and faculty. They are with him once more, perhaps even more fervently than before.

Chapter 15

# THE ABYSS

Lilith awakes in the squalor of her chamber at Rivka's place, unwilling—no, unable—to imagine facing one more day. Never knowing when another spell might manifest, she cannot even look at herself in the reflection. She neither bathes nor changes clothes. Rather, she gathers the torn pieces of the Scripture her wooden doll had borne for so many years—the so-called truth her father accepted with all that was within him.

What would he think of her now—who she is, what's become of her? She'd be unrecognizable to him. Is it true what others say—that she is actually possessed by demons? No question she can be violent, and victims accuse her of tearing their flesh. Do demons cause her excruciating headaches?

When had they overtaken her and become so much worse than those of her childhood? When she cursed God upon her father's death? When her mother's health so deteriorated that the young girl had to become the parent? When Mary was violated by the Roman? Had she somehow gotten what she deserved? And how was it that, even before she went to live in the Red Quarter, everyone seemed to know she was no longer bride potential?

How many times has she tried to repent, only to feel as if God Himself is repulsed by her? How she longs to return to her childhood wonder at the soothing words from the holy book!

But no. All is lost. Lilith cannot fathom a future with even one ray of hope. Is she sorry? Of course, she's sorry. Confused. Tortured. Without options.

"I repent! I repent!" she wails, but nothing ever changes. What more can she say or do? She can tidy her room, clean herself up, but to what end? She is what she is, and that's all she ever will be.

She has cried herself out and now kneels with the Scripture scraps balled in her fist. What would be the quickest way to end this, to end her, to do a favor to Sol and to Rivka and the others at the inn? Sol could concoct something to accomplish what she wants, but Lilith knows he will never do that. The irony of a eunuch being her only true male friend! What a nuisance she must be to him.

What is left to do, what scores need settling? She has left with Sol the last tie to her previous life and can only hope it might be of some amusement to one of his nephews. She tries to foresee any way to face one more tomorrow. But she won't be able to stomach even this room, let alone face herself. What must be done must be done now.

Lilith knows what to do and how to do it. Her last pleasant experience in this godforsaken city had been half a lifetime before, when she had first arrived. She'd heard of the spectacular view of the Sea of Galilee from a precipice fifty feet above one of the rocky inlets. She found even the climb invigorating, mostly due to the anticipation of the grandeur—which didn't disappoint.

The air had been bracing, the cloudless sky gleaming, the sea such a deep blue it took her breath away. She will not enjoy it today as she had then, because she is not the same person anymore. She doesn't even bear the same name. What beckons her to the cliff now are the jagged rocks below. They promise such sweet relief.

Lilith pauses in her doorway. How can she have endured this above-ground dungeon for an instant, let alone years? How close has she, or her visitors, come to death here? How she loathes every inch of this place, and how satisfying it is to shut the door on it forever!

• • •

The climb proves more treacherous, more difficult than when she was a teenager. Life has exacted such a toll on her body. But Lilith finds this only appropriate. She also finds it strangely gratifying that the weather is different too. With clouds stretching across the horizon, surely the view will be nothing like that first time.

As a young woman, Mary had been careful to stay at least fifteen feet from the edge. That will not be the case today. Lilith strides purposefully to the very limit of the precipice, hoping a gust of wind will propel her over the side. She peeks one last time at the scraps in her hand and lets them go. They jump and dance in the breeze toward the water.

Though she's sobbing now, knowing she will soon follow them offers a sense of closure. She regrets her life. There will be no regret in death. She closes her eyes and inhales deeply.

Her sandals hang half off the ledge, and she sways in the wind. One step and it'll be over. She leans forward, but a shadow moves across her face, and she peeks. A dove flaps above her, diving and soaring. Something compels her to follow it with her eyes. It flies lazily behind her, drawing her away from edge, away from the sea, away from the rocks.

## Chapter 16

# RUINED

As they walk through the city toward the tax booth, Simon is struck by Andrew's gloomy countenance. Simon says, "How much do you trust me?"

Andrew gives him a look. "With my life."

"Let *me* talk to the taxman."

"Talk to Matthew? I don't trust you that much."

"What if I told you I could save the boat and put us back in good standing?"

"Nope."

"You don't even know what I will say!"

"Don't care," Andrew says. "It's something foolish. And I'm finally ready to face this."

"You know, this affects me, too. Me and Eden."

"Maybe you should think of that the next time you feel like taking off for a week—"

Simon stops and glares. "That is so like you."

"—or playing knucklebones at The Hammer. Or cheating your brothers-in-law for some easy scratch!"

Simon leans and whispers in his ear, "I met a guy."

"Oh, really? Wow! Get the papyrus—Simon met a guy!" Andrew is loud enough to draw stares.

Simon's face clouds over and he points toward the square. "Okay, let's just go hand over our livelihood. I'm done."

"You're done?"

"As I'll ever be." The brothers join a long line of people waiting to pay their taxes, most appearing nervous, checking their documents or counting coins. Behind the bars of his booth, the collector hunches over his ledger. Gaius, the Roman guard, stands just outside, warily eyeing the line. Simon has fallen silent, determined to let Andrew fend for himself as they slowly edge toward Matthew. Finally, it's Andrew's turn, and Simon advances with him.

Andrew slides his receipt to Matthew, who carefully unfolds and studies it. "Your last tribute was collected the first month of summer?"

Andrew nods.

"Your account is therefore delinquent by"—he presses a thumb against his fingers, counting—"forty days. At a penalty rate of ten percent weekly—"

"Six weeks!" Andrew says.

Matthew's eyes are on the document and his ledger. "That's right. You're lucky to not be in jail."

Andrew looks stricken and turns to Simon, whispering, "He's saying sixty percent in penalties."

"What's that leave you with?"

"Simon, I came with about sixty percent of what I owe! I can't even pay the—we're ruined."

Simon smiles and nods. "Oh, now it's *we*?"

"It's a high number," Matthew says, finally looking up. "I say this based on your tribute history and"—with a knowing look at

Simon—"future prospects. How do you choose to square your account?"

Andrew hands him his change purse, which seems to repulse Matthew. He drapes a cloth napkin over it before hefting it. "Are there gems inside?"

"Just silver."

"Gold?"

Andrew hangs his head. Simon can't stand seeing him like this. He grouses to Matthew, "Just open the purse."

"This will cover about half of your penalty balance," Matthew says.

"Half the penalty?" Andrew says.

"My records indicate that you filed for an extension not once, not twice—"

Now Simon is engaged. "He just needed a couple of extra days, man."

Andrew whispers, "I'm ruined."

Matthew continues. "Extended rates compound at fifteen percent." He runs his finger across entries in his ledger. "As collateral, you've listed a fishing vessel and property at—"

Simon pushes Andrew aside. "All right, all right. I'm sorry, brother." He turns to Matthew, who still has his nose in the books. "What my brother didn't mention was our arrangement with Quintus."

That gets the guard's attention, as well as Matthew's. Matthew finally looks up from his work, as if seeing Simon for the first time. "You have business with Quintus?"

Simon nods. "Yeah, my brother's debt and a year *gratis*. For both of us."

Matthew looks rattled but also skeptical. "This will be verified with Quintus directly. If there's any inconsistency—"

"There won't be." The men lock eyes. "Now, can I get my brother's not-gold back, taxman?"

"This will be verified with Quintus. If you are misinformed—"

"I know, I know. You'll see."

Matthew uses the napkin again to hand back the purse. As the brothers turn from the booth, Andrew says, "What just happened?"

"Don't speak, just walk."

Chapter 17

# THE ARRANGEMENT

Simon and Andrew sit whispering under the cacophony of revelry at the crowded Hammer. Andrew has demanded to know what in the world Simon was talking about at the tax booth.

"Fishing didn't exactly go like I planned the other night," Simon says.

"What's that got to do with—?"

"I caught nothing. Net after net after net, empty. I catch a breeze around the point, and suddenly I know why the nets are empty—a merchant fleet. Six boats across. Netting everything."

"What'd you do?"

Simon leans closer and lowers his voice. "I followed them. Thought maybe I'd catch them sleeping, snatch a net during cleanup, but—it didn't work."

"Of course it didn't!"

"Desperate times, ya know? I even anchored and swam in, thinking maybe I could get scraps, but they loaded up like clockwork. Had carts with mules ready to move. So, I sail home, dock up, and wouldn't you know it? This sniveling Roman is standing on the shore. I couldn't believe it. They never bother patrolling on Shabbat."

"No, no, no."

"Yes, yes, yes. I didn't even bother trying to run."

"Good idea, considering how you run."

"Anyway—as he approaches me, I'm trying to figure out why he's even there. They don't care about any of our rules. Then I realize—they don't get the tax because we don't report any Shabbat catches. So, I tell him if he took me straight to Quintus, I'd let them know who caught more in one night than the guy they're arresting catches in a week."

Andrew holds up a hand. "Wait, wait, wait, wait! So—you offered to turn in fishermen?"

"No, not fishermen—merchants. And guess who walks up behind me—guess!"

Andrew stares, clearly not willing to bite.

"Quintus!" Simon says. "He's thorough, I guess. So, yes, we talked, and what I said to Matthew was real."

Andrew shakes his head, clearly disgusted. "I don't like it. It's dangerous."

"Yeah, well so is sleeping outside. Besides, what's a merchant ever done for you?"

"That doesn't matter. They are—!" He lowers his voice. "They are our people."

"We're clearing the way for the little guy—"

"*We*?"

"—leveling the playing field. Yeah, *we*!"

"*You* will be cursed if you inform on them. *We* are not doing anything."

Simon is done. "Andrew," he says, sneering, "that's fine.

Better get moving, though, if you want to catch the taxman. Might still be enough daylight to get out of the house before they take it." Simon stands abruptly and stomps out.

Andrew pounds his fist on the table and follows.

## Chapter 18

# REDEEMED

*Outside The Hammer*

Even after years of a squalid existence, Lilith has never felt so grimy. Her hair hangs in clumps; her face feels caked with grunge. Her woolen tunic is weeks past needing to be burned, let alone washed.

If anything, she is in a darker place than she had been at the precipice. She remains disgusted with her failure to follow through with that plan, and she's determined to return to the cliff, this time without hesitating. No memories, no contemplation. Just a rush to the edge and then over.

But her eyes are fixed on the sky. Lilith has been seeing that dove, the one that seemed to distract her from her resolve and lead her away. Or has it been just her imagination? It, or something, seems to lead her even now. But to The Hammer? Why? One of the few sympathetic faces in her life is there. But she already bade Sol farewell once.

She hesitates near the door, and a man rushes out. His face is clouded, his teeth gritted, and he's followed by another man who looks similar enough that Lilith guesses they might be brothers. The second man bumps her without a word and keeps moving. She wonders if these men can see what she sees in the sky. Not likely. She's gone, she fears, from worthless to crazy. Whatever diversion she finds in The Hammer, nothing will keep her from the cliff—and the rocks—this night.

The knock and the password get her in, and she moves directly to the bar, where she sits and lowers her head. Sol approaches, asking whether his concoction from last time brought her any relief. She shakes her head, a sob in her throat.

"I'm sorry, Lilith."

A swarthy tradesman staggers up, drink in hand, and leers. "Lilith?"

She eyes him. Not this again. "What?"

"We should—talk, eh?"

Even if she were what he thinks she is, why in the world would he want her, especially in her obvious state? She makes a face and turns away. "Leave me alone."

"Or what, huh?" he says, nudging her. "You gonna scratch me, too?"

Sol says, "Come on, not now."

"Sol, she's—"

"Not. Now."

The man hesitates, and Lilith fears he'll cause a row. But he takes a swig and says, "Fine. She smells anyway."

As the man toddles away, Sol gazes at her, sadness in his eyes. He whispers, "I don't know what else I can do to help you."

Lilith nods toward one of his jugs. "Give me that. Lots of it."

"That's not going to solve your problems. It's meant to distract from them."

She glares at him. "No more preaching. Just give it to me."

"Lilith. Please. Listen to what I'm say—"

"Please," she says, tears rolling now.

Sol shakes his head, pity in his eyes. He sighs and pours and sets the cup before her. But before she can reach for it, a man's hand covers hers. The drunk again? She turns. "I said leave me al—" But it's someone else. A bearded face with a kind, knowing expression.

With a slight shake of his head, he says, "That's not for you."

Lilith yanks her hand from under his. "Don't touch me!" She grimaces, pressing her palms to her forehead. "Oh!" The torment! What—or who—inside her is so repulsed by this man?

"Lili?" Sol says. "Lili? Are you okay?"

She's far from okay, but she massages her head and says, "Yes, I—" She stands and grabs her cup. "I have to go." She faces the stranger, her mind ablaze. Quietly now, she says, "Leave me alone."

She stumbles off, taking a big swallow from her cup while still clutching her head. At the exit, she glances back. The man follows her. These men! "Leave me alone!" Lilith rushes into the deserted street.

He calls after her. "Mary!"

Mary? She stops dead, her back to him, unable to move. How could he possibly …? Not a soul in Capernaum knows her real name.

"Mary of Magdala," he says.

She stops breathing and drops her cup. It smashes to pieces on the ground. Slowly, she turns and stares. This cannot be happening. He's looking at her in a way she has not felt since childhood. With compassion.

"Who are you?" she says. "How do you know my name?"

He gazes at her calmly, knowingly. What is this? *Who* is this? Who could have told him about her? He says, "Thus says the Lord who created you …"

He even knows the passage she'd memorized as a child! Is it sorcery? Her head feels about to burst. If ever she felt invaded—

"... and He who formed you ..."

This must stop! She cannot make sense of it, and she feels a spell coming on. Does this man, whoever he is, know he could be her next victim? Or a victim of whatever indwells her?

He slowly advances. She can't move. Her skull throbs. Everything in her opposes this man.

"Fear not, for I have redeemed you."

She stares in wonder. Is he claiming to be the one who created her? That's blasphemy, isn't it? Whatever is within her wants to attack him, and yet, in spite of herself, she feels bathed in love.

"I have called you by name."

Yes, he *has* called her by name! But how?

He reaches her, seeming to peer into her soul. "You are mine."

Despite the rage in her soul, still she cannot run or scream or fight. This is how she feels before her spells! But she also longs to belong to someone, to become someone's "mine."

He takes her face in his hands and she gasps, nearly collapsing. The bedlam marshalling inside her menaces as if it—they—want to destroy her, kill her, and him. But the stranger gently draws her to his chest and envelops her, making her his. He whispers urgently to everything, everyone, that has possessed her, "Be gone!"

And as she begins to sob, whatever has tormented her for so long gushes from her, leaving her empty and spent—and free from pain. Her knees give way. Buoyed in the embrace of her liberator, she is no longer Lilith. Never truly was. Never will be again. Despite her filth and stench and failure, she feels new. Wholly new. She's Mary again—cherished, forgiven, delivered, redeemed.

# PART 3
# Shabbat

## Chapter 19

# EVERY SEVEN DAYS

*Nearly 1,000 years prior*

The fenced city of Chinnereth lies south of Capernaum on the northwest shore of the Sea of Galilee, then known as the Sea of Chinnereth. In a nearby Bedouin valley camp, as the sun begins to set on a Friday, an extended family prepares tables outside their tents for dinner—as do their fellow tent dwellers up and down the ravine. A dozen men—young, middle-aged, old—mill about as the women busy themselves in last-minute preparations. Two tables are laden with challah bread and wine. These families, like their fellow Jews everywhere, will observe Shabbat from when the first star appears until three stars appear the following night.

A Rebbetzin lights candles as her eight-year-old grandson and her husband stand nearby. The boy points. "I see a star!"

His grandmother smiles but doesn't look. "And if you think I'll fall for that, Eli, you must think I was born yesterday."

"Was there a Shabbat when you were little?" Eli says.

"Of course! Since the time of the Covenant."

"Every seven days? Why so many, Savta?"

"Shabbat is a time for rest," she tells him. "And a time to honor three things—family, our people, and God."

"Family like Savta and Saba?"

She turns to him. "Yes, and you, Ima, and Abba, of course. Close friends are like family, too."

"Who else?"

"We honor our fellow citizens on Shabbat."

"Strangers, Savta?"

"We're all God's people. Even friends we haven't met. But most importantly of all, we honor God and all His works. We rest because He rested on the seventh day. We rest to refresh our souls to know Him better."

From behind her comes a voice she knows well. "Woman of valor!" her husband, the rabbi, says. "Who can find her?"

Work stops as the entire family listens. The Rebbetzin whispers to Eli, "This is the Eshet Chayil. An ode to women of valor."

Her husband continues, "Far beyond jewels is her value. Her husband's heart trusts in her, and he should lack no fortune."

Eli's eyes grow wide, and he points to the sky again. "There!"

As the others look and murmur, the Rebbetzin lays a hand on Eli. "May God make you like Ephraim and Manasseh."

A young man places his hand atop his daughter's head. "May God make you like Sarah, Rebecca, Rachel, and Leah."

Every man there pronounces the same blessing on his children, even grandfathers to their grown sons and daughters.

As they all sit, the rabbi stands and pours wine into his cup and passes the jug. As it makes its way around the table, he quotes the Scriptures about the heavens and the earth being completed on the sixth day and God resting on the seventh—blessing it and making it holy. He finishes, "Blessed are You, Lord our God, King of the universe, who creates the fruit of the vine. Amen."

Chapter 20

# BUTTERCUP

*Capernaum, circa A.D. 30*

Mary, even when hiding behind her Lilith alias, has always appreciated Rivka—has seen in her a core of decency, of compassion. Oh, the woman can be as tough as the jagged iron Tribulus the Romans use in battle. And the authorities largely ignore her, especially if they want to keep private their own visits to her establishment.

But Rivka is also fiercely loyal and watches over her tenants—regardless of the services she offers her patrons through them. She checks in on Lilith regularly and has never pressured her for more than hairdressing in exchange for meager lodging and enough shekels to eat on.

The morning after her encounter with the stranger, Mary gently taps on Rivka's door. "This had better be an emergency!" Rivka bellows.

"Oh, no, sorry!" Mary says. "It's only me. I can come back."

"Lilith!" Rivka calls out, suddenly softer. She sweeps open

the door. "You know you're always welcome. I just have to scare off intruders."

Rivka points to a chair. "Drink?" she says.

"No, thanks. I won't keep you long. Just want to talk."

Rivka studies Lilith's face. "What's got into you? You look different somehow. I didn't think you could look younger, but—"

"That's what I want to talk to you about."

Rivka sits across from her. "Tell me …"

Mary gushes her story, from her sad childhood to the deaths of her parents, the rape, all of it.

"I knew a lot of this," Rivka says, "but not all."

"You were so kind to let me stay here, even after my spells started scaring everyone and affecting your, um, business."

"Neither of us was very popular for a while," Rivka says. "But it wouldn't have been right to abandon you to the street."

"I would've understood. And I'll bet there were those who wish you had."

"I can't deny that, but you ought to know by now, I rarely do what I'm told. Now get to the good part. What's happened to you, Lilith?"

"First," Mary says, "I need you to call me by my real name." And she brings her story all the way to the night before.

Rivka furrows her brow. "You know I don't go in for demon possession and all that. The Pharisee they paraded in here proved that was a bunch of—"

"I didn't know what to think myself," Mary says. "But last night was different. You'd feel differently about all this if you were me."

"Well, the stranger at The Hammer had some kind of impact on you, that's clear."

"Stranger is right, Rivka. I don't even know his name."

"That's not good, Lil—Mary. How do you know he isn't some kind of—?"

"I was as suspicious as you are, but he knew me! He called me by name."

"But someone could have told him—"

"Rivka, no one knew. No one. If I'd have ever told anyone, it would have been you. But he went way beyond getting my attention by knowing my name. He delivered me. I felt not only cleansed, but also forgiven!"

"Careful now. I'm the last person to be mistaken for religious, but even I know a man cannot forgive—"

"I'm telling you how I feel, what happened to me. Whatever has been inside me is gone. My headaches, the turmoil, gone!"

Rivka looks dubious. "It hasn't been a full day yet. Let me keep an eye on y—"

"You said yourself you saw a difference in me."

"I do, but—"

"I beg of you, Rivka, don't diminish this."

"I don't mean to. I just care about you and—"

"I know."

"Can I at least meet this man?"

"I'd introduce him to everyone I know, but I have no idea if I'll ever even see him again. But, yes, of course, if I do …"

Mary stands to leave, and Rivka embraces her. "You need clothes that fit the new you." She digs a few coins out of a cup.

"Oh, no, you—"

"Come on now, let me do this," Rivka says, pressing them into her hand. "Clean yourself up. Make your hair as pretty as you make everyone else's. And get yourself a new tunic and mantle. I want you to look your best when I recommend you to the hairdressers near the market."

"Do you mean it?"

Rivka chuckles. "Don't I always say what I mean?"

• • •

*Three weeks later*

Mary of Magdala attends customers at a hair salon just off the Capernaum market, serving wine to patrons. The owner has hired her on Rivka's recommendation, certain her new, sunny countenance makes her an asset. And who knows, maybe one day she'll graduate from helper to hairdresser. Already she has earned enough to afford a small place of her own, away from the Red Quarter.

Mary watches an apprentice braid hair and whispers, "You're so good at that."

"Mary!" the young woman says with a smile. "You try."

"Oh, no! No, I can't—"

"Yes! I have seen you braid Leah's hair. You are wonderful. Go ahead."

Mary smiles sheepishly and takes over, secretly thrilled. When she finishes, she asks the apprentice, "How'd I do?"

The apprentice tells the patron, "Told you she was excellent! It's a shame only Ananias will see it." As Mary reapplies the woman's light gray veil, the apprentice says, "You know what would be great? Do we have any flowers?"

Mary loves the idea. "I'll get a buttercup," she says quickly, and to the patron, "Don't move." She rushes outside into the dissonance of the bustling marketplace, where merchants and buyers interrupt each other in a variety of languages. In her haste, Mary brushes into people in the crowd, apologizing as she goes. She's scouring the square for the flower of David, the hardy buttercup that flourishes even in this climate. One would look perfect in the woman's hair.

• • •

Yusef, student of Shmuel—chief rabbi at the Hebrew school—enters the marketplace in his pharisaical garb, striding deliberately, head high. Having to show subservience in his superior's presence, he can't deny he enjoys the attention here. As soon as people see him, they fall silent and make way for him, heads bowed. He pretends not to notice.

But now someone else has distracted the public. A beautiful woman seems in a hurry. She's picked a yellow flower and holds it briefly under her nose, smiling. As she works her way back through the crowd, he can't take his eyes off her.

It can't be, can it? So familiar! Finally, Yusef gets a clear view of her. Stunned, he can only stare. It's her! The woman from the inn who had caused such a disturbance that Nicodemus himself had been sent to try to deliver her.

But now she's glowing! She looks years younger, and while her garb is plain, it's also pristine. She shines head to toe.

He wants to speak with her, to ask her what has happened. But she's entered the hair salon where the patrons have their heads uncovered. Yet there's no doubt in his mind. It's Lilith. He hurries off, unable to contain this news.

Chapter 21

# DOMINUS

*The Roman Authority, Praetor of Capernaum's headquarters*

Gaius, as he does at the end of every tax-collecting day, escorts Matthew—laden with his bag, ledger, documents, and proceeds—to the crowded steps leading to the treasury, where the fastidious little man turns in his takings. Only today, Matthew insists Gaius gain him an audience with the praetor himself.

"Just let me see if Quintus can verify their story!" Matthew says.

More than exercised, Gaius is scared. Helmet tucked under one arm, his other hand on the hilt of his sword, he's determined to talk Matthew out of this lunacy. "If those Hebrew sea rats were lying, Quintus will have them killed and collect their tribute—from you!"

But plainly, Matthew will not be dissuaded. He continues to insist until finally they reach the ornate anteroom just outside the atrium. Gaius tells him to wait while he approaches a centurion captain. "We need to see Quintus immediately," Gaius whispers. "It's urgent, a matter of life and death."

Matthew fidgets, trying to avoid other Roman guards who roughly push past him. The captain shoots him a look of disgust. "See to your dog," he says to Gaius.

When Gaius returns, Matthew asks him what the captain said.

"He detests you as much as I do."

"And?"

Gaius shakes his head. "This was a horrible idea."

"Gaius, we must see Quintus!"

"Or what? He does not need to clarify anything for you. And do you have any idea who—no, clearly you do not. Dumb question."

"Idea of what?"

"Who you are dealing with!"

"Yes, I do!"

"Really."

"Yes," Matthew says. "He is the Roman occupying overseer of this region, and his primary responsibilities are to enforce the law and ensure financial stability."

"I am aware of his responsibilities! I don't think you know what he's capable of—"

"And if he's made a deal with this Simon person, I have valuable information related to his job."

"Have you ever heard of somebody making a decision based on a hunch?" Gaius says, sweating and peeking around like a trapped animal.

"If he has," Matthew says, "then I must let him know."

Incredible. How is it possible this man can be so naïve? He'll have to learn the hard way. "Yes. You must. But listen, I don't want to have to carry your corpse out, so I'm gonna wait outside for your replacement. Good luck!"

"I don't understand."

"You are a fool!"

Twenty feet down the hall, Gaius hears Quintus and slowly turns to face the praetor.

"Publicanus requests an audience?" Resplendent in his uniform and munching grapes just outside his lavishly appointed chamber, Quintus looks to Matthew. "Publicanus?"

"Yes, Dominus," Matthew says.

"Are you his escort, centurion?"

Caught, Gaius can barely speak. He whispers, "Yes."

With a haughty smirk, Quintus spreads his hands. "So, where are you going?"

Desperate to invent something, anything, Gaius haltingly tries, "Securing—the passageway, Praetor."

"Aah," Quintus says, dripping with sarcasm. "Well done!" He invites them in.

Convinced Matthew will not survive this, Gaius fears for his own future as they step into the candlelit office. A mural depicting the whole of the Roman Empire covers one wall. The captain Gaius had spoken with stations himself behind Quintus.

Standing at his desk, Quintus says, "So, a Jew tax collector and his escort demand to see the praetor of Judea. It's urgent, they say. A matter of life and death."

Gaius laments that he overstated their case with the captain. He can see his career hanging in the balance.

Quintus continues, "Last night burned very hot, and today I'm ash, so I'll get to the point. Why should I not kill you both?"

Gaius knew it. It's going to take everything in him to endure this, let alone to leave here alive. Matthew appears oblivious until Quintus points at him. "You first."

Gaius prays Matthew will know enough to just beg the praetor's pardon and slink away, but no. He clearly thinks this is his chance. "Dominus," he begins, "I was recently approached by a man while at my tax collection b—"

"Faster!" Quintus says, idly opening a small scroll.

"He was many months delinquent. To relieve the substantial amount of debt—"

"Skip to the end!"

"Did you hire a man to spy on Jewish merchant vessels fishing on Shabbat to avoid taxation?"

Quintus looks up slowly. "Yes. Simon. He's in your district?"

"He is."

"His debt's forgiven. Surprise!"

Gaius breathes relief and turns to go, pleading with the gods that Matthew will be wise enough to come as well. He wanted confirmation of Simon's claim, and now he has it. But of course, Matthew wants more. "As well as those of his brother?"

It's obvious Quintus can't believe the two are still here. "His br—? Yes. Forgiven. Goodbye!"

No one could miss that dismissal. Gaius bows. "Thank you for your time, Praetor."

"I do not find Simon reliable!" Matthew blurts, and Gaius closes his eyes. They had almost escaped! But Matthew speeds on. "Once he was deficient in his taxes, and when I pursued remedy, I discovered that he had spent an inordinate amount on games of chance at a local establishment." Quintus stares at him, visibly amazed at his audacity. But Matthew is not finished. "Additionally, based on his financial status, I question Simon's connections to the merchant class. In spite of his current intentions, I do not believe you have an accurate understanding of what he can deliver."

The centurion captain unsheathes his sword and rushes toward Matthew as Gaius drops to his knees. "I'm sorry for this dishonor, Praetor!"

“Say your last prayer, Jew!” the centurion barks.

“Stay there a moment, captain,” Quintus says, eyes remaining on Matthew. “Are you saying I made a bad deal?”

Gaius, still on his knees, prays Matthew will notice his shake of the head. Do *not* criticize the actions of this man!

“Yes,” Matthew says.

The silence seems eternal, and Gaius pictures his and Matthew’s hacked bodies hauled from the building.

But Quintus bursts into high-pitched giggles, staring at Matthew. He glances to the captain. “Where did he come from?”

Gaius wonders the same. Who speaks to an authority like this?

“Here,” Matthew answers. “Capernaum, Dominus.”

Quintus seems to study Matthew. Finally, he says, “My brothers across the world search for brave men to spare and recruit. But our power prohibits those very efforts, for what sane person would stand up to the Roman Empire?”

“I am sane,” Matthew says.

“Yes,” Quintus says, still obviously amused. “But a very different kind of sane.”

“I’m sorry, I don’t understand, uh—”

Quintus sits behind his desk as the captain steps back, replacing his sword, and Gaius stands.

“So,” the praetor says, “you say this Simon isn’t at the level of the merchant class at sea, but he claims they all spend time at the same establishments. Is that false?”

Gaius can’t believe Quintus converses with Matthew as if he’s other than a lunatic.

Matthew says, “I’m afraid I’m not aware of their social interactions. But even if that were true, it would be highly unusual for Jewish men to betray one another.”

"So says the Jew who collects taxes from them," Quintus says.

"Mine is a different circumstance, I—"

"Spare me, I admire it. Well, it won't surprise you to learn that, to date, Simon has not fulfilled his obligation to uncover the tax evaders."

"He's in breach of contract?"

"Not yet. But time may prove you out, uh—what are you called?"

"Matthew, Dominus."

"I may yet have need of your keen powers of observation, Matthew. A special assignment."

"I would relish the opportunity, Dominus."

"Of course you would," Quintus says, grinning. "I'll be in touch, Matthew of Capernaum."

"Thank you, Dominus."

"Thank *you*."

Matthew appears to want to say something more, so Gaius drags him out before he can utter another sound.

Chapter 22

# REPRIEVE

*The Hammer*

Simon turns from the bar, two drinks in one hand, one in the other, and announces to a group of merchants reveling over a game of knucklebones, "All right, a round for the table!" They cheer and tease him as he entertains them. "All you need is to have a good time!"

"What is this about?" one calls out.

"I can't celebrate my brothers"—he shrugs and points to one with long hair—"and sisters? Sol, make sure Amos gets a cider. He can't handle the good stuff! Tobias, Jason, you'll need this to drown your sorrows after you lose this game. And you, I don't know your name, you're new—but wow, huh? We're not afraid you'll steal our fish, we're afraid you'll steal our women! Look at this mane—like Absalom, no?"

Simon throws the dice.

"Hopefully he fares better than Absalom!" one shouts.

"Stay away from low-hanging branches, my boy," Simon says.

Jason laughs. "Stay away from steep staircases, old man."

"That's it, Sol, none for Jason!"

Baruch says, "Oh, what did he do this time?"

"Ask your wife!" Jason answers, and the rest roar.

Simon grabs two cups from Sol and turns to leave.

"Drinking alone again, Simon?" one says.

Simon smiles and lifts the cups. "Well, you merchants need twice the help at sea, I need twice the help on land."

Veteran fisherman Zebedee's sons enter, one tall, the other short. "John!" Simon coos. "I see The Hammer changed its rules on allowing children!"

"Go get caught in a net," John fires back.

"But you're here with a responsible adult! Sol, make sure James and John get some, too!"

He makes his way past them and joins Andrew at a table in the corner.

Andrew's disgusted eyes bore into Simon's. "What is that?"

"Whatever do you mean, brother?"

"Your face. You happy?"

"No," Simon says. "I'm handsome. I just happen to be wearing a happy face."

"Buying drinks for the merchants—you fattening your lambs before the slaughter?"

Simon shakes his head and affects a dour expression. "Better?"

"I don't want you to be miserable," Andrew says.

"You are, so I should be, too, no?"

Andrew leans forward. "I want you to be serious. This is not a game."

"Nothing wrong with enjoying a little financial freedom, a temporary reprieve from doom."

A heavyset fisherman claps Simon on the back. "That double knockout was a shame."

"Thanks, Hori," Simon says, trying to humor him.

"Get your footwork down and next time you'll see—"

"Yeah, I'll practice. Thank you, Hori, thank you."

The fisherman finally moves on.

Andrew gestures. "*Temporary* reprieve."

Simon grows serious, whispering urgently. "Believe it or not, I don't like it either. But these men, they're not family. You and Eden are my responsibility, not them. You two keep me up at night, not them."

Andrew stares at him. "And you want to be rich."

"Yeah, well, I thought I'd try the sentimental route. Maybe it's not my best look."

## Chapter 23

# SANHEDRIN AUDIENCE

*Torah room, Capernaum Hebrew school*

Nicodemus sits in a corner, bathed in the light of a half-dozen candles, reading and taking notes on demons and exorcism. He's startled when the chief rabbi shouts his name.

"Grief!" Nicodemus says, quickly stacking his documents as the man rushes in. "I'm studying! Was!"

"Apologies, Rabbi!"

"What is so urgent, Shmuel?"

"The judges of our Sanhedrin send for you."

Oh, no! Have they been told of his failure with the woman, Lilith?

"The Av Beit Din himself requests your presence," Shmuel adds, his eyes filling.

Nicodemus breathes in the news. The chief of the court, second only to the Nasi? His mind reels. After decades of service, building a pristine reputation—might it all end here in this little town? What might the Capernaum Sanhedrin tell the Great Sanhedrin in Jerusalem?

"God is good!" Shmuel adds.

How can the man consider this good news? "What happened?" Nicodemus says, but Shmuel appears too overcome to speak.

Dreading whatever is to come, Nicodemus determines to face it, head high. He rushes out and cuts across the quad to where Capernaum's council of judges meets. Shmuel follows closely, trailed by two other rabbis. Why they appear so buoyant, Nicodemus cannot fathom.

He enters to find six judges sitting in a half circle with Yusef—Shmuel's rabbinical student—kneeling before the chief. Has he reported Nicodemus' fiasco?

"Rabbi Nicodemus of the Great Sanhedrin, we are greatly honored by your presence."

"The honor is mine, Av Beit Din," Nicodemus says, eyes darting, trying to figure this out. "I was given the impression there was a matter of some—urgency?"

"We are considering a formal inquiry …"

So, he has been found out. But he's not about to see a lifetime of service to God dismissed without a fight. "What are the charges?"

The Av Beit Din appears nonplussed. "Wha—? A miracle, Rabbi of Rabbis!" He points to Yusef. "This man's testimony is clear, his account miraculous. The woman in the Red Quarter to whom you offered rites." He raises his hands. "She's redeemed!"

Nearly speechless, Nicodemus looks to Shmuel, then to Yusef. "You saw her?"

"Yes, Teacher," Yusef says, clearly overcome. "Perfectly restored and radiant—"

"Wait!"

"—at the hairdresser's salon at the market."

This is the last thing Nicodemus expected, and he's convinced it's not true. He's gone from dread to anger. "Men are not allowed at the hairdressers!"

"Of course, I did not go in, but she was on an errand. I believed my eyes betrayed me, so I followed until I was certain. There can be no doubt!"

"Teacher," Shmuel says, "it was successful! I told you—"

"Silence!" the Av Beit Din says. "This is unparalleled revelation. You yourself pointed out that the depth of her demonic oppression was beyond human aid. We want to send word to Jerusalem at once."

Oh, surely not yet! What if it proves false, or worse, temporary? Nicodemus fears he will look like a fool. "Av Beit Din," he says, trying to keep his voice from trembling, "with your permission, I would like to investigate this sighting myself—before you conduct a formal inquiry into this or have news of it spread."

Another judge attempts to whisper something to the Av Beit Din, but the chief judge waves him off. "We will, of course, yield to your request, but may we inquire as to the reason for your reticence?"

Nicodemus hesitates, knowing he must tell them something other than his own recollection of the incident, which would indicate that if anything happened, it wasn't *because* of him but *in spite* of him. He speaks deliberately, as if carefully thinking this through, while in truth, he's making it up as he goes along. "Just as this exorcism took some time to prove effective, it may have a tentative hold. It could come as a shock for a young woman of her station to be pored over by your learned judges, whereas mine is a familiar face."

The Av Beit Din studies him and nods. "It is decided. Conduct your investigation, but please, be efficient. News of this kind—it grows legs."

Chapter 24

# CHOICES

*Shore of the Sea of Galilee, 3 a.m.*

Simon sits in the sand next to Andrew under a brilliantly clear, star-filled sky, a shawl draped over his head against the cold. But a heavy fog has rolled in over the water, and he's trying to peer through it. His brother nods and dozes off, his head plopping onto Simon's shoulder.

"Andrew! Andrew, will you help me please!"

"Help you with *what*? I can barely see anything."

Simon can't argue with that. "Of course, it's the foggiest night in weeks." He sighs and stares out at the sea. "All right, we saw Hori, Chaim, and Baruch come in, offloading and cleaning their holds." The ghostly outline of a ship slowly glides toward the docks.

"Of course!" Andrew says. "Tomorrow is Shabbat."

"Well, there's still a fleet out there. They're sailing late because they're not cleaning out the holds tonight. They're definitely sailing tomorrow. I'm guessing it's Amos."

"This is all a waste of time if it is."

"What do you mean?" Simon says.

"What I mean is Gideon and Tobias sail with Amos."

That nearly silences Simon. Andrew clearly implies that they are friends, so Simon would never betray them to the Romans. *Well, I don't have to like it,* Simon tells himself. *But I can do it.* "I'm not saying it's Amos for sure. Whoever that is, they're definitely sailing tomorrow. We got 'em."

He can tell from Andrew's look that his brother can't believe what he just heard. And here it comes. "We got 'em? Those are our brothers! Tobias looks to you before his own father!"

Simon knows that's true, but he's beyond favoritism, beyond having a choice. He must keep his resolve. "So what? It's my fault a dumb kid doesn't know better?"

Andrew bores in on Simon, who can't meet his stare. "I keep waiting for you to tell me this is all part of a plan to double-cross the Romans."

"Andrew! There is a crew out there. That crew is stealing food out of Eden's mouth! They're gonna take our boat—maybe our lives!"

"Maybe. But we made our choices too."

Simon refuses to hear more. "You think this was a choice?" He flings off his head covering and stomps away.

## Chapter 25

# ONE LANGUAGE

*The Capernaum guesthouse, Friday morning*

Nicodemus finds Zohara applying lip color as he steps into the dressing chamber. Can he speak to her transparently, as he has enjoyed doing for decades? The Pharisee has never felt such angst.

"You're not teaching today?" she says.

"I have research." In truth, the last thing he wants to do is be the center of attention among guests. To think he used to actually enjoy the fawning, though of course he always feigned deep humility. But now the Red Quarter, and the woman there, have humiliated him.

"Now, don't be too long. Our guests will be arriving early."

He grunts, unable to hide his impatience.

"Nico! They are dear colleagues who admire you. They have been waiting weeks for the Teacher of teachers to lead Shabbat. It will be like sharing loaves with God Himself."

Had she really said that? Sharing loaves with God Himself? He sighs in disgust. "Am I the only one hearing this?"

“It’s a small gathering,” she says. “You’ll just go through it quickly.”

Oh, yes, speed through the ritual. That makes a lot of sense. “I’ll try to avoid spending too much time honoring God and our heritage.”

Zohara has apparently missed the sarcasm, applying gold dust to her hair. Nicodemus heads out toward the Hebrew school, where he plans to study in the Torah room.

• • •

The Roman guard Gaius strolls through the crowded market, snacking on fruit he steals from right under the nose of a merchant. What’s a Jew going to do about it? He quashes his own conscience, knowing that if he were consistent, he would speak out, even against his superiors, when necessary. Somehow, flaunting his bravado by cadging a bite or two from lowly Jews feeds his ego.

He spots another centurion trying to break up a fight by attempting to reason with scuffling men who ignore him. Gaius rushes toward them, nearly tripping when the blind beggar grabs his boot and shouts, “Are you the Messiah?”

Gaius jerks his foot away and moves in behind one of the combatants, drawing his sword. He lifts it high and thunders the hilt down onto the man’s head, dropping him like a stone. The other fighter appears to consider a move. Gaius points the blade at his face. “Do you want to lose that ugly nose of yours?”

The man runs off, and the other centurion says, “Thank you.”

“Only one language keeps their peace, Marcus,” Gaius says, replacing his weapon. “Learn to speak it.” Impressed with his own creativity, he wonders when he will be noticed, promoted.

Moments later he arrives for his duty at the collection booth, only to find the taxman nursing a battered face.

"Matthew!" he calls. "Another unhappy citizen expressing his disapproval?"

"I'll be fine," Matthew says, and Gaius can tell Matthew wants to blame the attack on him for being late—as usual. Matthew tries to scrub away feces someone has flung onto the hem of his tunic.

The smell reaches Gaius. "Oh! You're disgusting! Go home!"

"I have a job to do. My father never allowed me to shirk responsibility."

"Well, he raised you right. He must have Roman blood."

"We don't speak."

Gaius waits for more, but Matthew appears lost in reflection. "Jews are odd," Gaius says.

"People are," Matthew says.

"How can you not have a relationship with your own father?"

"He says he has no son," Matthew says, standing to face the citizens waiting in line. "Next!"

Chapter 26

# MEETING THE PHARISEE

Mary of Magdala enters the hair salon carrying a box. The proprietress, Leah, and her apprentice are preparing the place for the day's business. Mary says to Leah, "I got them. At least, I think they're right. It's what everyone else was getting."

"Oh, what did you get, Mary?" the apprentice says.

"Shabbat candles."

"Okay—I would not have guessed that."

Leah says, "It's Mary's first Shabbat dinner in a little while."

"In a *long* while," Mary says. "I barely remember how to do it."

Leah smiles at her. "You'll be great."

"I know how to make the bread," the apprentice says. She shrugs. "Part of it."

Leah laughs. "How do you make part of a loaf of bread?"

"If you're hosting Shabbat, sweetheart," the apprentice tells Mary, "you'd better get moving. Preparations might take you all afternoon."

"Really?" She remembers too little from years past.

"Just to be safe," Leah says.

"I haven't even swept," Mary says.

"Get out of here." The apprentice grins.

"Get the fire going, first thing," Leah says.

"I'm excited," Mary says. "And a little terrified."

"After you knead, rest the dough!" the apprentice says.

"With this kind of advice," Leah teases, "what could go wrong?"

Mary wishes them *Shabbat shalom* and ventures back into the street.

A man stops her. "It's you! It's real!" He's dressed in religious vestments and looks her up and down. "Lilith!"

Mary blanches. Not this again! She turns away.

"No, no, please! Don't be frightened. My name is Nicodemus. I—I ministered to you, Lilith."

She faces him, repulsed by the address alone. "I don't answer to that name. I am Mary. I was born Mary."

"But you were called Lilith, yes?"

Could this be the holy man from Jerusalem, the one who fled? She had vowed to never again even think of that horrible day. "Please, I must go."

"No, no, please! I am desperate for your help, Mary." He steps back, seeming to try to appear less threatening. "I'm a Pharisee. I'm visiting from Jerusalem. I'm a man of God. And I believe you have experienced a miracle, Mary."

He seems genuine. "Are you really a Pharisee?"

He adjusts his cloak to reveal his tallit. Is he even allowed to speak with her in public? Mary quickly covers her head. He apologizes and assures her he's not there to enforce Jewish law.

"So, how do you know who I am?" she says.

"You really don't remember me at all," he says, wonder in his voice. "I burned incense—"

"I don't remember. It's all a blur. I can't go back into that."

She moves away and he follows, sounding most earnest. "No, no, I don't want you to. I can't even imagine. But you are healed." That stops her. "That much is clear. I just want to understand how it happened."

"That makes two of us," she says, smiling.

"How long after my visit did you feel a change?"

She hesitates. Mary doesn't want to hurt his feelings, but she must be honest. "It wasn't anything you did. It was someone else."

The holy man appears thoroughly puzzled. "Someone else?"

This she does enjoy revisiting, and her eyes fill. "He called me Mary. He said I am his. I am redeemed."

Nicodemus stares. "And it was so?"

Overcome, Mary can only nod.

"Who did this?"

"I don't know his name," she says. "And even if I did, I could not tell you."

"Why not?"

Mary wants to remember what the man said, the way he said it. She recites, "His time for men to know has not yet come."

It's obvious this baffles the Pharisee. "'His time for men ...'?" he repeats. "He performs miracles and seeks no credit?" Questions rush from him. "What does he look like? Is he a member of Sanhedrin? Would you at least know him if you saw him again?"

That makes her chuckle. "I don't know why I am sharing this with you. I don't understand it myself. But here is what I can tell you. I was one way, and now I am completely different. And the thing that happened in between was him. So yes, I will know him for the rest of my life."

Nicodemus stares, wide-eyed.

"I have to be home to prepare for Shabbat," she says, "as I'm sure you do."

He shakes his head. "So mended you're even hosting Shabbat dinner!"

"It will be nothing like yours, I'm sure of that. But I'm going to try." She can tell she has rattled this man. She smiles. "Shabbat shalom, Nicodemus."

As she leaves him, she hears, quietly, "Shabbat shalom, Mary."

Chapter 27

# BAITING

Simon pads into the kitchen where Eden cuts vegetables, her knife loudly hitting the table with each chop. He knows she knows he's there, but she's not acknowledging him. How can he win her over? He sidles up behind her, rests his chin on her shoulder, and kisses her cheek. "Good morning, love," he coos.

"It's not morning," she says, still chopping.

*Uh-oh.* He'll try a compliment. "Good first-seeing-you, then," he says, reaching past her to break a piece of bread from a loaf and tuck it into his cheek. "Mm, your bread is wonderful."

"I know," she says, her back to him still. "How's fishing?"

"It's fine."

"Really?"

"You're surprised?" he says as he pulls on his sandals.

"Why would I be surprised?" she says.

"I don't know. You tell me."

"You haven't taken a catch to market for days."

He cherishes her like nothing else on earth, and he has always discussed business with her. So what's this? He nods toward the table filled with food. "And yet you have flour, vegetables. Did you sleep in a warm bed last night?"

"In fits," she says.

He's had enough. "Why are you baiting me?"

She turns to face him. "I don't understand what's happening."

"Nothing is happening."

"You don't sell to market, your hours are upside down, and your face is frozen in worry. Don't tell me nothing is happening!"

"We're—in a challenging season right now. I just need to work hard to get through it and I'll get caught up tonight and I'll be right on the way—"

"Tonight? What do you mean?"

"I'm not happy about this either. I need to work tonight so that—"

"You need to work on Shabbat!?"

"It's a special circumstance. I can't get into it right now. Andrew will be here for dinner as normal, and I'll just be gone for a few hours."

"Oh!" she says. "Well, would you like me to fix you a Shabbat plate to take with you?" Her words drip with sarcasm.

"Listen, love, I know this is not ideal—"

"Don't 'listen, love' me! I'm not a child."

"I just need you to trust me on this. Please?" She looks unbending. Simon steps toward her, pleading with his hands. "Look, I've—I've got this, Eden."

She stares him down and speaks evenly. "You answer to God, not me. But next time, you answer to the both of us. Because whatever this is, I don't have the strength for it twice."

## Chapter 28

# SURPRISE GUEST

Just before twilight, Matthew makes his way down a narrow alleyway, gingerly carrying a covered dish, napkins protecting his fingers. He's dressed down, more like the taxpayers he faces every day, and lost in thought. And longing. Might his parents and his sister welcome him to Shabbat dinner? A man can hope.

They had given him the Hebrew name Levi, no doubt intending that he grow up to become a revered priest. He was not cut out for that, he knew. And he grew weary of poverty. Unfortunately, most profitable professions involved more interactions with others than Levi found comfortable. But numbers and analysis came easily to him, and he found he could force himself to deal with people if he concentrated on their finances and government regulations. He focused on details and rarely even had to look anyone in the eye.

Levi thought he had done the family a favor, sparing them ridicule by using his Greek name, Matthew, upon becoming a tax collector. He needn't have bothered. Everyone knew who he was and what he was, and his family suffered the same scorn he endured every day.

But could they not forgive him? Could they not be proud of the child prodigy he once was? Was he not still their flesh and blood? Did they not still love him as he loved them? He remained a Jew, even an observant one. But that was not enough. Not nearly enough. His father, Alphaeus, had made that clear.

"Turning your back on us, extorting your own people …"

"It's not extortion! It's—"

But the man had stopped him with a raised hand. "Do not speak to me as if I am your father. I no longer have a son."

Time has not healed the breach, and Matthew can't deny his new station—and income—makes it almost worth the derision. Almost. The jeers he hates but can at least endure. Losing his family is another matter entirely. And so, on this Shabbat eve, as he has done every week for years, he ventures out toward the humble dwelling where he had been raised. Matthew has abandoned the illusion that his father might soften, but his mother? His sister? Might they not prevail upon Alphaeus?

He will not force his way in, intrude on their celebration, will not even knock. But he will be visible outside, bearing food to share. That has to say something, serve as a gesture, at least. Though it has never worked—in fact, most Shabbat evenings no one even glances out the window—he will not give up trying.

Near the end of his exclusive northern district neighborhood, Matthew hears a whine behind him and turns quickly to find his own large, black dog with its eyes on his dish. He stops, wondering how the dog escaped the house. He thrusts out a hand, palm up. The dog halts.

Matthew decides on a reasonable approach, which often works on irate citizens—though it hadn't that morning. In gentle, even tones, he says, "If there's any left when I come back, I'll give it to you." The dog cocks its head, and Matthew believes it has somehow understood. He turns back to his route, and the dog stays.

When he finally reaches his family's home, through the window he watches his mother set a steaming bowl on the candlelit table, and his sister sets down two loaves of challah. He's immediately transported to childhood Shabbat dinners—celebrations he took for granted, or wearied of, which now draw him like a moth to flame. What might he trade to be welcomed back to this weekly celebration?

His father takes his place at the other end of the table, facing the window. With one glance he would see his son, but he never looks up. And Matthew's mother and sister never turn. Matthew could not be more disappointed or feel any more rejected if one of them had come and closed the curtain in his face.

He trudges back toward home.

• • •

Meanwhile, at the Capernaum guesthouse across town, Nicodemus and Zohara are dressed resplendently. As servants set the Shabbat meal on the table, Zohara informs their guests of the history of many of the artifacts in the room.

Nicodemus stands apart, studying a tapestry on the wall. He's still smarting from his conversation with Zohara that morning, but he's even more conflicted by his encounter with Lilith, Mary, the once-demon-possessed woman from the Red Quarter. She is living proof that Shabbat should be all about God, not finery, not impressing guests.

Zohara says, "... from an artisan, this is the last from a long line of traditional works that his family has made." She points to the candelabras. "Solid gold from the finest goldsmiths." And the tableware. "I hope you will enjoy eating off these beautiful plates."

She excuses herself and approaches Nicodemus. "What's on your mind, love?"

He nods to the tapestry. "Do you know the significance?"

"Tell me," she says.

"Two hundred years ago we were ruled by the Greek King Antiochus the Fourth. He suppressed our religious observances. It wasn't until the Maccabees revolted and ushered in the Hasmonean dynasty that our worship was restored."

She gazes at him with a smile. "You're as smart as you are handsome."

He looks past her to the table, where guests of all ages take their seats. "So, who is responsible for suppressing our worship now? I fear I know the answer."

"Well," Zohara says, "it is a beautiful tapestry. Should the artist have made it less so?"

*Good question.*

"To what purpose?" she continues. "Sadness? A conquered people?"

She's good for him, he knows, softening. "You are as wise as you are beautiful."

A knock at the door draws Zohara away. A middle-aged couple greets her. "Shabbat shalom, Rabbanit."

Zohara returns the greeting, as does Nicodemus.

"Oh!" the man says. "Honored Rabbi! We are humbled and honored by your presence at Capernaum. You make us whole."

Again, more reverence for the man of God than for God Himself. Nicodemus waxes severe. "Only God can do that."

Zohara breaks back in, clearly eager to ease the tension. "Shall we join the others?"

"Thank you," the woman says.

Her husband whispers, "Try to get a seat at the head of the table."

Nicodemus shakes his head, grateful it's time to begin. "A woman of valor, who can find?"

• • •

Mary's small, sparse home—new to her—is night-and-day different from the squalid room at Rivka's inn that had been hers for years. She's spent the afternoon making it clean and tidy. She started a fire in the ancient fireplace and now finishes setting out chipped clay plates and mismatched wooden cups. Near the center of her table, she places a white rose in a tiny ceramic vase. She's ready, she thinks, but it certainly won't be fancy.

A wood-on-wood knock tells her who her first guest will be. "Oh, Barnaby!" she exults when she sees the one-legged beggar who has used his crutch to rap on the door.

"Mary!"

"Come in! I'm so glad you came."

"Oh, thank you, Miss Mary. This is a fine place!"

"Are we on?" a woman calls from outside, feeling her way to the door with her walking stick. "Is it still on?"

"Yes! Shula!" Mary says, reaching for her. "How did you find us?"

"I followed that mule, Barnaby. Not that he waited. Looking as handsome as ever, Barnaby."

"Lucky guess, Shula," he says, chuckling as she finds his shoulder and caresses it.

Mary hears a young man speak outside. "Is this the place?"

"If Mary's here, it is," another says.

She approaches. "Do I know you?"

"Sorry," the shorter one says. "I'm James. This is Thaddeus. We were told this would be a good place to come. We can leave if it's awkward."

"Oh, no, please come in," she says. "You are most welcome here."

"So, can we help?" James says.

"Ah, no. Well, yes, I don't know what I'm doing."

"I see food," Thaddeus says. "That's a victory."

"If I'm not doing something, or doing something wrong, please tell me."

"Oh, nonsense," James says. "It's already great."

Shula speaks. "I can't remember the last time I was invited to a Shabbat dinner."

"Me, never," Barnaby says, as all sit but Mary.

"You've never been to Shabbat?" Shula says.

"'Course I been to one. Been to lots. Just never got invited!" As everybody laughs, Barnaby adds, "Who's the extra seat for?"

"Oh, ah, for Elijah!" Mary responds. "Am I right? I remember my mother always setting an extra place for Elijah."

James whispers, "That's only for Passover."

"Just once a year at Seder," Thaddeus tells her.

Thoroughly embarrassed, Mary says, "Oh! When Seder comes, I'll have a head start on setting up."

She gathers up some crinkled bits of parchment. "I'll just take a look at my little notes. Let's see—"

Barnaby says, "Can I read it for you, Mary?"

"Stop it, Barnaby," Shula says. "*I* read better than you."

"My father taught me," Mary tells him.

"Very impressive."

She looks up from her notes. "Oh, is the first star out?"

"Yes!" Barnaby says. "Let's eat!"

A knock comes on the door. Barnaby grins. "You are very popular."

"Or," Shula says, nudging him, "it's a Pharisee here to shut us down for letting *you* be here."

Mary opens the door and freezes.

"Hello, Mary."

It's him. The man who healed her. "Hello," she manages, having wondered if she would ever see him again.

"It's good to see you," he says.

"Yes," she says, staring. "Yes." She smiles, unsure what to say or do next.

"I don't want to be rude," he says, "but would it be okay if I . . . ?"

"Oh! Yes, of course! Please, come in." As they approach the table, she adds, "I just never thought you'd, um—I have guests here, this is my first time, I don't know what I'm doing."

James and Thaddeus immediately stand and greet him, calling him Rabbi.

"You already know these men?" she says.

"They are students of mine," he says. "I trust they have been polite."

"Of course."

Another awkward pause passes as they all look at each other. Shula breaks the tension. "Your guest can take the empty seat, yes, Mary?"

"Of course! Yes, of course, please have a seat. I keep saying 'of course.' Um, friends, this is the man I told you about, who—" Mary pauses, "who helped me."

"Oh, yes!" Shula says. "Mary told us so much about you."

"I hope not too much," he says with a smile.

"I'm Barnaby. This is Shula." Then, in a whisper he adds, "She is blind."

"Aah."

"In case you couldn't tell," Shula says, elbowing Barnaby.

"I'm so sorry," Mary says. "I don't actually know your name."

"I'm Jesus," he says. "Of Nazareth."

"Well," Barnaby says, "apparently something good *can* come from Nazareth." He bursts into laughter.

But no one else laughs. James and Thaddeus look stricken, and Mary shakes her head at Barnaby. "What?"

Jesus winks at him and says to Mary, "I'm honored to be here. Why don't you begin?"

"Oh, no, I couldn't. Now that you are here, you must."

"Thank you, but this is your home, and I would love for you to do it."

Something about the way he speaks, with such compassion and understanding—and authority—floods her with peace. "Okay," she says. She sits and takes up her notes again. "I'll just, uh, I'll just read from this now. 'Now the heavens and the earth were completed and all their host. And God completed on the seventh day His work that He did …'"

• • •

At the Capernaum guesthouse, Nicodemus finishes the same passage, as does Andrew in Simon's home—as Simon sits fidgeting, eager to get going—and Matthew's father at his home: "'… and He abstained on the seventh day from all His work that He did. And God blessed the seventh day, and He hallowed it, for thereon He abstained from all His work that God created to do.' Blessed are You, Lord our God, Ruler of the universe, who creates the fruit of the vine. You have lovingly and willingly given us Your Shabbat as an inheritance and memory of creation, because this is the first day of our holy assemblies in memory of the Exodus from Egypt. Blessed are You, Lord our God, King of the universe, who brings forth the bread from the earth. Amen."

• • •

Simon rises and gives Eden a quick peck on the cheek, which she does not return. And he's gone.

• • •

And, no surprise to Matthew, the dog waits for him in the street near his home. Matthew presses his back against a wall and slides to sit on the ground. *How appropriate*, he thinks. The man his countrymen call a dog shares Shabbat dinner with his own kind.

# PART 4

# Jesus Loves the Little Children

Chapter 29

# ABIGAIL

The man who identified himself to Mary and the others at her Shabbat dinner as Jesus of Nazareth has informed his friends that he will be away, alone, for several days. He feels God, his Father, leading him to a time of solitude and prayer in preparation for the next phase of his calling—a public ministry. Jesus has found the perfect location, a clearing on the outskirts of Capernaum, near water and with plenty of wood. Here he can sustain himself and seek his Father's will for all that is to come.

He has brought his woodworking tools, a few clothes, and a tent. As he busies himself setting up camp, his heart is heavy, weighed down by the enormity of the task before him. He occupies his mind by erecting a tent and building a roaring fire, but he also looks forward to simply conversing with his Father in heaven. With everything in place, he assembles a fishing pole and sets out for the stream. After a sundown dinner of fried fish and berries, he finds himself weeping. He has seen such need from so many, and he can barely contain his love.

"Father," he cries out, lifting his eyes to the stars, "glorify me with Yourself. Speak through me." As he thanks God for both the privilege and the responsibility of the mission he has been called to, the monstrous nature of it makes him shudder and steady himself against a tent pole.

As the night wears on, he grows weary and reclines in his tent. The seclusion and isolation of this place magnify his loneliness as he drifts off to sleep.

• • •

*The following morning*

Nine-year-old Abigail bursts out the door of her parents' ramshackle home. She carries a doll made of yarn and skips through the yard, past a rooster and a tethered goat. She calls over her shoulder, "I'll be by the stream!"

"Do not swim!" her mother says.

"I won't!"

Abigail runs and hops and skips through the thigh-high grass behind the house, her long hair flowing in the breeze. She flits through familiar territory until she hears the gentle stream, then skids to a stop. Between the water and her lies a tidy campsite that hadn't been there the day before—tree stumps, branches, animal skins, and rocks neatly assembled. The remains of a fire smolder in a pit near a tent, but a work area draws Abigail. She looks around, approaches, and kneels before a leather pouch containing woodworking tools. Wood shavings and sawdust lie all around.

She toys with some of the tools, then replaces them and uses a wooden spoon to pretend to feed her doll. Near the firepit, she finds a tiny toy boat and plops her doll in it, pretending it's sailing away. A cloth sack contains berries, and she play-acts offering her doll the food. She's tempted to taste one herself but thinks better of it.

At the sound of footsteps and humming from beyond the tent, Abigail leaps up and runs for cover behind a rock outcropping. A pleasant-looking man about her father's age arrives, carrying a knapsack. As he pulls fruit from it to put on one of the makeshift tables, he stops humming and looks at Abigail.

She gasps and sprints away.

• • •

*That evening*

Jesus let his fire burn out as he worked during the day, and now he must start a new one to prepare his meal. He expertly spins a wood rod into a small hole and gently blows a spark into hay kindling. All the while, he's thinking of the cute little girl he'd seen that morning. How nice to have even her elusive company for a few minutes. He feels a deep affection for youngsters.

He cooks a stew of legumes and vegetables while slicing fruit. He places a small pan of bread directly into the fire, wishing he had someone with whom he could share this simple meal.

• • •

Abigail sits at dinner with her parents. She's amused by her mother, who doesn't seem to notice that her elaborate story about a friend is clearly not impressing Abigail's father.

"... and Joanna just isn't doing better," her mother says, "which will mean she will have to see if they will give her space to sell her headdresses at the market. And even if they do, which doesn't seem likely because last time I was at the market it looked full, she has to find time to make them.

"But she needs to focus her time on helping him get better so he can return to work before they give his job to someone else. Oh! She just seemed so scared. Do you think you could stop by tomorrow to see if she needs help with anything?"

Just as Abigail thought, it appears her father hasn't been listening closely. "Hm?" he says, mid-chew.

Her mother looks him full in the face and carefully repeats, "Can you stop tomorrow to see if she needs help with anything?"

"Joanna?"

"Mm-hm."

"I have to stay late myself," he tells her. "I don't have time to—" He sighs. "I will see."

"Thank you. It will mean so much to her. You know how she gets." She turns to her daughter. "Abigail, how was your day?"

Abigail doesn't dare mention the man camping by the stream. He looked harmless enough, but … "It was fine. Can I play with Joshua tomorrow?" She'd love to show him the man.

"Only after you finish your chores—"

"I know. I will get it all done first."

"Don't interrupt," her father tells her.

"I'm sorry, but after second meal, may I go?"

"I will ask his mother," her mother says. "And where will you go?"

"Um—just the field. Maybe the stream."

"No swimming."

"I know. And chores first."

Chapter 30

# JOSHUA

Abigail and her friend take the same route she had taken the day before, but she's in a real hurry now and jabbering away. "And there was one tool I've never seen before. I don't know what it's for. I think he was building stuff. I don't know. And there was some food, too, but even though I was hungry I didn't take any because that would be wrong, but maybe we could take a little bit this time, what do you think? But I'm glad I didn't, because that's when the man got there. Come on, go faster!"

"I'm trying, Abby," Joshua says, panting, "but your legs are going too fast."

"If he comes this time, shall we say something to him? I think, if you're with me, it's okay. I didn't see a sword or anything like that, so I don't think he'll kill us, and he seemed nice. Do you have a sword, just in case? Oh, we're almost there! Here it is!"

They crouch behind the rock outcropping and peer around it. The man sits at one of his little tables, bread in his hands. "Blessed are You, Lord our God, King of the universe, who gives forth bread from this earth." He breaks the bread into his lap.

"And I pray that if there are ever two children who come visit my home here …"

Joshua taps Abigail's arm and mouths, "Let's go!"

"No!" she whispers. "Stay!"

"… that You will give them the courage to say 'Shalom,' so that they will know they do not have to remain in hiding. Amen."

As Abigail whispers, "He's a good man!" the man grunts loudly. The children try to hide their giggles, but he quickly follows by blowing raspberries, making them laugh aloud.

He stands and says, "What's that sound I hear? Sheep don't sound like that!" He bursts forth with more sounds, and they laugh all the more. "No, that's definitely not sheep. Maybe a rooster?"

He moves toward the rocks, and finally Abigail stands, smiling. Joshua stays hidden.

"Greetings, children!" Jesus smiles at Abigail. "You know, it is not safe for a child to wander from her home. You never know if there are bad men around. You were wise to bring your friend this time."

"Joshua," Abigail tells him.

"Shalom, Joshua!" the man says. Joshua rises into sight but does not respond. "I admire your bravery to come here. You are a good friend. But don't worry, I'm not a bad man."

"See?" Abigail says. "I knew it."

"You are free to stay for a bit, but I'm afraid I have some work to do."

"Okay," Abigail says.

"And thank you for not taking any food yesterday." He hands her a bowl of fruit.

"See?" she says, grinning. "I knew it!"

Joshua steps out into the open but stays behind Abigail. "So," she says, munching, "what are you doing here?"

"I'm visiting for a time."

"Where are you from?"

"Nazareth."

"What is that wood for?"

"I'm building something."

"Are you a carpenter?"

"Sometimes, but I am also a craftsman. I build all kinds of things."

"So why don't you live in a house?"

"I travel a lot."

"How do you make money?"

"Abby!" Joshua whispers.

She shrugs. "I'm just asking him how he makes money."

"I know. You shouldn't!"

"It's okay," the man says. "I don't make money when I travel. So, for now I build things and trade them for my food and clothing."

Abigail points to the piece in the man's hand. "What is that?"

"This is going to be a lock and key."

"Joshua, ask him questions. He's nice."

"No, thank you."

"What else will you build?" she says.

"Wealthy people love decorations, and toys for their children."

"My family isn't wealthy," she tells him.

"Many times that's better."

"I don't know about that."

The man laughs. "You will."

She shows him her doll. "My mom made me this."

"Oh! What's her name?"

"Sarah."

"Very pretty."

"Okay," Abigail says, handing him back the fruit. "Time to go home. Bye!" Abigail and Joshua run off, leaving him laughing.

Chapter 31

# MORE QUESTIONS

*The next morning*

Jesus stirs from a sound sleep at the sound of whispers.

"Just leave him alone!"

"Is he dead?"

"Shh!"

He opens his eyes to half a dozen children staring down at him—two boys and two girls are new to him. He's groggy but amused. "You couldn't have waited half an hour, eh?"

"Can we be around today?" Abigail says. "These are my other friends. And Joshua again."

Jesus sits up. "Shalom, Abigail's friends. And 'Joshua again.'"

"Shalom," they say in unison.

"*Can* we be around today?"

In truth, he'd love the company. But he thinks about this. "I suppose. But I have some work to do. You might have to help." They all nod. "Good," he says.

Jesus approaches the stream, the kids a few feet behind, peppering him with more questions as he brushes his teeth with a rough cloth and washes his face.

One says, "How much longer are you going to stay here?"

"Until it is time for me to go."

"When's that?'

"Well, I have some work to do here and some people to meet, and then I will know the right time."

"You seem nice. Are you dangerous?"

"Hm, maybe to some. But no, not to you. And I won't harm anyone."

"Do you have friends?"

"A few. And more to come."

Jesus starts on a craft and assigns the children their own little chores.

"Abby said you travel a lot. Do you have a house?"

"My Father provides everything I need."

"Is your father rich?"

If they only knew. He chuckles. "Did Abigail tell you to ask me that?"

"No."

"That is a question for another time."

"What's your favorite food?"

"Oh, Joshua the Brave speaks!" Jesus says. "I like so many different foods, but I especially love bread. For many reasons. How are those spools coming along, girls? Good? The string, is it tight?"

He has to smile. They don't sound so sure. "Almost?" he teases.

"Almost."

"Okay. So, tell me, do you all know how to pray the Shema?"

"Yes."

"Oh, I would love to hear it." He points to one of the new boys. "You lead us."

As the lad begins and the others join him, Jesus is suddenly overcome by the precious little voices, and he mouths the words along with them, lips trembling. "Hear, Israel, the Lord is our God, the Lord is One. You shall love the Lord your God with all your heart and with all your soul and with all your might. And it shall come to pass if you surely listen to the commandments that I command you today, that you may gather in your grain, your wine, and your oil, and you will eat and you will be satisfied. I am the Lord, your God, who led you from the land of Egypt to be a God to you. I am the Lord, your God. Amen."

He can barely speak. "Beautiful," he whispers. "Very good."

As they continue working on their projects, Abigail says, "So, why don't you have a home?"

"My home is many places."

"Why?"

"Because I have a much larger job than just being a craftsman or teacher."

"You're a teacher, too?"

"I will be soon." He both looks forward to that and dreads it. Only those who have ears will hear, so to speak.

"What other job?"

"Everyone has a much larger job than just their trade. And you are more than just students. You are at school to show love to one another, and to take God's Word and to share it. And at home, to honor your father and mother. And most important, from the Law of Moses, to love who?"

"The Lord, your God," Joshua says. "With all your heart."

"Very good, Joshua the Brave! I will be doing my work in many places."

• • •

*Late that afternoon*

As Abigail leads the two younger girls, Joshua, and the two other boys across the fields toward their homes, they talk over each other, seeming to try to make sense of the kind man they're getting to know. "Maybe he's the best builder who ever lived!" one says.

"Or maybe he's stronger than Samson!"

Abigail says to the boys, "Maybe he's going to be your new teacher at synagogue school."

The youngest girl pipes up, "I think he's maybe a new prophet, and he'll show us the Word of God."

"No." Joshua shakes his head. "There's no new prophets. Rabbi Josiah said so."

"But maybe he's a murderer," one of the other boys says.

Abigail turns to face him. "He is not!"

"But maybe that's why he's by himself! He's running and hiding and—"

"Yeah, and probably he's pretending to be a builder so no one will know!"

"That's not true!" Abigail says. "He's building stuff *with* us! We're watching him do it!"

"Yeah, he's smart," the youngest girl says. "We should listen."

"But maybe we're even helping him build weapons," one of the other boys says, "and we don't even know it."

"No!" Abigail says. "He's a good man."

"I think so too."

"I like him," the boy says. He shrugs. "I'm just saying, maybe he's a criminal."

Abigail turns and the others stop behind her. "But no matter what, we all agree. We don't tell anyone about him. Right?"

Chapter 32

# "MY REASON"

Over the next several days, the children join Jesus daily. He works with them, teaches them, fishes with them, eats with them, prays with them, and even teaches them songs. When he tells them stories from the Scriptures, especially about other children, he dramatically acts out the parts, roaring like a lion or standing to lumber about like a bear. Their delight and laughter warm him, and they pepper him with questions for hours. How gratifying to have this time of preparation to speak to people of all ages. If he can make the children understand, adults should understand as well. He feels especially drawn to them, their inquisitiveness, their straightforwardness. He loves them.

Around a campfire at about midday, he teaches them a new prayer, which they repeat after him. "Our Father, who art in heaven, hallowed be Thy name …"

He finds himself melancholy each afternoon when they head back to their homes. He hears them as they retreat, telling each other what they learned and what they think about it all. How dear they have become to him! He loves their openness, their willingness to listen, their lack of guile. He smiles at the thought that with children, you always know what's on their minds.

They spend the better part of one day gathering up all the items he has crafted and loading them onto a wood sled he has built—which he uses to pull his wares into town the next morning to barter for food and clothing. It takes him all day and evening, and he misses his small companions.

When he finally returns after dark, he sits alone with just the sound of the wind, the water, and the fire. He dresses and wraps a gash on his forearm. His back and shoulders and arms ache from all the work, so he stretches as he prays for the children. He can hardly wait for dawn and their arrival. He also prays for the multitudes he will speak to before long, and then he sleeps soundly.

• • •

The next morning, the irrepressible Abigail—her five little friends in tow—asks him what they'll be working on today.

"Absolutely nothing!" he announces, a twinkle in his eye.

They moan. "Why? What will we do?"

"Today is a day of teaching and learning. Who should do the teaching?"

"You! You!"

"Oh, very good! Then who should do the learning?"

"We should!"

"Gather around. Make yourselves comfortable. And be ready to listen carefully."

"Can we ask questions?" Joshua says.

"You just did!" They all snicker. "But of course, you may! That's how the best learning happens. Just raise your hand whenever you want to ask me something."

In the middle of his teaching about the commandments, one of the boys raises his hand and tells of a recent fight for which he had been punished. He's animated, telling them how unfair it had been, because the other boy had been mean to him.

"So, what did you do?" Jesus says.

"I tried to walk away, but he wouldn't stop pushing me, so I pushed him so hard he fell down."

"And that's why you were punished," Jesus says. "Did you expect something different?"

"But even Torah says, 'eye for eye.' Why should I be punished too?"

"Yes, but that is for a judge! You were hardly in a court of law. And you—all of you—are to be special. You are to act differently from others."

Joshua raises his hand. "You tell us to be gentle, but Rabbi Josiah said Messiah would lead us against the Romans, that he would be a great military leader."

*Aah, religious leaders.* Jesus sighs and proceeds delicately. "It is important to respect your teachers and honor your parents. And Rabbi Josiah is a smart man." He lets that sink in. "But many times, smart men lack wisdom. Is there anything in Scripture that says Messiah will be a great military leader?" The kids are plainly puzzled. "There are many things about Scripture that you cannot understand yet, and that is fine. You have many years ahead of you, and God does not reveal all things at once. But, children, what if many of the things that our people think about how we are to behave, and how we are to treat one another, are wrong?"

Jesus points at the boy who told the story. "You want things to be fair. When someone wrongs you, you want to right it. You know who else loves justice?" He points to the sky. "But what does the Lord say in the Law of Moses about justice and vengeance?"

Abigail raises her hand. "Vengeance is Mine."

"Yes! Very good! Very good. Boys, pay attention. She doesn't even go to Torah class, eh?" He laughs. "The Lord loves justice. But maybe it is not ours to handle. Do you remember when David had the chance to kill King Saul, who was evil to him? But he didn't. Saul was God's anointed, and it was not the right time for justice. God says He will have compassion on His people when, what—?"

Abigail raises her hand, but Jesus winks at her. "Let's see if someone who studies this at school is learning, eh?"

"When their strength is gone," Joshua answers.

"Yes! Very good! So, maybe we let God provide the justice, hm? Maybe we handle these things in a different way, not trying to be the strongest all the time."

"Even Messiah?" one of the girls says.

Jesus shrugs. "You will have to see. But do not expect Messiah to arrive in Jerusalem on a tall horse, carrying weapons. And he will be most pleased with those of you who are the peacemakers."

"Where were you yesterday?"

"I had to stay in town late. There was a woman who needed my help."

"Did you build something for her?"

"No. You remember when I said that I have a job that is bigger than my trade? There is a woman who has had much pain in her life, and she was in trouble, so I helped her."

"Is she your friend?" Joshua says.

"She is now. I have chosen her, and others, and more soon, to join me in traveling."

"Do they know you?" Abigail says.

"Not yet."

"But what if they don't like you?"

Jesus laughs. How much to tell them? "Many won't. This is my reason for being here."

Abigail sighs. "I still don't understand. What is your reason for being here?"

So, there it is, the question of the day, and asked by a child. In truth, Jesus knows, it's the question of the ages. He pauses, praying they understand the weight of his answer. He lowers his voice to make them lean in and really listen. "I'm telling you this, because even though you are children and the elders in your life have lived longer, many times adults need the faith of children. And if you hold on to this faith, really tightly, someday soon you will understand all of what I am saying to you.

"But you ask an important question, Abigail. What is my reason for being here? The answer is for all of you." He pauses again. Then, just above a whisper but with conviction, he says, "The Spirit of the Lord is upon me, because he has anointed me to proclaim good news to the poor. He has sent me to proclaim liberty to the captives and recovering of sight to the blind, to set at liberty those who are oppressed, to proclaim the year of the Lord's favor."

"Isaiah," Joshua says.

Jesus nods. "Isaiah." He presses his lips together and gazes upon the six young faces, a sob in his throat. "I have loved spending this time with you. You are all so very special. I hope that my next students ask the same questions you do and that they listen to my answers." He smiles. "But I suspect they do not have the understanding you do." He looks directly into Abigail's eyes. "And I hope that when the time comes, they will tell others about me, as you have."

The children head home together, in silence.

Jesus works late into the night, knowing how deeply he will miss these little ones. When he finally retires, he includes in his prayer, "Should anyone cause them to sin, may he have a great millstone fastened around his neck and be drowned in the depth of the sea."

• • •

*Dawn, the next day*

Abigail, running alone with her doll, rounds the outcropping to find Jesus' campsite abandoned. Not far from the cold firepit, she comes upon a well-crafted dollhouse of wood, stone, and rope. It contains little carved animals, a tiny ladder, and a table with a swatch of cloth covering it. Atop the house, written in charcoal on a piece of wood:

*Abigail, I know you can read. You are very special. This is for you. I did not come only for the wealthy.*

# PART 5
# The Rock

## Chapter 33

# THE ACCIDENT

*Sea of Galilee, the wee hours of Shabbat*

Simon sits in the bow of his and Andrew's boat, the lifeline to their livelihood. He is repulsed by the presence of five Roman soldiers in brilliant red, four of them rowing. The other, a Quintus lackey, perches at his shoulder. The praetor of Capernaum has long since lost patience waiting for Simon to make good on his end of the deal. Simon and his brother have been forgiven their considerable tax debts and granted a year's reprieve in exchange for Simon's promise. So, he will lead them to real criminals—merchants who violate Shabbat to avoid paying their fair share.

Rome cares nothing about Shabbat, Simon knows. But for Jews to evade taxation, well …

The craft glides swiftly under the power of the massive arms of the soldiers. Simon would give anything for help like this while fishing, but he never hoped to have even one Roman aboard. It's as if he's invited poisonous snakes into his home. But it's his own fault. He stalled Quintus with excuse after excuse until the praetor assigned him this crew.

"Time to deliver, Simon," the man had said to him. "Or you and your brother will share a prison cell—or a grave."

This hadn't been Andrew's idea, though he would benefit from the arrangement. But Simon never considered bringing him on such a mission, so he alone has to satisfy the authorities. But can he really do it, turn in his Hebrew brothers for something he himself has done more than once? Is he no better than a tax collector, stepping on the necks of fellow Jews, men he has worked alongside for years?

He's spent his days in these waters since childhood. He senses things, smells things, long before laymen see them. Now, he feels boats nearby. He also spots something in the water no one else notices. Why does this night have to be so clear and quiet? "Whoa, whoa, whoa!" he says. "Slow down!"

The soldiers stop rowing, and the vessel drifts into a chunk of cork and its severed tether. If only his fishing comrades knew what he—and the Romans—were up to, they'd be more careful. They've left evidence in plain sight. Simon leans out and gathers it in.

"What is it?" the guard says.

"It's a fishing bobber."

"So?"

"So, that means we're close."

"Good job."

The compliment turns Simon's stomach. The last thing he wants is to be in league with these vipers. He's no better than they. His only advantage is that they are so far afield from their areas of expertise. The rowers caught on to their task quickly enough, and their brawn impresses, but they know nothing of this work.

In the light of the guard's oil lamp, Simon surreptitiously peeks at the bobber and turns it over. He and his cohorts carve their initials in these and agree to return any they find. His heart sinks when he sees the Z on this one. That means the delightful Zebedee is out with his sons, James and John, whom Simon and Andrew have known from childhood. Their fleet—or part of it—will be nearby with dozens of men.

*Am I really doing this?* Simon wonders. *Is it too late to continue misleading the enemy?* Eyes peeled to scan the dark horizon, he detects the ghostly outlines of three boats. All he has to do is tell the guard, and his future would be secure—his and Eden's and Andrew's.

But he can't. He just can't.

What becomes of Zebedee and James and John, not to mention all their men? And what of his own reputation? He would need that tax break for the rest of his life because his very name would be anathema on this sea. No one would work with him, buy from him, sell to him. Many would even sabotage him and Andrew—though this betrayal would all be on Simon.

"Hard to port!" he shouts, meaning away from where he's spotted their boats—and toward dangerous shallows. The guard looks back at the rowers, as if they should know what to do. But they look as puzzled as he. Simon points left in disgust. "This way!" How can they pretend to govern the waterways when they don't even know simple nautical terms? "Romans," he mutters.

Obviously believing they're on to something now, the soldiers pick up the pace in unison, racing through the water. Simon knows what's coming and braces himself.

*Crash!*

The rowers are thrown from their seats, the guard banging into Simon. "You stupid sea rat!"

"You hit a sandbar!" Simon says. "Why are you not listening to me? I told you to go this way!"

The guard is plainly not fooled. He orders his men into water up only to their knees to dislodge the boat and head for shore. Minutes later they're dragging Simon up the rocky beach. "Accidents happen, boys," he says jovially. "Nothing to be ashamed of."

The guard turns on him. "There was no accident. You know this sea better than anyone. That's why you smell of it." He draws his sword and presses it to the side of Simon's head. "I want you to remember this, Simon, son of Jonah. This is kindness." He flicks the blade and slices through Simon's ear. Simon cries out and yanks a hand free to stanch the gush of blood.

"Quintus, on the other hand," the guard says, nose to nose with him now, "is capable of savage violence against those who betray him. I can hold him off for a week perhaps." He smiles. "Think of Eden."

Simon narrows his eyes. He'll die before he lets anything happen to her. "If you even walk down the same road …"

The guard drives a fist into Simon's gut, doubling him over. "Make good on your promises, dog."

## Chapter 34

# CONFRONTATION

*The Hammer*

Simon has asked Zebedee and his sons to meet him for a drink. They join him and Andrew at the only table without a knucklebones or dice game in progress. Simon thanks the grizzled man for coming.

"Oh, the boys didn't have to twist my arm too hard to get me to have a drink." Zebedee gestures toward Simon's ravaged ear. "That business or pleasure?"

"Ah, this? No, ran out of bait. Figured I'd give my ear a try."

Young John and big James laugh before their father silences them with a look. "Maybe someone didn't like your sense of humor. Why are we here, Simon?"

*So that's how it's going to be.* Simon has long appreciated Zebedee's no-nonsense impatience with small talk. Might as well cut to the truth. "I made a deal with the Romans."

"Romans?" James echoes. "Simon—"

John breaks in. "He didn't say anything about any deal to us, Abba."

Zebedee shushes him. “You see the wound? Doesn’t look like Simon gave them what they wanted, does it? Use your brains!” He turns back to Simon. “Go on.”

“I owe taxes.”

“We all do.”

“A lot. They were set to take the boat, our houses …”

“Or?”

Simon hesitates. But this meeting was his idea, and there’s no way to soften it. “Or give up a fleet fishing on Shabbat.”

John wheels to face Andrew. “You knew about this?”

Andrew hangs his head, but Zebedee says, “Thank you for your honesty, Simon. If I may return the favor, I’m shocked you’d even show your face here, much less ask me to join you.”

Simon tries to avoid the older man’s glare. “I won’t argue that. I’m trapped, but”—he brightens—“it puts me in a valuable position.”

Zebedee chuckles. “Really? Now tell me, what’s the value of a dead traitor?”

Simon leans forward, insistent. “I’m not a traitor!”

John says, “You’re finished on the docks, Simon.”

“Leave him,” James says, standing. “C’mon, Abba.”

“I know their plans, Zebedee,” Simon says. “They’re coming for you.”

Zebedee shakes his head. “They’re playing you, kid.” He looks to Andrew and back at Simon. “Sorry. I can’t help you.” He rises to join his sons.

“You fished the Gregessa shore last night,” Simon says.

That stops the old man. He and James and John stare. He motions for them to sit back down. “Maybe I did. Maybe I didn’t. You dock six ships and pretty soon everyone in The Hammer knows where you were. What they can’t tell you is where I’ll be next time.”

"It was only three ships, Zebedee." Simon pulls from his lap the bobber he found in the sea. "I was practically in your wake with some soldiers. Many more were waiting on shore for you to offload."

The three look stunned. John says, "How did we make it out of there?"

"I made sure my boat had an unfortunate accident. Then lost part of my wife's favorite ear."

James smiles. "Thanks, friend!"

"No, don't thank him!" Zebedee says. "He chose to deal with Rome! So, what was your play gonna be, huh? Were you shopping around for an ally, someone to take you on in exchange for turning over *his* competitors?"

"No," Andrew says. "It's way stupider than that."

"I want you to turn over your catch," Simon says.

Zebedee looks to James and John. "What'd he say?"

"Wait," John says. "Turn it over to who?"

"To me! Then you stay off the sea on Shabbat—for a while anyway. I can tell Quintus the problem is solved."

The three burst into laughter, and Andrew grouses, "This is pointless."

"He's right," Zebedee says.

"It's just one night's work—" Simon says.

"*Forty* nights!" Zebedee says. "One for every man who made the sacrifice to be away from his family."

"And all forty went home in the morning because of me!"

"Yes, Simon, because you couldn't bear it if you ruined us as you've ruined yourself!" The man locks eyes with Simon, as if searching his soul. "We owe you a great debt for that." Simon wonders if he has somehow salvaged this mess. Yet Zebedee isn't finished. "But I cannot repay you by stealing food from the mouths of my men. I'm sorry."

• • •

*The Roman Authority headquarters*

A captain ushers Matthew into Quintus' office and announces him to the praetor.

Quintus stares out a large window, his back to Matthew. "The fruit here is incredible," he says. "Pomegranates, dates, figs, berries. The olives. Everything that grows here is immaculate."

Matthew shifts awkwardly. Quintus finally turns to face him, arms folded, grinning. "Except the people. You're such a miserable lot. You worship one god, and yet you're all divided. You see, people complain we Romans run the world, but I know a dirty secret. You people *want* to be ruled. You *want* an excuse to complain. It's part of your nature. Do you understand that, Matthew?"

"I don't know."

Quintus is obviously amused. "No, you wouldn't. You're a single-minded machine. These things are beneath you." He looks past Matthew. "Where's your escort?"

Matthew hesitates. He knows where Gaius is. Waiting outside, certain Matthew is going to mess this up. "He didn't want to enter. He feels that my lack of social graces—"

"He thinks you'll get him killed."

*Exactly*, Matthew thinks. "Yes."

Quintus laughs. "Not today, Matthew, no. Today I am in need—and you heard me right. I am in need of your machine."

"My machine?"

"Your mind, Matthew. Keep up." He opens a document. "You might have been right about Simon. He double-crossed me. Maybe. Probably. Truth is, I don't have many seaworthy troops here. It might have been an accident."

"Dominus?"

"Follow Simon. I want to know where he goes, with whom he meets. Tell me what they're talking about, what he's drinking. Anything."

"The latter may prove difficult. In fact, all of what you request, Dominus, may prove difficult."

"But you're a resourceful man. Goal oriented …"

"I am not accepted."

"Where?"

"Anywhere. I'm a tax collector."

"Viewed with jealousy?"

"Hated. Everyone hates tax collectors. We're worse than the Romans." Matthew realizes what he's said. "You were born a Roman. I made the choice."

Quintus stares at Matthew and shrugs. "So, go in disguise. I don't care." He hands Matthew a wax tablet. "You can write, can't you?"

"Yes."

"Write everything. Every detail. Is your booth protected?"

"Yes, Dominus. My dog guards it while I'm away."

Quintus laughs aloud. "Oh, Matthew, you are a priceless treasure! Of course you have a dog!"

Chapter 35

# THE WILD MAN

*Capernaum Hebrew school*

Nicodemus has called a brief meeting with Shmuel, Shmuel's protégé Yusef, and two other leading Pharisees. They stand in a small circle in the foyer as an exercised Shmuel regales them. "I saw it with my own eyes. The line stretched from the edge of the Jordan into the acacia groves, as far as the eye could see. All of them awaiting an immersion in the river by a loud man wearing camel skin."

"And not for purification?" one says.

Shmuel shakes his head. "He called it a baptism of repentance—a forgiveness of sin!"

"What exactly did he say? Have you seen him before?"

"I have not. That is what he said." He turns to Nicodemus. "Rabbi, is there precedent for this?"

Nicodemus is lost in thought. Could this be the man Lilith—Mary—spoke of? But she said nothing of his being loud or wearing skins. Maybe it's another whom Nicodemus has heard about. "What of his speech?"

Shmuel looks puzzled. "Rabbi?"

"His words—the message! Did he advocate rabbinic law? Did he call for revolution? Violence?"

"Not violence. But I haven't told you the worst part. One of our own approached him, and he called all of us snakes."

"Us?" another says.

"Yes! Religious leaders."

"Snakes?"

"He ranted like a madman about how worthless we were."

"What else?" Nicodemus says.

"What else? What can be worse than that?"

"It depends—on who he is."

"He told tax collectors and soldiers not to extort money or collect more than they're authorized to."

"They were present as he said this?"

"Yes! And he told the commoners to share food and clothing with those who have none."

"Aah," a Pharisee says, "he's preaching a populist message."

Nicodemus silences the rest with a gesture. "In Jerusalem, I heard talk of a wild man who entered the king's court with a list of evils done by Herod Antipas and his family."

"What should be done, Rabbi?" Yusef says. "Can we bring him in for questioning by the Sanhedrin?"

Nicodemus shakes his head. "If it is the same person, he does not answer to Sanhedrin. We are not his only targets anyway. He seems to relish rejecting anything with tradition, or anyone with influence." He turns to Shmuel. "Do they say he performs miracles?"

"I don't know."

The others seem to wait for more from Nicodemus, but he merely says, "This meeting's adjourned," and leaves them.

## Chapter 36

# THE CONFESSION

Simon arrives home to find his brothers-in-law huddled with Eden in the kitchen, whispering. "What's this?" he says.

The men, plainly surprised, turn and smile—too broadly, especially considering they're the characters he's fist-fought almost weekly for so long. "Aha!" the elder says, sounding like anything but a combatant today. "There he is!"

Wary, Simon responds flatly. "Jehoshaphat. Abrahim."

"Simon!" Jehoshaphat says. "What happened to your ear?"

"There is a cut on it." Eden appears near tears. "What's going on?"

"Simon," Jehoshaphat says, still seeming to force a smile, "we are brothers here …"

"Yes!" Abrahim says. "If you ever find yourself in need of *anything* …"

Enough of this. Simon blurts, "Look, if this is about what's going on at the docks—I don't know what you've heard. It's just a misunderstanding, all right? It's business."

Eden perks up. "What's wrong at the docks?"

So, it's not about his trouble with the Romans. What is this? Simon stutters, stalling till something comes to mind. "I—uh, I lost a lure. What's happened?"

"Ima is sick," Eden says.

"Dasha? What happened?"

"She's coughing in fits," Jehoshaphat says. "She has no strength to do anything."

"And yet, she does not sleep," Abrahim adds.

"She's spitting up blood."

"I don't understand," Simon says. "We just saw her last—"

"Month!" Eden says. "Simon, it's been a month since you have visited Dasha."

Is that possible? He scrambles to cover. "You know how it's been—work and … I know. I haven't been a good—" It suddenly hits him. He nods at her brothers. "Wait, why are they here?"

As the three look awkwardly at each other, he hears coughing from the other room. So that's it. They have brought his mother-in-law here! "No, no, no, no, no. Look, I love your Ima like she was my own, but—"

"She loves *you*!" Jehoshaphat says.

"—but we can't take her."

"Abrahim and his family are all in my home already," Jehoshaphat says.

"This is really bad timing," Simon says.

"When is a good time to fall ill, Simon?" Abrahim says.

"Guys," Simon whispers, "the answer is no."

The siblings stare wide-eyed at each other, then the brothers approach, demanding, "What kind of man are you?"

"You have no honor, son of Jonah!"

"It was so sweet punching your head—"

"Sucker punching my head!" Simon barks. "Yeah, where's the honor in that, huh?"

Eden shouts, "Stop it!" They fall silent. "Jehoshaphat, Abrahim," she says quietly, "if Simon says it's a bad time, he has good reason. It's a bad time."

"Thank you, Eden," Simon says.

"A bad time for you," she says. "Not for me."

"Honey."

"No! If I can't be there for my own Ima when she's sick, what am I? I'm nothing. I'm not a daughter. I'm not a sister. Nothing!"

"You'll always be—"

"Nothing!"

She will not be coddled. "Abrahim, Jeho," Simon says, trying to keep his tone even, "please. Go be with your Ima or go outside. We need some privacy."

They look at each other, then to Eden. They're not moving. "Eden?" Abrahim says.

Simon's had it. He faces them, serious as leprosy. "I'm not talking to your sister. I'm talking to my wife in my own home, and if you're not out of this room in three seconds, I will beat you both with my bare hands!"

They retreat. He turns back to Eden. Tears stream down her face. "I can't do this anymore," he says. "Please. Please listen to me. I haven't been honest with you." Her eyes widen. "There's no woman, it's not gambling—" He has her attention. "Look, a few days ago I looked you in the eyes and I told you, 'I've got this.' I lied."

"What do you mean?"

"I've been fishing on Shabbat because I've had no choice. Andrew has tax debts. I've got tax debts. We haven't been able to keep up. I did some things I'm not proud of to fix it, and now it's gone bad, and—we're in trouble."

"We? What do you mean?"

"*I. I'm* in trouble, but I say *we* because I need a miracle, or I could be in *big* trouble."

"I'm not a child. Stop speaking in riddles. Tell me what's happening."

He mouths, "I could go to prison. We could lose the house."

She recoils. "What?"

"The cut on my ear—it's from a Roman."

She gasps. "Simon!"

"If I don't catch a ton of fish, or get some help somehow, they'll arrest me."

"Or kill you!" she says. "They are Romans!"

"Yeah, so I need to go now."

"Go where?"

"To fish. I've got to spend the rest of the week doing nothing but catch every fish I can and hope I can fix this somehow." She turns away, but he continues. "That's why we can't take your Ima. It's just not possible right n—"

She spins back to face him. "No! She has nothing to do with this! I will not let you punish her for your sins!"

"Eden, you can't do this alone."

"You can't tell me what I can or can't do. You have had your eyes closed around here! And God is with me, even if you aren't."

That cuts him deeply. "I'm sorry."

She seems to study him. "Where is your faith? Hm?"

"What?" Surely, she's not accusing him …

"You heard me."

"Faith isn't gonna get me more fish."

"I'm not talking about tonight. I am talking about long before tonight. You've been different. Before it was gambling, and now it's working and trying to do everything yourself. The popular Simon, fixing everything and charming everyone, all by yourself! And fishing on holy days without even thinking about it, with no respect for our God."

"What about the *pikuach nefesh*? We can break a commandment to save a life. Our lives are at stake here."

"You don't know that because you have not pursued the Lord lately. You're not the man I met and married." She has stunned him to silence, and she's not finished. "*That* is why you are stuck, and you feel desperate, and now you are off to try to fix it yourself again."

He has no defense. He knows she's right. How he longs to be reconciled to her!

"So, go," she says, sobbing now. "I don't want you here tonight anyway."

"I'm sorry," he whispers.

She can't seem to hide her love for him. "I know you're sorry. I know. And I'm glad you were at least honest with me. But no more talking. Maybe God can get your attention now."

• • •

Simon trudges out, as dejected as he's ever been. He's brought all this on himself, he knows, and he's wounded the woman he loves more than anyone else on earth. He punches one of the tables where he repairs fishing gear, wishing he could injure himself as deeply as he deserves. But the skin on his hands is thick as leather, and he barely feels it.

"Simon!"

That's Andrew's voice, and he sounds excited. Perfect timing. Simon would rather wallow in his shame than have to talk to anyone, even his brother. He wants to channel his guilt into a bedrock of resolve to do whatever he has to do to win back Eden's faith, satisfy his debts, willingly take in his mother-in-law, regain his reputation with the other fishermen, restore Andrew's trust—all of it.

Andrew bounds into the yard, smiling like a maniac. The

poor man has been so troubled for so long, this is a side of him Simon hasn't seen for ages. And it's all been his fault. His crazy schemes. His willingness to skirt the laws.

"Simon!" Andrew calls out, breathless, supporting himself on a wood railing. "It's happened! It's happened, Simon!"

He can't wait to hear this.

Chapter 37

# GOING FISHING

Andrew pants, gasping, clearly trying to gather himself. His beatific grin makes him look drunk, but Simon knows better than that. "What are you talking about? Did you run all the way from Jerusalem?"

Andrew finally blurts, "We're saved!"

Oh, brother! Simon has no idea what this is about. "We're saved?"

Andrew nods, tears in his eyes, joy all over him. It's as if the weight of the world has lifted from his shoulders. Simon doesn't have time for this. Does Andrew not realize the desperate straits they're in?

"I saw him! With my own eyes, Simon!"

"Who?"

"It was incredible!"

"Andrew! Who did you see?"

His brother pauses, looking as earnest as he ever has. Simon has to admit, it's better to see Andrew enthused over something, anything, rather than as troubled as he's been for weeks. But what is this?

"The Lamb of God!" Andrew says.

*Great,* Simon thinks, *just what we need right now—little brother's had some ecstatic religious experience.* They'd both been devout since birth, but the prophets have been silent for 400 years. And now Andrew's convinced he's encountered the very Lamb of God?

But he's only just begun. As if Simon doesn't recognize the language of Scripture, or might not get that he's referring to the long-prophesied Messiah, Andrew says—his voice still full of emotion: "He who takes away the sin of the world!"

Simon shakes his head and turns away. Whatever this is, whoever this is, it changes nothing about their situation. Simon still has to get going, to get the boat and the oars and the nets into the water and start producing his only real hope of staying out of prison—or staying alive.

Plainly put off by his brother's less-than-enthusiastic response, Andrew says, "Simon! We were standing by the Jordan, and John the Baptizer pointed at the man who was walking and—Simon! Are you listening?"

Simon has wandered to the table where he's now deftly mending nets. His life as he knows it—not to mention Eden's and Andrew's—dangles over a terrifying abyss. "Yeah! You're just not saying anything."

Andrew approaches, a sob in his voice. "I saw the Messiah today, the man all of us, including you, have been praying for our whole lives! Don't you even care?"

Simon doesn't know whether to laugh or cry. He doesn't look up from his chore. "Was he a big man?"

"Big?" Andrew says. "No."

"Rich?"

"No."

"It didn't seem he could bail us out of this debt to Rome?" He finally looks up at Andrew. "Maybe, maybe he was a doctor. No? Well, then he can't help with Eden's Ima—who's now living with us, Andrew!"

Andrew looks stricken. "Dasha?"

"So, pardon me if I'm not exactly jumping out of my sandals because creepy John pointed at someone!"

Andrew steps closer, seeming to study Simon's face. "You're scared," he says softly.

*That's not the half of it.* "I've lost everything. Burned every bridge."

Andrew grips Simon's shoulders and whispers hoarsely, "It doesn't matter! The Romans don't matter if the Messiah has arrived!" He takes Simon's face in his hands. "Anything is possible now! Don't you see?"

Simon can't deny Andrew really believes this. He smiles condescendingly and pats his brother on the shoulder. "That'd be nice." He pulls away and heads toward his storage shed.

Andrew sounds incredulous. "Where are you going?"

Simon points back to the house. "Go help Eden. Her brothers are trying to cook. I can smell it."

• • •

Andrew can't help but wonder what just happened. Simon had to know he was serious, that he hadn't made this up. He'll just have to introduce him to the Messiah.

But what's this? Halfway down the block, the tax collector peers at him over the top of his tablet. No cover. Right out in the open.

Andrew pretends not to notice and moves a few steps one

way and then the other. The taxman keeps him in sight. What a terrible spy.

• • •

Simon emerges from the shed, laden with everything he needs for a night of fishing. Unless he's successful, this may be the last he sees of his own home. He hurries toward the sea, only to walk directly into the path of the tax collector. "You're following me now, huh?"

Matthew smiles. "It's a matter of accountability."

"You're here to make sure Quintus knows where to go when it's time to hurt me."

The little man looks proud of himself. "To settle your debt. I keep track of things. I do it well. Quintus knows I do it well."

That makes Simon smile. "You're a little—off, aren't you?"

Matthew looks uncomfortable, as if he's been caught—not spying, but being strange. "You should turn yourself in. We can accompany you."

"Nah," Simon says. "Still pursuing every option." He turns to keep moving.

"There are no options," Matthew calls after him. "You must provide information implicating the guilty fishermen or balance the books. Somehow."

Simon stops and sets down his gear, returning to face Matthew. "Andrew says anything's possible."

"Not mathematically."

"Yeah, but—what if? You know?"

"You'd only be subjecting your family and friends to needless anguish by prolonging the inevitable."

"You use a lot of big words."

Matthew looks as if he's been complimented. "But no one listens to me—not like they do you. You have a singular talent."

Amused, Simon nods. “That’s something at least.” He picks up his gear again.

“Can I assume you are not headed to the authorities?” Matthew says.

“Going fishing.”

“Ha! Variables. People are always adding variables.”

Simon ignores him, ready to get going. Matthew seems to try a new tack. “Does it change anything to know you have only until sunup?”

Simon feels the color drain from his face. “Sunup? But Shabbat’s not for three days!”

“Quintus is convinced you’ve double-crossed him. He’s coming.”

Simon is thrown. There’s no way he can catch enough fish in one night, even working till dawn, to put a dent in his and Andrew’s debt. But he has no choice. “I’m still going fishing.”

“Turn yourself in! You have no feasible plan.”

“I just told you my plan. If I’m going down, it will be doing what God built me to do. Tell your boss he can come get me off the water.”

Chapter 38

# OPPORTUNITY KNOCKS

*The Capernaum guesthouse*

Nicodemus sits across from Zohara at dinner as servants scurry about, trying to anticipate their every need. The elder Pharisee still enjoys gazing at the bride of his youth, his partner for decades.

"We should be counting our blessings," she says.

*Just what I've been doing*, he thinks. "Adonai is great, indeed."

"This trip could not have gone any better if we had planned every moment," she says. Zohara raises her spoon to her lips.

In truth, Nicodemus has wearied of the constant adulation, the bowing and scraping when people can tell by his raiment who he is. But he also knows it's his responsibility to deflect praise that belongs to God. "My eyes are always opened anew in this land."

"Not to mention the new opportunities our successes here will no doubt unlock."

She means back in Jerusalem, of course, but he privately rues the idea of some triumphal return, especially after his failure with Lilith—Mary. Better to lower Zohara's expectations. "We will stay another fortnight or until all my research is concluded."

He can tell by her look that was not what she wanted to hear. "But, Nico," she says, passing him the bread, "surely you can conclude your research in Jerusalem. And the archives are there—"

"The matter is decided."

A knock at the door interrupts them. Zohara looks puzzled. "I'm expecting no one."

It's Yusef, telling a servant, "It's important. I need to see him."

Nicodemus approaches.

"I'm sorry to interrupt at this hour, Rabbi," Yusef says. "I bring news regarding the heretic called John."

"The baptizer?"

"The Romans have taken him into custody."

"How did you hear of this?"

"Shmuel, Rabbi."

Nicodemus wonders why Shmuel himself has not brought him this information.

"I believe Shmuel may have given the Romans his location," Yusef adds.

That had better not be true. "We do not lightly turn Jews over to the Romans," Nicodemus says. "Did the Sanhedrin order this?"

"No, Teacher."

It strikes Nicodemus that this may be one instance where it might be appropriate for him to exploit his position to gain access to someone he'd desperately like to meet. "I want to question the baptizer myself. I'll make inquiries. Thank you, Yusef."

"Yes, Rabbi."

"And I will discuss this with Shmuel myself, eh?"

• • •

*The Sea of Galilee*

Despite years of oppression and exorbitant taxation at the hands of the Romans, Simon has always loved his work. He's been on the water since infancy, loved working with his father and his brother, not to mention numerous other friends who have become like family. He loves the outdoors, the water, the sun—especially the sun. He enjoys even being known as a fisherman.

He's good at it, too—can recite the more than thirty different species that fill these waters. Hard work has been his life for so long that his hands and feet, even his fingers and toes, have been conditioned to deftly handle every chore. Though not a big man, he bears limbs hardened and toned, and he prides himself on having mastered every task on the water.

Simon does not particularly enjoy fishing at night, however, especially alone. Even empty nets are waterlogged and heavy, and repeatedly casting them into the sea and dragging them into the boat makes for a long night. But he loves the moon on the water, the gentle lapping of the waves against the vessel, and the relative silence.

Simon is optimistic, though he's also a realist and knows that even a successful haul this night won't come close to satisfying his debt. But with his gift of talking his way out of the worst of trouble, he believes a decent catch will at least buy him a little more time. If he can produce one full load overnight, imagine what he could do with a couple of more days. Even Quintus would have to be impressed, wouldn't he?

But as the night wears on and he pulls in nothing—not so much as a sardine—his confidence wanes. He's had bad runs before, but nothing? How can this be? This sea, which has fed not only all of Capernaum but also the entire surrounding area for as long as anyone can remember, is completely devoid of fish tonight? Impossible.

Despair turns to anger as he grunts and groans with the solitary effort. He tries both sides of the boat, even front and back. He tries coves and inlets, favorite spots, even areas he's left to other fishermen the last few years. He sets the oars in place and propels himself over a mile to a position that has always delivered for him. But no. He's found nothing but more fatigue for his effort.

All Simon knows to do is to cast and cast and cast his net into the sea and drag it back in. Slowly he begins to boil. And now he seethes—throwing equipment, stomping about, ferociously cutting through snagged and tangled nets. Finally, he cries out, bellowing in rage. As the hours pass, he spends himself. At one point he simply sits, shoulders drooping. An onlooker might assume he's merely taking a break. But he's about to explode.

What will all this mean if he fails? For Eden? Her Ima? Andrew? Their home? Their future? Their dreams? It all seems to sink into the black expanse of this sea he has cherished his whole life. Is he being punished? Has Eden been right when she accuses him of no longer seeking the Lord? He's willing to try anything now.

• • •

On the shore, Matthew sits with his dog, which starts at a cry from off the water. He calms the animal, telling him softly, "People bark sometimes too."

He has been watching Simon's boat for hours, wondering if the man is making progress. On the horizon beyond, he espies a tiny speck of firelight. Another boat? Who else would be out here now?

The craft moves slowly toward Simon.

• • •

Simon sits on the thwart of his boat, exhausted, studying his hands. It's been years since he's ripped open callouses and developed new blisters. But he can live with that, work through it, if only he could find the right place—anywhere that produces fish.

His sodden net lies at his feet, but for the moment he can't bring himself to rise and toss it in one more time. The boat drifts, its wood gently creaking. "Cast after cast," he mutters and stares at the sky. Such a beautiful, clear night! Under any other circumstance, he would revel in such a sight. What was it God promised Abraham? "'And I will make your descendants as many as the stars in the heavens.' And then what, huh?" he says aloud.

Simon struggles to his feet and snatches up the net. "Make the Chosen as many as the stars, only to let Egypt enslave us for generations?" With a grunt, he flings the net into the water yet again. "Bring us out of Egypt, part the Red Sea, only to let us wander in the desert for forty years? Give us the land, only to let us be exiled in Babylon? Bring us back, only to be crushed by Rome? *This* is the God I've served so faithfully for my entire life! You're the God I'm supposed to thank! You know, if I didn't know any better, I'd say You enjoy yanking us around like goats and can't decide whether we're chosen or not! Which one is it? Huh?"

"Simon!"

He wheels around to find a boat drawing near. "Andrew?"

"Who are you talking to?"

Simon shakes his head. "Apparently no one."

"You shouldn't joke like that, my friend," another says.

"Yeah," says yet another. "Your friends might think you've lost faith."

"James and John, I presume," Simon says. Even in his fury, he's deeply touched that they're here. As their boat pulls next to his, he sees their father as well. "And who brought the old man?"

"I heard you need a real fisherman," Zebedee says.

Simon extends an oar to Zebedee's boat and pulls Andrew aboard. "How'd you know I was here?"

"Eden may be angry," Andrew says, "but she's not too proud to ask for help."

"Oh," John says. "So, you told her the whole story, huh?"

James grunts. "How'd she take it?"

"Let's just say it's my last night as a free man," Simon tells them—"and I'm fishing."

A look of concern washes over Andrew. "Your last night?"

"Quintus," Simon says. He need say no more.

The others look at each other. Zebedee rises, tossing a rope from his boat to Simon's. "Well, there are only so many hours in a night, huh? Let's fish!"

Simon is no more optimistic, but he's profoundly grateful for the company and stirred by how his brother and their friends—the very ones he nearly exposed to the authorities—swing into action. With military precision, the five put their years of experience to work. They secure the boats together, add their nets to Simon's, and set about casting in a huge circle around both vessels. Whether they succeed or not, Simon will enjoy laboring with men who know how to work and how to fish.

• • •

An hour later, Simon's joy has vanished, and so, it seems, has the energy of his brother and the others. As they pull in empty net after empty net, coordination has been sacrificed. The whole crew begins to slow, to grow sloppy, and their moods seem to match Simon's. Neither boat has landed a single fish, not even a throwback. Without a word, they move the boats to another spot and reorganize the nets for another pass.

After several more minutes of futility, they sit, heads

hanging, pulling in the nets and quietly straightening them. John says, "If we catch nothing, in the morning maybe you could hide in the merchant caravans. Escape to Egypt."

James nods. "Fish the Nile."

"They've got perch the size of children," Zebedee says.

"Egypt is a Roman province now," Andrew adds.

"Nah," Simon says. "Eden hates Egypt."

"So?" Zebedee says. "She can wait for you to send money."

Everyone chuckles but Simon. "I'm hoping if I let Quintus and his boys take out their frustrations on me, he'll eventually allow me visitors." The nets are ready again. "Let down," he says, and they cast yet again. The water laps against the hulls as a lazy breeze cools Simon's drooping hair.

As they sit motionless, waiting for any activity in the sea, Andrew turns to Simon. "So, about the news I was trying to tell you. I was walking with John, the one they call the Baptizer—"

Simon doesn't want to hear it. "Andrew—"

"What's he on about?" Zebedee says.

"… and he pointed at a man," Andrew continues.

"No more!"

"And he said, 'Behold the Lamb—'"

"Andrew! I said—just, please. Not another word from you about this Lamb of yours. We don't need a lamb. We need fish."

## Chapter 39

# IT'S HIM

The sky turns a grayish blue as the faintest hint of light illuminates the eastern horizon. The men have been silently fishing for hours. Zebedee idly coils a length of rope, and Simon can tell he's done. The others sit still, appearing ready to nod off.

Simon begins untethering his boat from Zebedee's. Andrew sits nearby. His brother whispers, "Maybe John was right. You have a chance. You could sneak into a merchant caravan and get away."

"I won't leave the land of our father. And they'd find me, I'm sure." The game is up. "Maybe the baptizer could make me a disguise out of an old camel's hide."

Clearly not amused, Andrew stands to pull the last net from the water, and everyone pitches in except James, who dozes. Simon and John holler for his help, and he rouses. Both boats lie full of nothing but nets as the sky brightens. A hundred yards from shore, the men sit slumped, and in their resigned faces Simon sees what he feels deep in his soul.

He's not just devastated. He's angry. Defeated. "Zeb!" he says. "Come around."

The old man deftly brings his craft into position on the other side of Simon's. "Sometimes the sea bests all of us. It's not your night."

Simon appreciates Zebedee's effort, but he can't muster a response. "All right," he says finally. "Time to be done."

James and John settle in at the oars on their father's boat. Andrew and Simon do the same on their own. But as they set their sights on the shore, Zebedee yells, "Boys!"

To a small band of people in the sand near the water's edge, James shouts, "Roman scum couldn't even wait!"

*This is it*, Simon decides. No running, no hiding, no escaping. He's exhausted his every chance.

Zebedee assures him, "We're right with you!"

Simon wishes he could persuade Zebedee and his sons and Andrew to flee to another shore. The Romans want him, not them. "Make sure Eden is safe," he whispers. "Do you hear me, Andrew?"

"Hey!" John says, staring. "Those aren't soldiers."

Simon squints. They're not! No uniforms. A man pacing the shore with his back to the sea appears to be addressing a small crowd. "I might still have time to see Eden."

"Don't clean our nets," Zebedee says. "We'll stick around to make sure you can leave."

As they row toward shore, Simon sees Matthew down the beach, sitting next to a black dog. The taxman seems to intently take this all in, watching the crowd, then the boats.

Zebedee leaps to secure his boat as it runs aground, and Simon and Andrew prepare to do the same, when the man addressing the crowd turns to face them.

"Simon!" Andrew says, grabbing his shoulder. "It's him!"

"Excuse me," the man says.

"Simon, it's him!"

"No time for this, Andrew."

"It's him, Simon, it's the man John said—he's here. Right now!"

Chapter 40

# THE CATCH

"May I ask a favor?" the man says. "I'm teaching these people, and apparently they're having trouble hearing me. If I could stand on your boat, that would be helpful."

Simon snorts. "Having trouble hearing you, huh?"

Andrew says, "Yes! Yes, of course! Please! Please stand on our boat, thank you."

This is the man Andrew has been so excited about? He appears to be nothing special. "I need to go," Simon says. "I'm sorry, no time for this today."

"Stay a few moments longer," the man says. He climbs into the boat.

Simon is nonplussed. *This stranger thinks he can just tell me …*

He looks into Simon's eyes. "I have something for you."

"For me? Uh, I'm in a hurry."

"Yes, I know."

*He knows? What could he possibly know?*

"Just allow me a few moments, please."

"Simon," Andrew whispers. "Trust me as I have trusted you. This man is the Messiah."

*Well, that remains to be seen.*

The man turns to Simon's brother. "It's good to see you again, Andrew."

"Yes," Andrew says, his face flushed. He can't stop smiling.

Simon's brother called him the Messiah, and the man didn't even correct him. For Andrew's sake, Simon nods and offers his hand.

"I'm Jesus. Thanks for this."

"Simon."

Jesus turns to face the crowd. "In my last moments with you, I want to share another story. Can everyone hear me?" They assure him they can, and he says, "Well, let's thank our friends for this strong boat, eh?"

The crowd applauds.

"Trust me, my yelling voice is not easy on the ears. Because I'm on this boat, my final parable should be about fishing, yes? Simon, please hand me that net. When this net is thrown into the sea, what happens, Simon?"

Boy, did he pick the wrong day to ask that! "Well—"

"I mean most of the time."

"It gathers."

"A little louder."

Simon looks past Jesus to the crowd. "It gathers fish!"

"Yes, this net gathers fish." He turns again to Simon. "All kinds of fish, yes?"

"Yes, all kinds of fish."

"And the kingdom of heaven is like what happens next. After the net is full, Simon and the others draw it to the shore, sit down, and sort out the fish. The good fish go into the barrels, the bad fish," he drops the net, "are thrown away. So it will be at the end of the age. Angels will come and separate the evil from the righteous and throw them into a fiery furnace. Do you understand? Therefore, every scribe who has been trained for the kingdom of heaven, like you all are now, is like the master of a house who brings forth his treasures, both new and old. You are to do the same with this knowledge. These parables I tell you make sense to some, not to others. Be patient. That is all for today. I have some business to attend to with my new friend."

As the crowd disperses, Jesus hands the net back to Simon and steps out of the boat into the water. "Put that down for a catch," he says. "A little farther out."

Andrew leaps into action, scurrying to the back of the boat. But Simon has had enough of fishing. "Look," he says. "I don't have a quarrel with you, Teacher. But we've been doing this all night. Nothing."

Jesus just looks at Simon. Apparently, he will not be dissuaded. "All right," Simon says at last. "At your word."

He and Andrew row a short distance from shore and throw out the net. Simon cocks his head at Jesus. Now what? Jesus cocks his head too and smiles. Suddenly the boat nearly capsizes, and Simon grabs the side to keep from being pitched into the sea. He frantically struggles with the net, stretching and straining under the weight of fish that fill it to overflowing.

"Grab it!" Simon hollers. "Grab the net! Grab it! Make that tighter!" He steals a glance at Jesus, who laughs with delight.

Andrew scrambles to hang on to his end of the net. "Help! Help!"

Simon yells down to Zebedee and his sons, three dozen yards away. "Help! Help! Come on!"

Amazingly, Zebedee sprints through the water ahead of James and John, who yells, "Let's go!"

They reach Simon and Andrew, and all hands fight to keep

the net from bursting as Simon shouts instructions. With a giant heave, they finally push the mass of twisting, flying fish past the tipping point, and they cascade into the boat, filling every nook and cranny. Everyone laughs, whoops, and shouts.

Andrew grins at Simon. "I told you! I told you! I told you!"

"The boat!" Zebedee cries. "It's sinking! Get out!"

Simon and Andrew jump into the water, and the boat levels. With help from Zebedee and his sons, they drag it to shore. Exhausted and euphoric, knowing his trouble with Quintus will soon easily be past, Simon finds himself facing Jesus. He drops to his knees, sobbing. "My brother, and the baptizer—they—you are the Lamb of God, yes?"

"I am."

"Depart from me! I am a sinful man! You don't know who I am and the things I've done!"

"Don't be afraid, Simon."

"I'm sorry! We've waited for you for so long! We believed, but my faith—I'm sorry!"

"Lift up your head, fisherman."

Simon can do nothing but what this man says. He stares into the kindest face he has ever seen. "What do you want from me? Anything you ask I will do!"

Jesus gazes down on him, then squats to look deep into Simon's eyes. He says simply, "Follow me."

Simon is transfixed, every trace of doubt obliterated. "I will."

Andrew approaches. "Rabbi."

Jesus calls out to Zebedee's sons. "You as well! Yes, you, James and John! Come, follow me!"

John lurches forward, but James stops him and looks to his father as if for permission.

"I'll take the fish to market and settle up Simon's debt," Zebedee says. "I'll get some help to fill both of these boats."

John says, "Are you sure?"

"Yes! Go!"

"What will you tell Ima?" James says.

Zebedee laughs. "You've just been called by the man we've prayed for our entire lives, and you ask me what will I say when you miss supper? Go on! Now!"

• • •

Mary of Magdala has been in the crowd at the shore, along with the other James and Thaddeus, who shared Shabbat at her home. The three of them already follow Jesus. She's intrigued by these new followers, the four fishermen. Simon and Andrew walk alongside Jesus. James and John run to catch up.

"So," Simon is saying, "you sure you don't want to do this just a few more times? We would make a great team on a boat."

Jesus laughs, but Andrew scolds, "Simon!"

"Joking!" Simon says.

Jesus stops and allows everyone to gather around him. He puts a hand on Simon's shoulder. "Fish are nothing. You have much bigger things ahead of you, Simon, son of Jonah. Did you understand that parable I told earlier? From now on, I will make you fishers of men. You are to gather as many as possible, all kinds. I will sort them out later."

Mary can hardly wait.

Chapter 41

# THE IMPOSSIBLE

Matthew has been with his dog on the shore all night. For hours he kept an eye on Simon. Simon the gambler. Simon the talker. Simon the tax evader. When the dog dozed, Matthew did too. But he has seen enough. He knew the old man and his sons, the ones who brought Simon's brother out to help. How nice it must be to have friends and family who care that much.

But Matthew can't deny he took secret pleasure in the initial failure of these fishermen. Making promises they could not keep, trying to talk their way out of danger, arranging side deals with the praetor himself.

Matthew has been just close enough to hear the teaching of the man known as Jesus. What strange and confusing things he said! Who was he to sound so authoritative and knowledgeable, so convincing and persuasive? And yet so mysterious? He was attractive and engaging—not to look at, but to hear. Matthew would have to keep an eye on him, too. He wonders if the man pays his taxes.

How did he know where the fish would be? But Matthew

knows this was about more than knowing. This man made those fish appear. Matthew makes his way down the beach to where the old man tends both boats, one low in the water under the weight of writhing, silvery fish.

"Hello," Zebedee says to Matthew.

"This catch is worth a lot."

Zebedee nods and chuckles. "It's amazing."

"It's impossible."

• • •

*The next morning*

Nicodemus has not felt this out of place since the Red Quarter. Legionnaires lead him to a dank underground dungeon where he tiptoes in past men wallowing in their own filth. The Pharisee's regalia makes him no more courageous in here, where he holds his breath as long as he can. Is the man he seeks nearby?

He gingerly approaches the bars of a cell and peers through the darkness at a silhouette. It speaks first. "You are supposed to be the powerful one. Yet you are more frightened here than I am."

"Are you the one they call John the Baptizer?"

The silhouette emerges from the shadows and approaches the bars. Hair and beard long and unkempt, he's dressed in camel hair. "Yes."

"I have questions for you about miracles."

# PART 6
# The Wedding Gift

Chapter 42

# MISSING

*Jerusalem, two decades earlier*

Mary had been certain Jesus was with others in their party. At least, she had been certain until a day into the journey back from the Feast of Passover, when she couldn't find him anywhere. Now she's been back in the city of David two more full days and has barely slept. Her husband, Joseph, has gone one way to search, she the other, and she is near collapse.

Breathless and pouring sweat, she races through the narrow streets, looking for any sign of her son, pleading for news from anyone. How can it be that she has been entrusted with God's own son and has lost him? "Father, please!" she wails. Surely his heavenly Father will not let anything happen to him.

Mary knows she must appear a madwoman, dusty face streaming with tears, eyes frantic. She enters a small square and grabs the first merchant she sees. "Please! Have you seen my son?"

The man recoils. "Why are you alone, woman?"

"My son! He's only twelve!"

The merchant laughs. "There are kids all over! It's Jerusalem! Are you from here?"

"No, we came for the Passover Feast. We thought he was in the caravan."

"The feast was three days ago!"

She hurries past him, crying out, "Jesus!"

And here comes Joseph, their son in tow. "Ima!"

Mary rushes to the boy and pulls him to her as if she'll never let him go. She pulls back and cups his face in her hands. "We looked everywhere, day and night! We were so scared!"

"I told him," Joseph says. "He's all right."

"Why is everyone so upset?" Jesus says.

"Mary." Joseph nods toward the synagogue. "He was in there."

"You were supposed to ride in the caravan with Uncle Abijah!" Mary says.

"I was supposed to be with my Father."

"Then why weren't you?"

"I was."

She looks to Joseph. He nods again.

"You were in the temple?"

"It was incredible, Mary!" Joseph says. "You should have seen him. He was teaching on the prophets. The rabbis, the scribes, the scholars—they could not believe their ears. They really listened!"

"Didn't you know I must be in my Father's house?"

*Oh, no*, she thinks. *Already?* "It's too early for all—this."

Jesus puts a hand on her shoulder, and she's stunned by his earnest little face. "If not now, when?"

She shakes her head and whispers, "Just help us get through all this. With you. Please."

Jesus nods, and Joseph says, "Maybe we should get going

before they make a formal inquiry, hm? Jesus, please don't do that again, eh?"

"Yes, Abba. May I read?"

"We'll see. Come now. We've got a long journey." As they head back to the caravan, Joseph teases, "What are you going to do for your mother for this transgression? I'm going to make you rub her feet."

"Abba!"

Chapter 43

# PREPARATIONS

*Cana, A.D. 30*

A woman with a spring in her step enters a synagogue courtyard and beams at all the activity as servants prepare for a grand event. She's surprised to hear someone call out "Dinah!" and whirls to see an old friend.

"Mary!" She runs to embrace her, laughing. "What are you doing here?"

"I heard someone is celebrating a marriage."

"I mean so early!"

Mary grins. "I came here to help."

"All the way from Nazareth? You must have been riding in the dark." Dinah raises a hand to her mouth, overcome.

"When your best friend is mother of the bridegroom," Mary says, "you'll be early for the feast too. Now, come on, give me a broom or something."

## Chapter 44

# IN THE DUNGEON

Nicodemus lets his request hang in the air as he peers at the man in the cell.

"Miracles?" the baptizer says, his hair ratty, an animal fur covering his body.

"Yes, John. Signs and wonders."

"From who?"

"You," the Pharisee leader says.

John grins, showing discolored teeth. "Are you adding those to my list of infractions? Only a Pharisee … You would have labeled Moses a lunatic for talking to a shrub."

Is this man as insane as he looks? "Do you consider yourself to be like Moses?"

John rolls his eyes, and Nicodemus sighs, reaching for a wood stool. He might as well humor John. He fluffs out his vestment and sits before the man, slowing removing his head covering. "Tell me about your ministry."

John hesitates, seeming to study his visitor. "Do you remember when Caesar traveled through Judea?"

"Yes."

"He sent all these men to clear logs and debris for the coming king. 'Make straight the way for the king,' they'd shout. 'Prepare the way!'"

"The roads in Jerusalem do not have the same problem," Nicodemus says, "but I remember the visit."

"I had to move. Romans aren't kind to the homeless. Lost all my possessions."

"Many in Jerusalem were frightened as well."

This appears to amuse John. "Oh, and they were lucky to have you to comfort them—for a price, of course."

"Should we be clearing the road for you, John?" Nicodemus says, snorting. "Is that the point of this story?"

"I don't like your frock! The cost of the vestments alone could feed three children in Nazareth for a month."

"Do you hail from Nazareth?"

"Mm-hm. And Jericho. And Bethlehem. Jaffa. Hebron."

"I see," Nicodemus says dismissively, glancing around at the squalor. "Well, you have a new home now. Whatever your mission was, I hope you completed it." He rises.

"But you're here to ask about miracles."

Nicodemus slowly sits again. "First, I wanted to tell you of a miracle that I've seen but cannot comprehend."

"And *then* to make accusations."

"This is pointless." Nicodemus rises abruptly. "Clearly you are not a frothing madman, but every bit as unreasonable."

"You imprison me and accuse me of being ill-tempered?"

"I am not your captor! Do you not understand? This is a *Roman* cell! I came here to speak to the warden on *your* behalf!"

"On my behalf," John scoffs. "Why are you really here, old man?"

"The official reason? You are a Jewish citizen. If you have

broken Jewish law, it sets a dangerous precedent to allow Rome to adjudicate."

John waves him off. "And the real reason?"

Nicodemus sits yet again. "The truth? I am far from home. I am looking in places I would never go, because I am searching for an explanation for something I cannot unsee."

This seems to reach John somehow. "No one else knows you're here?"

Nicodemus shakes his head.

John appears to see him with new eyes and slowly nods. "Tell me from the beginning."

## Chapter 45

# TELLING EDEN

*Capernaum*

In the cool shade of the leeward side of their home, Simon's barefoot wife treads grapes she has released from a sack above. To keep her balance, she holds a loop of rope dangling overhead. Her feet are just sensitive and pliable enough to crush the grapes and release their juice, which she will store to ferment, without also smashing the seeds—which would make the wine bitter. The sweet aroma pleases her, as does the cool sensation under her feet.

The squishing makes her oblivious to the chirping of birds and the wind, but from behind comes a familiar voice. "Eden."

So he's home. Finally. She turns.

Simon stands there looking plaintive. "We need to talk," he says.

"So I hear." She releases the rope and stands ankle deep in the grapes.

"What have you heard?"

She spreads her hands and shakes her head. "Nothing that makes sense."

Simon smiles ruefully and lowers his head. Eden puts her hands on her hips and sighs. "Last night you told me the truth," she says. "Let's continue with that."

He approaches and sits on a stool before her, beginning slowly. "I worked for hours last night, and I couldn't even catch one fish the entire night. Andrew and the boys showed up—thank you for that, by the way—and *none* of us could catch one fish the entire night. It was horrible. This morning we finally gave up, and we went ashore. But there was this teacher on the shore—and Andrew knew who he was, but I'll talk about that later. He told me to cast one more time, which made no sense, but I did it anyway because of the way he looked at me!

"And then so many fish showed up, they were pouring into the boat. So many kept coming that Zebedee ended up filling both of our boats—enough to pay off the whole debt."

Eden hardly knows what to say. She stares at him wide-eyed. "What?" Simon should be leaping for joy. "Why don't you seem happy?"

He sits there, eyes cast down. "This is hard to explain."

"More than what you just told me?"

"No, it's like the story of Elijah and Elisha."

She's familiar with it, of course. "Yes?"

"Elisha was plowing with twelve yoke of oxen, and Elijah the prophet walked up and threw his cloak over him, right? A calling to follow him."

"And without delay," she says, as if reciting, "Elisha slaughtered the oxen, burned the plow, and left everything behind."

"Yes!" Simon looks her full in the face now, eyes shining. "The teacher—Andrew told me, but I didn't believe him at first—he's the Messiah."

Eden stares at him, speechless.

Simon rises. "I know it sounds impossible, but I saw it with my own eyes! He made boatfuls of fish appear out of nowhere! And the words he spoke! The one John told Andrew was the Lamb of God who takes away the sin of the world, it was him! And then he called me to follow him. And Andrew, James, and John, to go where he goes and to learn from him. He said I wouldn't be a fisherman anymore, but that I would catch people instead!"

Her husband grins. "I don't even know what that means!" he says. He grows serious. "But I'm sure of what I saw. He's the one we've been waiting for all our lives, and I want to quit fishing and leave the sea behind to go—"

Eden quickly turns away from him, covering her face with both hands.

"I know! I know!" Simon says. "I know it makes no sense, and I knew it would upset you. All I can tell you is that this is—"

"I'm not upset!" she says, turning back to him. "Oh, why would I be upset? Come here! Come here!" Looking stunned, he steps close to the treading platform. Eden pulls his face to hers, whispering, "This is the man that I married."

"And you believe me?"

"You couldn't make this up." She's weeping now. "Of course he chose you."

"I don't know why he did. I tried to tell him I'm a sinful man."

"Everyone is sinful."

"I don't know what this means. I don't know yet how I'm going to provide."

"Oh, I don't care about that," Eden says, knowing that this is real and God Himself will take care of them.

"Then why are you crying?" he says.

"Because someone finally sees in you what I have always seen. You're more than a fisherman."

"You know, I will travel sometimes. I don't want you to feel abandoned."

"You have to go with him. How could I feel abandoned? I feel saved!"

"It's not going to be easy," Simon says.

"When have we ever had anything easy? It's not our people's way." They chuckle. She reaches again for the rope. "So, were you going to help me?"

"Actually, I could watch you do that all day."

She smiles. "Wash your feet."

As he removes his sandals, he says, "We leave for Cana today."

"What's in Cana?"

"A wedding."

"What does a wedding have to do with the liberation of Israel?"

"I'm about to find out." As he steps into the winepress, he adds, "Come on, don't you think our wedding was a kind of liberation?"

"From your fear that I would be bald?"

"Well, my father is nearly blind."

She laughs. "Remember how cold it was?"

"No."

"Remember Andrew's toast?"

He looks puzzled, shaking his head. She can tell he's teasing.

"Remember the rabbi lost his place?" she says.

He begins to nod, then shakes his head. "No."

"What? He made everyone stand up, then, 'Please be seated,' twice in a row. You don't remember?"

"What I will remember, for the rest of my life, is lifting your veil. I'd fight tigers for that memory." His voice lowers and he leans closer, putting an arm around her waist and pulling her to him.

"You'd fight tigers?" she says, raising her brows.

"Well, unless it was as cold as our wedding day right before the sun came up and you got tangled in our chuppah."

She giggles. "You do remember!"

## Chapter 46

# ANTICIPATION

*Outside Cana*

Young wedding supplier Thomas and his even younger vintner, Ramah, load a donkey-pulled wagon with all manner of savory cheeses, vegetables, and spices from the supply house run by his twin brother. "The lamb meat will be there before or after we arrive?" he asks her.

"After. They don't have a good place to keep it, so I didn't want it there too early."

"But are they going to show up?"

She rolls her eyes. "With plenty of time for you to roast it your way. Yes."

He's not convinced, but he wants—needs—to appear to trust her. His brother had introduced her as a potential employee, appearing to suppress a smile as he told her, "He's a good businessman, but you may tire of his whining."

"I don't whine!" Thomas insisted.

"Call it what you will," his brother teased, "but it's why we're looking for someone to work banquets with you so I can stay back."

Ramah had proved the perfect solution, the daughter of a renowned vineyard owner and eager to establish herself. Thomas hasn't been able to keep his eyes off her since the day she was hired. So enamored had he become of her that he resolved to keep from showing her the side of him that drew such taunting—and sometimes actual ridicule—from his family.

He has since childhood been one to question things. He doesn't understand himself. His brother is not this way. Raised in Galilee by devout Jews, Thomas can't seem to take anything at face value—even the teaching of the Torah. He doesn't feel contentious. He just wants evidence, proof, answers. He frankly wonders if the prophecies of old, especially concerning the Messiah, should be viewed less literally and more allegorically, considering that Yahweh seems to have stopped communicating directly with His people.

Despite Thomas's determination to hide this negative side of himself, he can't help himself, even today when he and Ramah have landed what should be a profitable assignment. It has come through Ramah's father, whose longtime friend is throwing a wedding celebration in Cana for his son and daughter-in-law.

"Wait," Thomas says as he surveys the wine load. "There are only three jars."

"Yes! That's what they asked for."

"Ramah, I am very concerned we won't be able to get all three all the way to Cana intact! I told you, we need a fourth from your vineyard to be safe."

"I told *you* the wedding family can't afford it."

"I would have paid you out of my own pocket."

"Thomas! That would almost erase your whole margin. Why would you do that?"

He's warmed by her concern, though she shows it through good-natured scolding. He stares into her beautiful eyes. "I—I mean, we're a team," he says, pointing to himself and to her. "Right?"

She falls silent, and he can tell from her look he has pushed too far, made assumptions. Angry and embarrassed, he busies himself rearranging things, only to cause a basket to tumble, forcing her to catch it.

"Well," she says finally, "I think everything will arrive intact." She offers what he takes as an apologetic smile. "Especially with how carefully you drive."

"I just want to be certain that everyth—"

"Thomas! It's going to be fine." She gives him a long look, and they smile.

• • •

*Synagogue Courtyard, Cana*

Dinah hugs a woman who has brought her a vase and returns to a table where Mary assembles strings of wildflowers. "I'm glad you got some hired help," Mary says. "There's much to do."

"Oh, Tereza? She's a neighbor. We couldn't afford anyone extra, so she volunteered. On her only day off."

"And here I was, thinking how lucky you were to have me."

Dinah smiles. "My son just married his love, and I'm surrounded by friends. Couldn't be luckier."

Mary squeezes her hand. "What is she like?"

"Oh, Sarah is lovely. And respectful. And just—wonderful!" She pauses. "Her parents, Hayele and Abner, are not so convinced."

"About Asher?"

"About Rafi and me, as in-laws. Abner especially. But he's very successful and influential, so maybe that will be good for the kids' future."

"You don't have to grovel to anybody, Dinah. They'll come around."

Dinah forces a smile, as if hoping Mary is right. "I should go find Rafi."

Mary's own smile fades as loneliness comes over her.

## Chapter 47

# FIRST FORAY

*Outskirts of Capernaum, late morning*

Simon and Andrew leave Eden, who has sent them off with their lunches in cloth bags. Andrew looks uncomfortable, out of sorts. "You could have shown a little gratitude," Simon says.

"I *do* appreciate it. You heard me tell Eden how grateful I was."

"I heard your words. But I also watched your movements."

Andrew shifts the bag from one hand to the other. "I don't know what to do with it! I don't go on long trips. Do I hold it like this? If I had a stick, I could sling it over my shoulder."

Simon stops and helps him arrange the bag over a shoulder, then shrugs. "We'll see what the others do."

"What if they didn't pack lunch? Will we look stupid?" He stops. "What if it comes off as ungrateful?"

Simon makes him keep moving. "I don't know, maybe it'll look like we never traveled with the Messiah before and we don't know what we're doing!"

They walk on, the weight of this new life washing over

Simon like a wave. At the top of a grassy knoll, Andrew says, “I’m a bit nervous.”

“Come on, don’t be nervous. If you’re nervous, I’ll come on too strong.”

“Don’t tell me *you’re* not nervous,” Andrew says.

“I said I was.”

“No, you said, if *I’m* nervous, you—”

“I know what I said!” Simon shakes his head and looks away. “I don’t want to let him down.”

“I don’t want to do it wrong.”

“C’mon, we’ll probably both do it wrong. It’s like fishing. Remember when Abba taught us?”

“Dad didn’t teach us anything,” Andrew says. “We just sat there—”

“And watched! And then it was our turn and we made our own mistakes.”

Simon holds Andrew by the shoulders and cackles. “Can you believe this?”

Andrew shakes his head. From across the path, Thaddeus calls out, “Well, you guys are great!” He’s standing there with Mary of Magdala, the other James, and John. The four of them grin at the brothers, and Simon blushes. He separates from Andrew and says hello. “You been here long?”

They nod, and James says, “Oh, yeah.”

“Perfect day for a wedding, huh?” Jesus says, approaching.

“Master,” Simon says.

“Simon, Andrew, Mary, James, John, Thaddeus. But where is, uh—”

Fruit falls from above, and they look up to see John’s brother, James, in a tree. “Uh-oh,” Jesus says.

“Figs!” James says, perched on a branch. “For the journey!”

"Ah!" Jesus says, smiling. "Now we won't even need to stop for lunch."

Simon glances at Andrew, feeling as if everyone is staring at their cloth bags. James drops down from the tree, and Jesus says, "Thank you, James."

The other James looks up. "Yes, Master?"

"Aah," Jesus says, "two Jameses. How will we solve this dilemma?"

John's brother towers over the other James. "Well, how about if I go by Big James?"

"Is that acceptable to you, young James?" Jesus says.

"Yes, I think that's fair, Master."

"A sense of justice too, eh? Then it's settled. Now, to the road, my friends. The bride and bridegroom await."

## Chapter 48

# AWKWARD

*Cana*

Mary, brow furrowed, stands next to Dinah, both staring up at a crudely framed wood support for what would become the chuppah. "Hm. I think—I think it might be a little roomier on this side—"

"Perfect!" Dinah says.

"No?" Mary says.

"Yes, no. It's perfect." Dinah feels one of the support poles. "And sturdy!" But the structure wobbles at her touch.

Mary knows Dinah is making the best of the situation and doesn't want to go to any further expense. "Let me speak to the carpenters. I know their language."

"It will be fine! Will you help me decorate it?"

"Dinah, please! Let me do this for you."

"Mary, I love you, but Rafi and I got what we paid for. I'm embarrassed how few timbers we could afford."

"That's no reason to settle."

"Who's settling? It will be perfect. There are many other things to do today, Mary." Dinah smiles again. "You said so yourself."

"Always on the bright side."

"Someone has to be." Dinah looks distracted as an exquisitely dressed woman approaches. "Will you start on gathering more flowers?" Dinah asks Mary quickly.

"Of course."

• • •

As Mary steps away, Dinah says, "Shalom, Hayele," and moves to embrace her.

But the other woman merely bows and says, "Dinah."

Dinah gathers herself and returns the bow. "I'm delighted to share this special day. Is Abner here? I'd love to tell Rafi we have time for a special prayer tod—"

"Abner sent me on ahead. He'll come with friends before the ceremony. He asked me to select his table."

"Oh! Well, we have arrangements for everyone's seating already."

"Abner likes things his way. I'm here to see that they are."

Dinah's smile fades. "Even at our children's wedding feast?"

"Dinah, Abner is set in his ways. It's not personal."

"Well, it should be!" Dinah regrets her words as soon as they escape her lips, and Hayele surprises her with a look of empathy.

"On certain important occasions, I have been able to prevail on him."

"I hope this is important enough," Dinah says. She begins to move away, but Hayele stops her.

"Dinah, Sarah is unwavering in her love for your family."

Dinah nods, eager to ease the tension. "We love Sarah. And all of you. Very much."

"Sarah knows you do."

Hayele seems to notice the rickety wood structure for the first time. "Chuppah's crooked," she says.

Chapter 49

# ENTOURAGE

As Jesus leads Simon and Andrew, followed by Thaddeus, Mary, the two Jameses, and John, on the long walk toward Cana, Simon chews vigorously on an apple. He has an idea.

"I know that look," Andrew says as Simon presses the fruit into his brother's hands and hurries next to Jesus.

"Master!"

"Yes, Simon?"

"I was thinking. If this wedding is worth the journey for you, who has so much to do, perhaps it is also worth the journey for many wealthy Jews."

Jesus shoots him a glance. "You believe important and powerful Hebrews will be there."

"Possibly."

"You're very keen, Simon. The most important and powerful person I know will be there."

"Yeah?"

"My mother."

"Isn't your mother from Nazareth?" Andrew calls out from behind them. But his joke falls flat.

"You should announce yourself to the guests," Simon says. "Right? There'll be no Romans. Seems like the perfect place to gather more followers, get this whole thing moving."

"It's not my special day, Simon," Jesus tells him. "It's the special day of the couple, Asher and Sarah."

"They are blessed to have you at their wedding!" Andrew says. "Do they know what a remarkable thing it is?"

"Well, considering that I was the clumsy teenager who cracked my head open at Asher's when he was a child, I don't think he finds me remarkable." Jesus looks at Andrew. "Do you think much of your childhood friends?"

Simon says, "He didn't have any," making Jesus laugh.

"That's not true!" Andrew says.

"I stand corrected." Simon holds up his hands. "He had me. Compulsory service."

"I don't remember kids exactly lining up around the block to—"

"Mary!" Jesus says. "Did you think that having brothers would be like this?"

"Ha! I always wanted brothers as a little girl."

"When you have twelve, then tell me how you like it."

"Twelve?" Andrew says.

"You'll see. Ah! We're getting close now. Cana is just over the next rise."

Chapter 50

# ON TIME

Mary and Dinah garnish the chuppah with garlands of greenery and flowers. As they work, Dinah asks why Mary and Joseph had not celebrated their own marriage.

"We had a wedding," Mary says. "It just wasn't like everyone else's."

"Why not?"

"You know why," she says, drawing an imaginary bulge at her torso.

"I would have gone," Dinah says.

"I know. If Joseph were here, he would be so proud of you and Rafi. So happy for you."

"You don't think I'm overdoing it?"

"I would have said so."

"It's just that Hayele's canopy for their son's feast had exquisite and extravagant—"

"It doesn't even matter," Mary says. "Sarah and Asher will love it."

"Have you heard from your special guest?"

"He's coming!" Mary says, beaming. "He may bring several others. Is that okay?"

"He can bring everybody he wants. I haven't seen him in ages. How is he?"

"He's good. He's always good."

"I'm ecstatic for you. I imagine he's a fine craftsman."

Mary nods. "Well, he's not working." Dinah looks puzzled. Mary adds, "He has a calling. I seldom know where it will take him. He's bringing students."

"I'll bet he's handsome."

Mary demurs.

"I'll bet he *is*," Dinah says.

"Dinah!" Rafi calls out from across the courtyard. "Dinah, they're here!"

"Moment of truth," she whispers to Mary. "I made Rafi spend everything we had left for good wine, so wish me luck."

• • •

"You must be Thomas. I am Rafi, and this is my wife, Dinah."

Thomas bows. "Many blessings to you on this joyous day. And may I present the finest, most beautiful vintner in all of Galilee, Ramah bat Kafni of the Kafni Vineyards on the plains of Sharon."

"It is an honor to meet you at last," Rafi tells her. "You will give my regards to the old scoundrel upon your return." He turns to his wife. "Ramah is the daughter of my old friend Kaf."

"The wine is here on time," Dinah says. "A good start to a joyous day!"

"Of course," Ramah says. "Thomas is never late. My father sends his warmest regards—with this." She uncorks a clay jar. Rafi and Dinah lean in to sniff. "Pressed in the year Augustus died. Cut with seawater, honey from Mount Hermon, black pepper, and pine from Tyre."

"Divine!" Rafi says.

Ramah pours a cup, and Thomas hands it to Dinah.

"I certainly won't refuse that," she says. "Blessed are You, Lord our God, King of the universe, who brings forth the fruit of the vine." She sips it and looks rapturous. "Oh, my! Thank heaven on Asher's day." She turns to Rafi. "Abner and Hayele will be pleased." She adds in a whisper, "Maybe a little jealous even."

Ramah grins, but Rafi shakes his head. "Abner and Hayele. I'm now in debt because of wine for Abner and Hayele."

Dinah hushes him and asks Ramah, "How much is there?"

"Of the special vintage there are two amphorae, and one of a lesser. Of course, we intend to serve the best wine first, when the guests are fresh."

"Later," Thomas says, "when everyone is stuffed and senses dulled, we'll serve the remaining jar. Do you understand?"

"Yes, son," Rafi says. "It's the oldest trick in the book. We are in good hands!"

"And I assume the head count is still the same, forty or so at the time we bring the weak?"

"Is it?" Rafi says.

"I'm asking," Thomas says.

"I'm sure it's right," Dinah says.

"Perfect. Where would you like us to set up?"

"This way," Rafi says, pointing. "The master of the banquet will walk you through it."

• • •

As Rafi leads Thomas and Ramah away, Dinah turns at the sound of Jesus' voice. "Knock-knock," he says, laughing. "May we come in?"

She watches, smiling, as Mary races to him, tossing a handful of flowers aside. They wrap their arms around each other, and Jesus lifts her off the ground, grunting. “Hi, Ima! Oh, how are you? I missed you!”

“I have missed you!” He sets her down, and Mary takes his face in her hands. “Look at you! It’s been a while. Have you been eating?”

“I *have* been eating. And these people have been helping me to eat.” He gestures to the friends he has brought. His mother warmly greets them.

Chapter 51

# "WHAT'S HIS NAME?"

*The dungeon*

Nicodemus has recited the entire harrowing incident from his horrifying encounter in the Red Quarter, and John the Baptizer has appeared a preternaturally rapt listener. The bravado that had so annoyed the Pharisee seems a distant memory now. John stands stock-still, the color drained from his face. "Multiple demons?" he says.

"I saw it myself. They jeered at me from inside her mouth. Nothing could be done for her, short of a miracle."

"And she won't say who restored her?"

"He did not reveal his name to her."

Now John paces, his breath coming in short bursts.

"What?" Nicodemus says. "What?"

"It has begun!"

"*What* has?"

"If he's healing in secret now, the public signs cannot be far off!"

"Public signs? What? You *know* him?"

John stops and grips the bars, smiling at the Pharisee. "You can say that!"

"What's his name?"

John points skyward, grinning. "'Who has ascended into heaven and come back down?'"

"I asked his *name*!"

Excited, John continues. "'Who has gathered the wind in his fist . . . ?'"

Nicodemus fires back. "Don't quote Solomon to me, you wild mongrel!"

"'Who has wrapped up the waters in a garment . . . ?' Finish it!"

"No! You answer me first!"

"Teacher of Israel! Finish the oracle of Agur, son of Jakeh! 'Who has established all the ends of the earth?'"

And so, Nicodemus finishes it. "'What is his name, and what is the name of his son?'"

Breathless, John shakes his head, smiling. "Surely you know!"

"You are careless with Torah!" Nicodemus says. "God does not have a son except Israel! *Israel* is His only son!" Incensed at John's condescending grin, he adds, "All of us!"

"Suit yourself," the baptizer says, seeming to gloat, as if he knows something no one else does.

"You know, they'll put a man to death for blasphemy like that!"

"Who will? You? It would be a terrible precedent for Rome to adjudicate."

Nicodemus thrusts his stool aside and turns toward the door. "I should never have come here!"

"All your life you've been asleep," John says. "'Make straight the way for the King! He's here—to awaken the earth! But some will not want to waken. They're in love with the dark.' I wonder which one you'll be."

Nicodemus glares at him. "If this man is anything like you believe, or if he exists at all, you should leave this region. Your presence alone puts him in danger."

"If you think he needs my help, you've heard nothing."

As Nicodemus stalks out, John sounds ecstatic, panting. What so thrills him?

Chapter 52

# RUNNING LOW

*Cana*

Busy in the food preparation room, Thomas instructs the servants as a traditional wedding song wafts in from the courtyard, where guests sing and dance. "When the song is over, bring out the olives and the cheeses, and set them on the long table between the loaves of bread and the cucumbers."

• • •

Outside, Ramah tries to count the crowd as they dance around the tables, arms about each other's shoulders. In a panic, she rushes inside to find Thomas seasoning the lamb. "Am I going mad, or has forty been the magic number all along?"

"For the head count?" he says. "Why? Are we over? They always do this. I've got food enough for more." He turns back to the lamb.

"The last count was eighty!"

He spins back. "You made a mistake."

"Maybe by a few, but even if I'm off by five, the wine—"

"I did advocate for a fourth," he says, but she shoots him a look as if he's not helping. "But three," he adds timidly, "is still enough. For sixty."

• • •

Outside, the song ends to applause and laughter, and the banquet master raises a cup of wine. "Blessed are You, Lord our God, King of the universe, who brings forth the fruit of the vine."

*Amens* ring out, and everyone seems to imbibe at once. Cup after cup after cup.

• • •

Thomas demonstrates with a pitcher. "Lighten your pours," he tells the servants. "Like this, three quarters full. If they ask for more, tell them you'll be right back. But guess what? You won't be. Understand? Go!"

As the servants exit, the master of the banquet enters. "Well!" he says, and Thomas quickly straightens. "The guests seem to be happy so far. The servants do not. How are we doing?"

Thomas, dying inside, shrugs. "Nothing to worry about. And you are one of the finest banquet masters we have ever seen. Keep up the good work." Ramah nods, smiling.

The man's self-satisfied grin tells Thomas his flattery has worked. Hands clasped before him, the master grunts, "Hmm!" and walks out.

Thomas's smile fades, and he sighs. "What now?"

"I have an idea," Ramah says.

• • •

At the chuppah, Dinah and Rafi are thanking guests who offer congratulations and small talk. The crowd parts as the parents of the bridegroom approach in beautiful silk raiments. Dinah dreads what might be coming.

"Rafi! Dinah!" Abner calls out in his *basso profundo.* They greet him and he gazes at them, wine cup in his hand. "Well," he says, and pauses so long that even Hayele affects an awkward expression. Finally, he announces, "This is the best party I've been to in a long while!" Dinah is at first relieved, but then Abner laughs loudly and grabs Rafi's neck, pulling him close and planting a kiss on each cheek and one more for good measure, shouting "Mwah!" with each smack.

"You honor us, Abner," Dinah manages. "We are blessed to have two children so in love."

"Aah, I'm happy too," Abner says. "I'll be honest, I was not always happy about this. You may not have known that."

"Yes," Rafi says. "We know."

Dinah just wishes Abner would keep his voice down. But no such luck.

"You were born in *Nazareth*, Dinah," the man adds, as if it pains him to have to bring up such a distasteful subject. "Rafi, your people are *travelers,* and your trade, Rafi, hasn't brought you much success. And while Asher seems like a nice young man, he has not—"

"Yes, Abner," Rafi says. "We get it."

"Aah, I don't mean to insult."

*Too late*, Dinah thinks.

"My family have been powerful traders in this region for years!" Abner continues. "I believe success has made my generation arrogant."

*My sentiments exactly*. Could he be sincere? Abner gazes at the late afternoon sky, brow furrowed, and she waits for whatever else is coming.

"I lost my line of thought," he says at last. He gestures

toward the chuppah and turns to Hayele. "I thought you said this was crooked. Looks fine to me."

Dinah can't resist a triumphant glance at the woman. Abner and Hayele raise their wine cups and turn away, only to have Abner wheel back around and announce, "And this wine is delicious! I must know the vineyard."

It's all Dinah and Rafi can do to stifle their giggles.

• • •

Ramah leads Thomas to a cavernous storage room bearing six stone jars. "Purification water," she tells him. "There's still some left in these."

"Dilute the wine," he says, catching on. "But people will notice. Whispers will spread."

"If they did, I feel like this family would die of shame."

*This family?* Thomas thinks. "What about us? We'd be ruined."

"It's not a great option, I agree," Ramah says. "So, help me think!"

"We could serve the guests extra date cakes," he says. "Oversalt the food? Make them thirst for water?" He sighs. "I don't know. This is humiliating."

"Let's keep looking."

Chapter 53

# SURPRISE

As the day wears on into evening, the wedding feast guests laugh, eat, drink, and dance. Jesus sits with a group of children, delighting them with a shell game. They cackle and squeal at his reveals.

Simon sits with Andrew, Mary the Magdalene, Little James, and Thaddeus, eating and watching the festivities. Simon nods toward Jesus and the children. "They have no idea who sits before them." The master has stacked cups before the boys and girls, and when they tumble, the children laugh.

Thaddeus says, "To be a child again, yes?"

"I think we are the lucky ones," Mary says. "They have to go home with their parents tonight. We get to stay with him and his mother."

"Where will that be?" Andrew says.

Mary lifts her cup. "Who knows? With him I have learned to stop worrying about those things."

"I haven't," Andrew says. "It's cold in this region."

Little James says, "Do you think he would let you freeze?"

“My brother has many worries,” Simon says. “I keep reminding him of when our abba taught us how to fish. We sat there and watched until we became fishermen.”

“We will watch him,” Mary says. “And watch and watch and watch. Forever, I think.”

They fall silent until Andrew says, “I’m going to get more wine.”

“Get two.” Simon raises his empty cup but playfully pulls away when Andrew reaches for it. He finally lets him take it and says to the others, “I don’t even know why I’m here. It’s usually the students who choose the rabbi, not the other way around. And I’m not even a student.”

“Neither was I,” James tells them. “Thaddeus introduced me to him.”

“How did you meet?” Mary asks Thaddeus.

The young man looks embarrassed. “On a, uh, construction job. In Bethsaida. He hasn’t exactly been picking the best and brightest students.”

The others chuckle, but Simon is confused. “Wait. He works?”

“Well, until recently,” Mary says. “He’s not a professional rabbi.”

“Yeah, but I thought he has no home and no job?”

“No permanent home,” she says.

*Aha!* Simon thinks. “He’s a stonemason.” He looks to Thaddeus. “Like you.”

“A craftsman,” Thaddeus says. “He taught as well. He asked me to follow him. He said he was building a kingdom. A fortress stronger than stone. I believed him.”

“What were you building in Bethsaida?” Simon says.

“Uh, a public amenity.”

“An aqueduct?”

"No, uh, but something, ah, humbler."

"What then, man?"

"It's not proper to say in front of a woman," Thaddeus says.

Mary looks sober. "I have seen and heard things that would turn your blood to ice."

"A latrine?" Simon says. "Wait," he adds, looking to Mary. "Ice?"

She nods.

And Thaddeus says, "Yes."

"Our master," Simon says, "building a privy!"

"A job is a job," Thaddeus says. "I was cutting stone for the retaining wall. He was building a ramp of cedar planks so the crippled and the elderly could get to it without climbing the steep stairs."

"Why didn't he heal them so they could mount the steps themselves?"

"He's always saying," Mary says, "his time has not yet come."

"But calling you by name," Simon says. "The catch of fish. Why was it his time for miracles then, and not others?"

"Because those were private," Little James says. "He hasn't shown his signs to others publicly yet."

"What's keeping him from making his ministry public?"

Mary shrugs. "The wind blows to the south or to the east and you cannot say why."

That arrests Simon. "A latrine," he says, and they all laugh. "We'd better not spread that around."

"He doesn't hide where he's from," Mary says.

"Don't tell Andrew," Simon says. "That will—well, he'll be surprised."

"And now, friends!" the master of the banquet shouts. "The Dance of Miriam!"

The guests cheer and prepare to dance. Simon notices Jesus

has left the children, so when Andrew returns, they set off to find him.

• • •

On his knees in the wine room, Thomas reaches a ladle deep into an overturned jar and comes up empty. *What in the world are we going to do?* Just then Dinah enters. He freezes.

"Thomas," she says, her tone pregnant with dread. "Talk to me."

## Chapter 54

# CRISIS

Night has fallen, and torches and flaming cauldrons illuminate the courtyard of revelry. Simon, Andrew in tow, looks for Jesus. He hears the rabbi finishing a joke— "Just watch out for the frogs this time!" —and laughing before he appears around a corner. "Oh!" Jesus exults. "Sons of Jonah!"

"We were just looking for you," Simon says, then tells him the Dance of Miriam has been announced. "We thought you wouldn't want to miss it."

"Of course! Let's the three of us show 'em how it's done, huh?"

Andrew hesitates. "I don't think that's such a good idea."

"Why?"

"Well," Simon says, "Andrew has four left feet."

"Four?" Jesus says, clearly amused. "Why four?"

"When he tries to dance, he looks like a donkey walking on hot coals."

Jesus roars. "Oh, Andrew! Do you deny it?"

"I've never seen a donkey walking on hot coals," Andrew

says, glaring at Simon. "Actually, that would be a terrible thing to behold."

"My son!" Mary rushes to them, panic on her face. Thomas and Ramah stop several feet behind her.

"Aah, Andrew, you see? Even my own mother will join us in the Song of Miriam!"

"They've run out of wine," Mary tells Jesus.

Silence.

Finally, Andrew says, "But it's only the first day."

"Yes. And it's all gone. Not a drop left."

"Why are you telling *me* this?" Jesus asks her.

Mary whispers, "We can't let the celebration end like this, with Asher's family humiliated."

Jesus stares at her, then reaches for Simon and Andrew. "Brothers, go join the others. I'll be right there."

• • •

Jesus pulls Mary a few steps from where Thomas and Ramah watch. He lays a hand on her shoulder and whispers, "Mother, my time has not yet come."

She covers his hand with her own and holds his gaze. "If not now, when? Please."

He softens and sighs, allowing a hint of a smile. She grins and pulls away, hurrying to Thomas and Ramah. "Do whatever he tells you," she says.

• • •

Thomas has no idea what to make of this. Do whatever this stranger says? He leads the man to the storeroom where the six stone water jars lie. He turns up his palms, as if resigned.

The man folds his arms and rests his chin in his hand. He appears to study the vessels. "Fill these jars with water."

Thomas shoots him a look. "I'm not sure you heard her clearly. We've run out of wine, not water."

"These are similar in size to your amphorae."

*So what*? Thomas wonders. "To the prudent marks, yes. Equal if filled all the way to the brim."

He feels the man's eyes on him. "You are a very responsible person, aren't you?"

*What does that have to do with anything*? "We are in a crisis," Thomas says. "And I was led to understand you have a solution?"

"Do you know why jars for purification rites are made of stone?"

Thomas laughs. "What?"

"You heard me," the stranger says, not unkindly.

Thomas lets his smile fade and looks past the man to Ramah. She nods. He swallows and turns back. "Because the stone is pure," he says quietly. "Less likely to stain or break. It can't be made unclean."

"Yes. Fill these jars with water, all the way to the brim."

Thomas still doesn't get it. "Why?"

Ramah turns to the servants crowding the doorway and peering in. "You heard him. Start drawing water. Quickly. Tell anyone you find to stop what they're doing and help."

Thomas shakes his head at her, but she just nods back and follows the others out. Alone with the man now, Thomas covers his face with his hands. "From the directions you have provided, I see no logical solution to the problem."

"It's going to be like that sometimes, Thomas."

He had not told this man his name and hadn't heard anyone else tell him either. Thomas looks at him, stunned. "What did you say?"

"I do not rebuke you. It is good to ask questions. To seek understanding."

The man speaks with such quiet authority. But— "There's no time for this," Thomas says.

"I know of a man like you in Capernaum. Always counting. Always measuring."

"That's my job," Thomas tells him, "one that people will think I have not done well tonight."

The man steps closer. "Join me," he says, "and I will show you a new way to count. And measure. A different way of seeing time."

What could he possibly mean? "Go with you where? I don't understand."

The man stares at him, as if into his soul. "Keep watching," he says.

## Chapter 55

# THE MIRACLE

Abner munches salty seeds from the bottom of his bowl, lifts his wine cup to his lips, and stares at Hayele. Empty. He struggles unsteadily to his feet. "Dinah!"

She hurries over. "Abner! I do hope you are enjoying yourself."

"Where are the servers?"

"I don't know, but I'll go find them right away."

The banquet master approaches. "It is far past time for another round of wine," he tells her. "The last one was nearly an hour ago."

"Yes! Well, you see—"

"Surely there is more coming, Dinah," Abner says.

She seems to find it hard to speak and just nods.

"I'm very sorry," the banquet master says. "Please do not worry. This will be taken care of immed—"

Dinah's close friend, the widow she calls Mary, arrives and takes Dinah by the shoulder. "Next round of wine right away," she announces to Abner. "Thank you for reminding us. It's all under control."

• • •

Mary of Magdala sits with Thaddeus. "Was your father a stonemason as well?"

"No," he says. "A smith. I think it broke his heart, but I apprenticed under a stonecutter when I was nine—and every man must leave his father."

She smiles. "Masonry seems like harder work."

"It isn't harder. It's just more, ah, final. If the smith wants to change the horseshoe or the plowshare or the pothook, he has only to put the iron back into the fire and reshape it to fit his designs."

Mary of Magdala is intrigued by the thoughtfulness of young Thaddeus. "Once you make that first cut into the stone," he says, "it can't be undone. It sets in motion a series of choices. What used to be a shapeless block of limestone or granite begins its long journey of transformation, and it will never again be the same as it was."

• • •

Thomas remains dumbfounded—not to mention skeptical—standing next to the stranger and, along with a couple of servants, watching as Ramah finishes pouring the last jug into the sixth purification water jar. She turns to him and the man. "They're full," she says, seeming not to breathe, eyes wide.

*What is the point of all this?* Thomas wonders as the man gazes at Ramah and the servants.

"Everyone, please step outside," the man says softly. Ramah leads them out, but Thomas stays. "Just for a moment, Thomas," the man adds.

With a last suspicious look at the jars of water, then at the man, Thomas heads for the door.

• • •

Jesus leans over the mouth of one of the vessels, his candlelit reflection gazing back from the water. He looks up, as if past the ceiling into the heavens. A great weight washes over him as he realizes the step he's about to take. This act will begin a new existence for him—at least in the eyes of others. His role, his calling, his destiny will become known to all. No turning back.

He closes his eyes, lowers his head, and sighs. "I'm ready, Father."

Jesus lays his left hand on the rim of the jar and reaches into the water with his right. He slowly cups his palm and raises his hand, closing his fist as a deep red liquid splashes back into the jar, its rich, heavy aroma filling the room.

• • •

Thomas stands with Ramah, two servants behind them, and watches the doorway. What could this man be doing? Does he fancy himself some sort of a magician? Or does he have a secret concoction, something to add to the water that will fool drunken guests? Suddenly the man steps out with a solemn look. "Go draw some out," he says, "and serve it to the master of the banquet."

What? Is he serious? Ramah looks at Thomas, but he can't move. She rushes past the man, carrying the empty pot she had used to pour the last of the water into the jar. The servants follow. Thomas can only stare at the man until Ramah and the servants exult, hollering from the other room. The man smiles at him and walks away.

• • •

Dinah stands with Jesus' mother, listening to the crowd, who have been without wine for much too long now, murmur over the music. She's sick at heart, dreading an end of the feast before the first night is done. Yet Mary has announced to Abner that more wine is coming, and she seems so sure.

Ramah, holding a goblet, advances upon the master of the banquet. Where could this new wine have come from? Had the hosts held some back or found some substitute? Oh, please let it be close to acceptable!

From across the courtyard, Dinah hears Abner grouse to Hayele, "It's about time!"

Ramah pours from the goblet into the master of the banquet's cup. "The latter vintage, sir," she whispers.

"Good, let's have a taste."

He lifts it to his lips and appears dumbfounded. "Stop the music! Stop the music! Everyone! Listen! I have something I would like to say! I would like to address the bridegroom and the bride's families. At every wedding I've ever overseen, they serve the best wine first. And then, when the people have drunk freely, much later in the feast, they serve the poorer wine—the cheap stuff!"

The people laugh knowingly, and Dinah wonders where this is going. Is the man trying to distance himself from this disaster?

"Because by then," he continues, "who is going to notice?" He grins as they laugh more. "Am I right? But you," he says, looking to Rafi and then to Dinah, "you have chosen now to serve the best wine I have ever tasted! Let us thank them for this unnecessary but honorable gesture!"

Applause erupts, and Abner points at Rafi with a huge grin.

The servants bring out trays of full cups and begin passing them out.

The master of the banquet isn't finished. "May the wedding of Asher, son of Rafi and Dinah, to Sarah, daughter of Abner and Hayele, be as pure and as fruitful as this wine. Blessed are You, Lord our God, King of the universe, who brings forth the fruit of the vine. To Asher and Sarah!"

The crowd lifts their cups and shouts in unison, "To Asher and Sarah!"

Dinah beams with pride as guests sip the wine and seem astonished to the point of silence. Except for Abner, of course. He's drunk from his cup and now stares at it, his face a mystery.

"Something wrong?" his wife says.

"Yes. I was."

Dinah sees Mary catch her son's eye from across the courtyard and mouth thank-you.

• • •

Back in the storeroom, Thomas stands still as a statue, staring at the vessels full of wine.

• • •

Outside, Simon stares at Jesus. "Fish," he says. "Wine. What will be next?"

Jesus shrugs. "Any suggestions?"

"Anything. And everything. Let's do this." He claps. "I'll go with you to the ends of the earth."

Jesus steps forward, suddenly solemn. "I hope so, Simon." And now with a gleam in his eye, "But I seem to remember there was a problem."

*A problem?* Simon thinks. *What is he talking about?*

"Something about Andrew's feet."

Simon grins. "Andrew's feet!"

Andrew apparently overhears and approaches with their other friends.

"But first," Jesus says, "we must evaluate, no?"

"No," Andrew objects. "No, no, no, I can't."

"I think we have to."

Andrew continues to demur, but Simon and the rest join in. "Come on, Andrew!" They circle him, raising their arms and pulling him in. Soon, they're all shouting and singing and dancing, Jesus and his followers reveling to the music. The bridal families join in, and Abner grabs Rafi, dancing with him alone.

The mothers and the two Marys dance with the bride in the middle of it all.

In the large circle, Simon shouts to Jesus, "So, will you help him?"

Jesus laughs, watching Andrew hop around. "Ah, some things even I cannot do!" bringing the others nearly to their knees.

• • •

Thomas wanders outside as the merriment dies and people stand around talking. He gazes across the way at the man they call Jesus, chatting with others.

Ramah joins Thomas. "That should be it for the night," she says. She follows his gaze. "Who is he?" Thomas does not respond. She adds, "We cannot pretend we didn't see a miracle. He gave us even more than we need."

"He invited me to join him," Thomas tells her. "He wants us to meet him in Samaria. In twelve days."

"Samaria," she whispers.

Thomas shakes his head. "I don't know what to think."

She pauses. "So, don't." When he finally turns to look at her, she says, "Maybe for once in your life, don't think."

PART 7

# Indescribable Compassion

Chapter 56

# EXPOSED

A stonemason with a terrible secret stands in line for hours outside a pawnbroker's shop in a sparsely populated village in the Galilean countryside. He's hoping against hope that by coming to this godforsaken place, he will be able to slip in and out unnoticed, perhaps pocketing a few shekels for the treasures he bears. Others in the line appear to be the dregs of society—the lame, the crippled, the ill. They carry odds and ends, random objects they apparently hope will net them something to survive on for another week. The mason dresses lavishly compared to the others, though his unseasonably long sage green tunic and yellow turban make him pour sweat like a man at hard labor under a hot sun.

The woman in the shop before him stomps out. "You're a liar!" she cries, throwing a handful of rocks to the ground.

The mason enters casually, fighting to keep his composure, bearing a rolled stretch of leather. Used items of widely varying value cram the place.

"She was crazy," the broker states, as if he'd been asked. "Just because I run a charity does not mean I have to buy rocks from every old lady."

What a laugh. "Charity?"

The broker, leaning on an ornately carved cane, says, "Just like everything Roman, it's part of business. We lend to the poor proceeds seized from criminals." He looks the stonemason up and down. "And others, as well. You are passing through. I do not recall seeing you before."

"I come from Tyre," he says, opening the leather roll, revealing his tools. "The mallet is carved of maple from Sidon. The chisels are bronze. The trowel is tin from Phoenician ore."

The pawnbroker looks impressed. "My, my," he says. "Why would anyone want to part with these?"

"I'm on my way to the Dead Sea," the mason says, knowing it's not much of an explanation.

"Shalom, pilgrim! Lucky me! I do not often see items of such quality." He frowns. "If only they were not brought in by some stranger passing through."

"They weren't stolen, if that's what you're saying."

The broker raises his brows and reaches into a bowl of coins, transferring a few to a bowl closer to the customer. "I can justify twenty denarii."

"You're joking! That's a fraction of what they're worth!" He gestures toward the tools, causing his sleeve to rise, exposing festering sores.

The broker leaps back and covers his mouth. "Hades and Styx!"

"I beg you—"

"Leper!" He pokes the mason in the chest with his cane, sending him sprawling. "You are marked! You couldn't just die? You had to take us all to hell?"

The mason struggles to his feet.

"You are forbidden to come within four cubits of me!" the proprietor yells.

The leper scoops the denarii from the bowl.

"Take it and go!"

"I didn't mean you any harm. My tools were all I had left."

• • •

*Outside Matthew's tax booth, Capernaum*

The taxman and his assigned guard, Gaius, peer into a huge chest on the ground, filled with gold and silver and other treasures—Simon and Andrew's payment. Those in line also stare. Paranoid, Gaius slams it shut and whispers, "I never knew those little skiffs could hold so many fish."

"They can't," Matthew says. "The weight of the catch and the sailors caused the boat to sink. They had to jump. They ended up filling two boats. Should we put this inside the booth?"

"They'll be here any minute," Gaius says, referring to his compatriots who will accompany him and the payment to the Roman Authority headquarters.

"At least you have your sword," Matthew says. "Should I have a weapon?"

*Oh, for the love ... That's all we need, this man with a weapon.* Gaius shoots him a look. "This can't be the first time you've been saddled with a couple months' worth of—"

"Two years and seven weeks."

"Two *years* and seven weeks?" Gaius says, realizing immediately he has invited yet another endless explanation.

And here it comes. "Simon and Andrew were each granted one year gratis. That totals one year and seven weeks, plus another year, less marital credit for Simon—"

Gaius tries to stop him with a gesture. "Okay, that's—"

"... plus penalties."

"Okay, that's good." Gaius surveys the crowd, knowing he and Matthew—one of their own who has turned on them—are hated above all others. "We're sitting ducks here." Matthew isn't helping, leaning over the box with fingers entwined. "Just try to—try to look natural."

"I am natural. I look exactly how I feel."

That's for sure, but the frustrating little man incenses Gaius. "Try to act like a normal person under normal circumstances!" he says. Matthew looks puzzled. Gaius adds, "Forget I said normal."

Gaius' colleague approaches with two other legionnaires. "Gaius!" he says.

"Yes, Marcus."

Marcus whistles as he eyes the box. "Thought it was a joke."

"You could say it was comical when the men leapt from their boats," Matthew says in his matter-of-fact tone.

"Leapt from their boats?"

"They were sinking from the weight."

Marcus turns to Gaius. "Told you it was made up. Can't catch this many fish that fast—"

"Captain!" Gaius says. "Can we continue this conversation on the road?"

"Oh, Gaius, don't tell me you're nervous about guarding a couple of months' taxes."

• • •

*Capernaum Sanhedrin, that evening*

Nicodemus stands front and center, addressing the leader and a gallery of others, including Shmuel and Yusef.

"I've just returned from questioning at length the man known as John the Baptizer, while in Roman custody, Av Beit Din. Though his appearance is unconventional and his teachings ignorant, I've concluded he presents no material threat to Herod or to the public peace."

This causes a stir among the assembled. The Av Beit Din calls for order, then says, "The man has a following. We've heard as much from brother Shmuel's testimony. Is that not a matter of concern?"

Nicodemus smiles. "I believe these followers are simply investigating, as one would a loud noise—and on inspection, they will find that his words bear as much substance. He seeks attention. They do not gather on the Jordan to be immersed as we understand ritual cleansing. They stand in line because others are standing in line." He steals a glance at Shmuel, knowing his own magnanimity toward John serves as a rebuke to Shmuel's bitterness. "We only legitimized him by ordering his detention. The very effort to keep him silent gives him a pedestal."

The Av Beit Din looks baffled, and the other judges also appear confused. Except Shmuel. Nicodemus knows why, of course.

"But, Nicodemus," the chief judge says, "we issued no such order."

"Oh? I was shown sworn statements from the arresting soldiers saying a Pharisee had ordered his detention. Perhaps they were mistaken."

Shmuel rises. "It was me! I turned him in."

The Av Beit Din frowns. "Brother Shmuel!"

"'He who justifies the wicked,'" Shmuel insists, "'and he who condemns the righteous are both alike an abomination to the Lord!'"

The Av Beit Din looks exasperated. "Quoting the proverbs of Solomon is not an explanation."

"I will not turn a blind eye to his sins, even when all others do!"

"What sins?"

"He called us a brood of vipers!"

Nicodemus chuckles. "He uses coarse language to attract attention."

"Do you know how vipers are born?" Shmuel demands. "They hatch inside their mothers! The Law of Moses says, 'You shall not hate your brother in your heart!'"

Nicodemus grows serious and responds, "Were he a member of our congregation or our faction, we would admonish him! But he's not! He's a rogue who answers to no one."

"Brother Shmuel," the Av Beit Din says, "your rash actions have inflated the importance of a trivial outlier and drawn undue attention to our sect by Rome."

"But he—"

"And I'm astonished that any student of the great and learned Nicodemus would have the temerity to bypass his approval."

Shmuel lowers his head, and Nicodemus says, "I'll talk to him, Av Beit Din."

"You will defer to your teacher," the leader continues, "on all matters of polity and practice. Do I make myself clear?"

Shmuel sighs and raises his head. "Yes, your honor."

"This council is adjourned."

Nicodemus bows to the Av Beit Din, but Shmuel storms out past his mentor.

Chapter 57

# THE PROMOTION

*Outside Cana, morning*

Jesus' followers are breaking camp. Simon, used to long days and nights fishing, finds himself exhausted by this work. As he and Little James dismantle a tent, the latter doubles over, panting. Simon supports himself on a tent pole to catch his breath but says, "I'm glad I'm not the only one."

James grins. "I thought I was prepared for life on the road. Snakes, hunger, floods."

"Torah doesn't mention the blisters, huh?"

"What, you never read the book on constant, low-level aches?"

"The sermon on dust in your nose?" Simon says.

They continue packing. Simon says, "So, what'd you do before you met him?"

"I, um, I was on my way to join the two-eighty-eight."

Simon squints at him. "The Jerusalem Temple Choir?"

James nods.

*Very funny*, Simon thinks. "Right, okay. Yeah, I was Caesar's favorite gladiator."

James laughs, and then breaks into song. "My soul thirsts for you, my flesh longs for You, in a dry and weary land where there is no water."

The others stop what they're doing, appearing awed. They applaud, and Simon nods. "Hey! Wow! I stand corrected."

"Thank you."

"It's clear why Jesus asked you to join him."

Little James scratches his head as they go back to work. "I don't know if anything's clear. You know, maybe I'll sing, maybe not. He's the only one who knows who I'll become. More than anything, he's a teacher, and we are his students."

Jesus approaches. "Good voice," he says to Little James. "Simon?"

"Rabbi?"

"I'm going to escort my mother back to Nazareth. I'll catch up with the others at our camp in Capernaum."

"I understand. I'll make sure everyone arrives safely."

"I want you to go on ahead."

"Ahead of the others?"

"Yes," Jesus whispers. "You have some business to tend to at home."

"But, Teacher, I can protect the others."

Jesus grips Simon's shoulders. "In time you will. The others don't have families. You do. Look at me," he adds. "I'm leaving all this fun to escort my Ima."

• • •

*Roman Authority headquarters, Capernaum*

Gaius waits, breathless, with Matthew and a centurion captain as Praetor Quintus inspects a ledger. Gaius has never been comfortable in Quintus' presence.

"Remarkable," the praetor says, grinning. "For the first time in a year, quarterly collections will have exceeded Pilate's projections. And if the fishermen are no longer fishing on Shabbat . . ." He tosses an olive, catches it in his mouth, and slides the bowl across his desk. "Have an olive, Matthew. You've earned it."

"Thank you, Dominus." Matthew grimaces and uses a handkerchief to fetch one.

"Simon the cheat," Quintus says. "Simon the fraud. Simon, the man who delivered when it mattered most. I wonder if there's a way to make him do it again."

Gaius wishes Matthew would just let the praetor talk. But no. It's as if he can't help himself.

"It wasn't Simon, Dominus," Matthew says.

"What if I told him it wasn't enough?" Quintus says. "He obviously performs well under pressure, and I do have a knack for creating stakes."

*Shut up, Matthew*, Gaius pleads with a look. Again, hopeless.

"Simon wasn't responsible for this, Dominus."

"Oh, I don't care who he conscripts into his schemes."

"Forgive me, Dominus, if my report was unclear. There was a man—"

"Yes! You are a fine reporter, Matthew. But you're also a bit of a rube. I read your report. It's clear Simon and his accomplice tricked you."

"But there were others—"

"Accomplices, fine."

*Let it go, taxman*! Gaius wishes.

But it's obvious the praetor's comments make no sense to Matthew. "To what end?"

"Who can say?" Quintus says. "Maybe Simon wanted the other fishermen off his back. You said yourself, word of his disloyalty had spread. Or maybe he wanted to spook anyone who'd fish on Shabbat. He is a wily one."

"The fishermen have taken notice."

"Aah, it couldn't have worked out better." He pauses, appearing to study Matthew. "Don't tell me you're spooked?"

"I'm neither sophisticated nor subtle, Dominus. But I am observant. I detected no subterfuge. I recorded everything I witnessed—however impossible it seems."

"You did well, Matthew," Quintus says soothingly. "Fortunately, you have me to interpret for you."

A messenger bursts in, pushing between Gaius and Matthew. "Forgive me, Praetor!" he says. "It's urgent!"

"No kidding," the praetor says, as if the man should know he could be killed for such an intrusion.

"King Herod's envoy approaches."

That sobers Quintus. "Spotted where?"

"Outside Gennesaret. Riding north."

Quintus rises, appearing giddy. "Captain!" he calls over his shoulder. "Silvius Gamalius, son of Senator Gamalius, will be arriving in one hour."

"Yes, Dominus."

"Prepare my guard for inspection."

The captain bows and exits, and Gaius wonders if he should drag Matthew away too. But not until he's dismissed.

Quintus strides to his wardrobe and riffles through his dress options. He slowly turns, clearly amused. "How long would you have stood there?"

*Probably forever*, Gaius decides, but neither he nor Matthew respond.

"Things turned out very well with Simon," the praetor says, "and I'm grateful. Gaius! I've reviewed your service records. You're Germanic."

"My people *were*." *Surely he won't hold that against me.*

"Powerful warriors. Even if they did surrender."

"I believe they sensibly joined the winning team, Dominus."

"Sensibly."

What does the praetor want to hear, need to hear? "My only allegiance is to Rome. I have trained to fight for her since I was a boy."

"And now you will lead."

What? What could he mean?

"I hereby promote you to the rank of primi."

Gaius drops to one knee, head bowed. "Thank you for this honor, Praetor!"

"Don't slobber. And Matthew, you're so wonderfully—odd! Keenly intelligent, but it's your reactions to the world I love." Gaius rises, wondering how Matthew will respond to such insulting praise. Quintus continues, "Like right now! How you're not a stain on a cartwheel is a mystery we will have many moons to unravel, my new friend."

"I saw no ruse or deception at the seashore, Dominus."

"Because you have no guile. Give me your first reaction to this scenario: You will shortly be visited by a childhood rival whose father gave him everything, while yours gave you nothing, and yet you've risen to a higher rank." Gaius recognizes the praetor is talking about his own upcoming meeting, but there's no way Matthew could decipher this. Quintus adds, "You want to make it clear you won, that it's your meeting, even if he arrived unannounced."

Amazingly, Matthew does seem to catch on. "I would show him my plans for infrastructure," he says. "Conquest is not simply conquering nations but imposing a way of life."

Quintus appears frozen by the genius of it. "Unbelievable. So simple." He rushes to his desk and opens a scroll of technical sketches. "You're dismissed."

"Thank you, Praetor," Gaius says with a bow. Matthew appears to want to say more. Gaius yanks him away.

Chapter 58

# THE LEPER

Mary of Magdala walks with Jesus and several of his other disciples, approaching the edge of Capernaum. She can't help but wonder at her new life and new friends, including men she actually admires and trusts. Of course, she's learning—it seems every moment—from Jesus, but those he has called impress her too with their curiosity, their obedience, their devotion to him. And for the first time in how long, she feels honored and respected. These men evidence no ulterior motives.

They chat as they pass others on the road, and as they come into a clearing, they happen upon a striking black woman on her knees, filling a basket with flowers. "Hello!" Mary calls out, and the woman rises. She wears an ornate headdress of various metallic pendants and a broad necklace of polished wood.

"Hello," the woman says. "Shalom."

"It's a beautiful day for picking flowers," Mary says.

The woman smiles. "Well, if you like Gilboa iris, lupine, and anemone, I sell them in the market."

Jesus gestures toward the woman's necklace. "Is that Egyptian?"

"Yes, I grew up there. My father was from Ethiopia."

Mary is stunned when Jesus breaks into a foreign language. The beautiful woman responds in kind. After a brief exchange, she switches back to Aramaic. "Shalom to you all!"

As she departs, John approaches Jesus. "You were speaking Egyptian?"

"Yes, I told her I grew up in Egypt too and that her necklace reminds me of things I saw in my childhood. She told me she was Tamar of Heliopolis, and I told her who I was and wished peace to her. She thanked me."

Mary looks to the others and knows they're thinking what she's thinking: Of course he speaks Egyptian. "Why were you there?" she says.

"We had to leave Bethlehem when I was two years old because of Herod."

"You lived in Bethlehem?" Big James seems surprised. "During the massacre of the innocents?"

"I did."

"I know the story," Big James says. "Herod had every boy in the area under the age of two killed."

"Yes. It was very sad." Jesus sighs. "Not to spoil this beautiful day or anything, eh? Come on."

But as they set out again, Mary screams, and the others stop. A gaunt man in a ragged, sage green tunic and filthy, yellow turban staggers toward them, his breath coming in rasps, his skin ravaged.

John pulls a knife. "It's a leper! Stay back!"

"Cover your mouths!" Little James shouts. "Don't breathe his air!"

"Don't come any closer!" John says, menacing with his blade.

"It's okay, John," Jesus says, a hand on his arm. "It's okay." He sheds his own pack and approaches the man.

The others reach out to Jesus, calling, "Rabbi! Rabbi! No! His disease!" Jesus silences them with a look and a raised hand.

As he turns back toward the man, the leper cries, "Please! Please!" He drops to his knees. "Please don't turn away from me."

Jesus stands over him. "I won't."

"Lord! If you are willing, you can make me clean! Only if you want to. I submit to you." He's sobbing now. "My sister, she was a servant at the wedding. She told me what you could do. I know you can heal me if you are willing."

Jesus kneels before him. "I am willing."

Panting, laughing, crying, the man trembles as Jesus lays a hand on his shoulder. Mary and the others gasp as they see the man's rotting flesh become new. He reaches for Jesus, and they embrace as he gushes, "I knew it! I knew it! I knew it! What can I ever do to—"

Jesus shakes his head. "Do not say anything to anyone."

The man looks stunned. "You don't seek your own honor?"

"Please, just do me this one thing."

"But what do I tell people?"

Jesus stands, lifting the man to his feet. "Go, show yourself to the priest. Let him inspect you to see that you are cleansed. Make the proper offering in the temple, as Moses commanded, and go on your way."

The man just shakes his head, beaming.

Jesus turns to his disciples. "Who has an extra tunic?" Mary watches as the men who just moments before had feared for their lives all begin digging into their packs. "Just one of you," Jesus says. "That's enough."

Thaddeus rushes forward and helps Jesus dress the man in a fresh garment. Jesus chuckles. "Green is definitely your color. Not too shabby."

As the man hurries off, Mary and the others regroup to continue their journey toward Big James and John's home. She notices that Tamar has left her basket and flowers on the ground.

Chapter 59

# THE QUESTION

*Capernaum*

Zebedee would rather be fishing, though his profession has become lonely since his sons James and John abandoned it. He and his wife, Salome, had given James and John their blessing on that decision, yet still he misses their raucous days together on the Sea of Galilee.

But their sons are expected home today, along with the man they all believe is the Messiah himself. Zebedee has promised his wife he will help her prepare. He stands on the roof at one end of a pulley, like those atop the houses of his neighbors in the fishing district. It feeds down into the house through a trapdoor, allowing the fishermen to raise equipment, supplies, sometimes even catches, to the roof without having to haul them up the steps at the side of the house.

Today his wife is making use of the convenience. A tug on the rope tells him Salome has filled another basket of foodstuffs ready to be hoisted aloft and cured in the sun before the boys and their guest arrive. As Zebedee begins the careful lift, she calls up to him, "Spread out the flax! It dries faster!"

Does she not realize he knows that? "Okay!" he bellows.

"Zebedee!"

What now? "Yes?"

"Can you check the grapes, please?"

"Aah! I forgot!" How he has grown to love this woman! But on the sea, he needs no constant instruction. He secures the dangling basket. Then, to himself, "We no longer have anyone on raisin duty." James and John used to help with all this. He's heard that Jesus fondly refers to them as the Sons of Thunder. *But if that's what they are*, he thinks, smiling, *what does that make me?*

Salome has been a great wife and devoted mother, but not much of a cook. She has only nuts, seeds, fruit, and a little bread for their soon-arriving guests. At least she'll finally get to meet the man he and the boys had met on the shore the day of the miracle of the fish.

Zebedee lifts a cloth off the grapes and bites into one. "Too tart," he mumbles, tossing the seed over the wall. His eye drawn to the horizon, he smiles. "Salome! They're coming!" He skips to the edge of the roof and down the stairs.

"Zeb! Be careful!"

His sons lead a small contingent, and he rushes to them, grunting and laughing and pulling them in, kissing them.

• • •

Salome steps out just in time to find herself face-to-face with the man Zebedee had described as Jesus.

"Hello," he says, and she finds herself staring, speechless. It's not that he's striking or even handsome in a conventional sense. There's just something about him. She doesn't know whether to laugh or cry. Jesus appears amused by her reaction.

She's aware her sons have pulled away from her husband and approached. A woman stands there too. But Salome's eyes are still on Jesus. "James," she manages. "John."

"Yes, Ima."

"Listen to him. Please. And stay by his side."

"We will."

Jesus smiles. "It's a pleasure to meet you, too, Salome. I'm Jesus of Nazareth."

"Of course you are."

"And hello again, Zebedee."

"It's an honor, Rabbi."

Salome still gazes at Jesus.

"Ima," John says. "Ima!"

She finally turns, laughing. "Where are my manners? Please, come in."

"Are you certain?" Jesus says. "There will be others joining us."

"I insist! Everyone, please."

• • •

As his wife leads the others inside, Zebedee pulls his sons aside. "Hey, where's Simon?" It would be just like him to have already caused some ruckus and lost his place among Jesus' followers.

James points down the street. "He's taking care of some things at home. Andrew is getting him now."

"Mm. Good. I thought maybe he got cold feet, or I'd have to go drag him out of The Hammer."

"Are you kidding?" John says, grinning. "He's the teacher's pet."

"You would hardly recognize him now," James adds, and Zebedee laughs.

• • •

Not far away, Simon sits next to his mother-in-law's bed and sings a lullaby as he dabs at her arms and hands with a cool, damp cloth. He presses it against her forehead, then adjusts her blanket. He emerges to find Andrew regaling Eden with what happened at Cana.

"The wine! Oh! He introduced us to all of his friends. It—it really was unlike anything. We danced. He danced!"

"He danced?" Eden says.

"Yes!"

The account reminds Simon of the miracle. But his mind is on Eden's mother. "She's asleep," he says. "Breathing is labored but steady."

"Okay," Eden says. "Good."

Andrew nods, then casts a mischievous look with which Simon is all too familiar. "That was some soulful singing, my man."

Simon looks to Eden, who's obviously trying to stifle a grin.

Andrew tells Simon the others are at Zebedee's, so they say their goodbyes and head outside. They joke about Salome's cooking, and Simon says, "Don't tell Eden I said that."

In the yard, Matthew rocks on the balls of his feet and averts his gaze as Simon approaches. "Taxman!"

"Simon. Andrew."

The cheek of this man! "I guess no one told you the good news," Simon says.

"We squared our debts with Quintus," Andrew tells him.

"Isn't that great?" Simon says, drawing near. He whispers, "So go back to your cage. And stop following us."

They leave him, but he calls after them. "It's not you!" They stop, their backs to him. "I'm here about the man."

That's it for Simon. This dog had better not be talking about— "What man?"

"The man at the shore who made the fish appear."

Simon has never felt so protective. He whirls and glares. "The man at the shore—" Advancing on the tax collector, he grabs Matthew's tunic in both hands and pulls him close. "You saw no man at the shore! You hear me?"

"Yes, I did! I was there! I saw!"

"And the first thing you did was tell Rome, huh?"

"They don't believe me!"

So, he did tell them! "You really are a traitor." Simon rears back to throw a punch.

"Simon!" Andrew cries, wrapping him in his arms.

"Best for you to forget it," Simon spits as his brother holds him back.

"Go home, Matthew," Andrew adds.

The man cowers, but then seems to muster his courage. "They don't believe what I saw. But I do. I need to know. Am I deceived?"

Simon is too disgusted to respond.

Andrew says, "What good is our answer if you don't even listen to yourself?"

Chapter 60

# CROWDED

It's not lost on Nicodemus that only Shmuel remains seated when he enters the Capernaum synagogue to address pharisaical students. He has considered the younger man a protégé for years, but having dismissed what he considered Shmuel's overreaction to the wilderness baptizer has clearly embarrassed Shmuel before the local Sanhedrin. He will have to develop thicker skin if he's to continue his rise among the Pharisees, Nicodemus thinks.

Shmuel's student Yusef stands at the lectern, preparing the scrolls for Nicodemus, and the others bow to the dignitary from Jerusalem.

"Welcome, Rabbi," Yusef says.

"Greetings!"

"Everything is prepared, Teacher. The scrolls of Isaiah and Malachi. Would you like us to get you any water, Teacher, or—?"

"No, thank you. Actually, I'd like to do the readings a little later. Would you mind giving me a little time to myself?"

"Of course, Teacher."

Shmuel finally rises as the others file out, but Nicodemus says, "Shmuel! Would you join me please?"

Nicodemus' former protégé stops, looking as if it's the last thing he wants to do.

• • •

Simon already misses Eden, but he can't deny it feels good to be back in the presence of Jesus. He and the others sit at Salome's table, and Jesus munches on walnuts from a plate of various roasted nuts. When Zebedee passes the plate to Simon, he says, "Salome didn't cook?"

"No."

Still Simon refrains and tries to hand the plate to Andrew, who also demurs.

Salome shows Mary the Magdalene around. "Oh, your herbs are beautiful." Mary points at the vegetation hanging here and there. "Rosemary. Dill."

"Mint," Salome adds. "Coriander. And sage for Zebedee's indigestion."

The other men grin at Zebedee, who says, "Thank you for sharing that, dear wife." He turns to Jesus. "So, your father was a fisherman?"

"Carpenter," Jesus says.

"Oh. Is he back in Nazareth?"

"No. He's in heaven."

"What was your father's lineage?"

"Josiah, father of Jeconiah at the time of the Exile."

"But before the Exile, what tribe?"

"Abba!" John says.

"I like genealogies," Zebedee whispers. "It's what we talk about."

"I would imagine from the tribe of Judah," Salome says. "Yes?"

This seems to intrigue Jesus. "Why would you guess the tribe of Judah?"

"Well—"

A pert woman with narrow-set eyes rushes in, a man behind her. Simon recognizes them from the neighborhood. "Are you having a party?" she says.

"We heard voices," her husband adds.

Big James rises. "Rabbi, these are our neighbors Mara and Eliel."

Mara sits across from Jesus. "We've heard about you," she says.

"Have you?"

She and Eliel say in unison, "The parable of the net." She pops a walnut in her mouth. "I have a question about that."

"Please," Simon says. "Our master is tired. He's had a long day of walking."

"It's all right," Jesus tells him.

"You said angels would come and separate the evil from the righteous. How soon do you think they will come, Rabbi?"

Jesus appears to study her, and it intrigues Simon that—rather than answering her directly—he launches into yet another story. "My friends and I recently returned from a wedding. The father of the bride was a man of great wealth—Abner. As the night got longer, near the end of the feast, what do you think his servants were doing back home?"

No one seems to want to answer, so Simon says, "Waiting. If they're good at their jobs."

"Waiting where? In their rooms? In the kitchen?"

"At the gate," Mary says.

"Aah." Jesus nods. "At the gate. Doing what? Just standing there in the dark?"

"Holding lamps," Andrew says.

"But why? Why wouldn't they just relax?"

"Because," Mary says, "they don't know when he's coming back."

"Suppose they figured the master was delayed in coming. So, they took a nap on his bed, got drunk on his wine, and let their lamps burn down."

"That's easy," comes a voice from the big window that looks out onto the street. "They would be fired and then kicked out, called a name, and told that if they ever showed their faces around here again—"

Jesus grins. "My friends! Shalom, shalom!" It's Barnaby, the one-legged beggar, and his friend Shula, the blind woman. Simon had heard the story of Jesus' meeting them at Mary's Shabbat dinner.

"We were just passing by," Shula says, "and heard a familiar voice."

"We heard about the wedding," Barnaby tells Jesus. "Can you do that to the well by my house?"

The others roar in laughter, and Zebedee says, "You know them?"

"Yes," Jesus says. "Mary introduced them to me."

"Hm. Stick around," Zebedee tells them. "Why not?"

Big James speaks up, "You were saying, Teacher?"

"Aah, yes, thank you, James. The servants. So it will be at the end of all things. Neither the angels in heaven nor the Son of Man know the day or the hour, but only the Father. So, you must always be ready, with your lamps trimmed and burning brightly."

Simon silently signals John and beckons him to the door. "What's wrong?" John says.

"It's getting too crowded."

"Don't worry about it. You know Ima and Abba love the company."

"I'm not worried about them." Simon looks out to the street, where people have gathered, pushing closer to the door and the window.

John follows Simon's gaze. "Oh, okay." His voice lowers. "What do you want to do?"

"Let try to make sure the path out of your back garden is clear."

"What do you think is going to happen?" John seems amused.

"Anything could happen. All these people, word spreading, the wrong people stop by …"

"Simon," John tells him with a smile, "you don't have to be his bodyguard. I think he can handle anything."

"Yeah, well, he called me, and if we're not fighting the Romans yet, I want to do something until that time comes."

"He called you to catch men!"

"I don't know what that means."

"Exactly!" John places a hand on Simon's shoulder. "And if he needed you to know what that meant, he would have told you. So, just—just be you. Okay? And hey, maybe you already know."

What it means to catch men? Simon isn't so sure.

• • •

"Shmuel," Nicodemus says, moving past him to sit. He rests his head back against the wall. "My eyes are tired. Would you mind reading to me from the scroll of the prophet Isaiah?"

Shmuel trudges to the lectern and opens the scroll, using

a stylus to find his place. "'Comfort, comfort my people,' says our—"

"A bit further down, a few lines."

"A voice cries in the wilderness, 'Prepare the way of Adonai; make straight in the desert a highway for our God.'"

"Hmm," Nicodemus says. "Who does that sound like?"

Shmuel turns to face him and raises his chin. "The heretic John."

"And what heresy do you find in those words, being that Isaiah said them?"

"The heresy is that John has appropriated Isaiah's words by taking a spiritual description of God in heaven and applying it to John's physical successor on earth."

"Successor?"

"John said, 'After me comes he who is mightier than I, the strap of whose sandals I am not worthy to stoop down and untie.'"

"And?"

"God has no body. He cannot wear sandals. God cannot take human form. To say so is blasphemy."

Nicodemus chuckles and stands. "Where does it say God cannot take human form?"

"In the scroll of Deuteronomy. 'You saw no face the day Adonai spoke to you at Horeb.'"

Nicodemus moves into full teaching mode. "Just because they saw no form doesn't mean God cannot take one."

"In Exodus! 'You cannot see my face, for no man shall see me and live.' This person would have to walk around with his face covered!"

"So, you would place limits on the Almighty?"

"None that are not written in Law," Shmuel says.

"And if God did something that you felt contradicted the Torah, would you tell Him to get back in that box that you have carved for Him? Or would you question your interpretation of the Torah?"

"When I was a student," Shmuel says, more softly now, "I knew all your sayings. I read every word you wrote. Your teachings were so sturdy, so reasoned and pure."

"We are still students, Shmuel. All of us! Our understanding will never be complete."

"It frightens me that I can no longer predict your rulings."

"And fear alone ensures we remain ignorant, asleep in the safety of rigid tradition. Take the Sadducees. They take the first five books, the Law of Moses, as inspired Scripture. The rest they disregard. Ha! To them, God stopped speaking when Moses died. Think of all they have missed—the psalms of David, the stories of Ruth and Boaz, Esther and Mordecai. I don't want to live in some bleak past where God cannot do anything new. Do you?"

"Why is that your concern? God gave us His Law. We must uphold it!"

"We can do both! Let's look to the ancient roads 'where the good way is, and walk in it,' as Jeremiah said, and still keep our eyes open to the startling and the unexpected. Can we agree on that?"

Shmuel pauses. "Yes."

"You and I, we can lead the others in this."

Nicodemus looks up as Yusef hurries in. "I beg your pardon, Teacher of teachers."

"What's happened?" Shmuel says.

"A crowd has gathered in the east side to see a man preaching."

"A Pharisee?"

"No, a common person. It's not John. Someone normal. He has commanded the attention of the entire area."

Shmuel turns to Nicodemus, who says, "We will investigate."

## Chapter 61

# TEACHING

Mary of Magdala barely recognizes herself anymore. Delivered, redeemed, and cherished by the man she believes with all her heart is the Messiah himself, she feels like an entirely new being. Fulfilled, happy, joyous to the soles of her feet, she has purpose now. She has been called to follow him, to learn from him, to bring others under his influence.

She is drawn to him, captivated by him, but not in any conventional romantic way. From the day he called her by name and cast out her demons, she knew he was not of this world. Plainly a man, of course, but of God, from God, sent here for a purpose far beyond common reason. His aura draws others as it had her. And while he can have fun, it seems his every serious comment is so earnest, so deep, so fraught with truth that she savors every syllable.

Even now, at Zebedee's house—while she so loved meeting her new friends' mother, Salome, and even their neighbors Eliel and Mara—she finds herself rapt as Jesus teaches by merely quietly conversing. He's not preaching. He's simply exuding truth.

And as Mary helps her hosts while the place silently fills, she's careful not to move out of earshot of the master. What a privilege, she decides. For her and for everyone else close enough to hear him.

He converses with Eliel, who asks questions, and Jesus speaks just loudly enough to be heard by the crowd in the street, now five, six, ten people deep. Some who tried to go around seem to have been captivated by the quiet authority of the man to whom they were listening.

"So," Jesus says, "you think because Pilate killed them, they must have been worse sinners than others?"

Eliel shrugs. "I know Pilate wasn't doing it for that reason, but God must have been punishing them for something."

"No, no, God does not see some as worse than others. All must repent or perish. You know of the tower in Siloam that fell and killed the eighteen, yes? Do you think they were worse than those who lived in Jerusalem? No. All must repent or perish."

Mary carries empty platters outside to the small table in the alley where Salome stands with Mara. Salome whispers to Mara, "I'm out of pistachios, walnuts, bread, and water. Can you please go next door and ask Deborah for some bread to feed this crowd?"

"Deborah's at the door," Mara tells her, pointing.

Mary tells Salome, "They're already being fed."

Pressed near the front window, the blind woman with Barnaby says loudly, "What about prayer?"

"What about it, Shula?" Jesus says.

"I don't like to pray out loud because I feel embarrassed around the leaders who know how to do it so much better."

"Aah, big words don't matter. A lot of that's for show anyway. Don't worry about doing it in public. It's better to go into your room, shut the door, and pray to your Father who sees you in secret. The same is true for giving to the needy. Do not let your left hand know what your right hand is doing."

Barnaby looks puzzled. "How can my right hand do something and my left hand not know?"

"I mean give generously without thinking about it," Jesus says. "Do not do it for show, to impress others. Don't even congratulate yourself in private. Give in humility."

• • •

Tamar, the Ethiopian flower seller, rounds a corner and comes upon the crowd outside Zebedee's. This has to be the place. She turns and whispers urgently, "Come! Come!"

Four African men bearing a man on a stretcher slowly make their way behind her.

## Chapter 62

# "A SITUATION"

On guard at his usual station outside the tax collection booth, Primi Ordine Gaius can't deny he's proud of his new rank as one of the most senior centurions. While he knows Matthew's success with the fisherman Simon has as much to do with his elevation as Gaius' own performance, he also believes he deserves the role—in fact, that it was overdue.

The market lies oddly quiet today. No one waits to see Matthew, whose writing tablet stands open before him. And he has that blamed dog next to him, inside the booth.

"When was your last customer?" Gaius asks the strange little man. "Matthew. Hello?"

Matthew grimaces. "Sorry, what?"

Gaius switches to speak as if to a child. "How long has it been since you've had a customer?"

"I don't have customers."

Now he quibbles over semantics? "When was your last citizen?"

"One hour. Perhaps two."

"Is there a Jewish holiday that I don't know about?"

"There are many you don't know about, Gaius."

What is with him today? "Snap out of it."

At the sound of footsteps, Gaius turns to find Marcus approach. They whisper. Finally, Gaius steps back toward the tax collector. "Matthew, close the booth and go home."

"It's not time yet."

"There is a situation! Lock up and get out of here."

"What situation would require we abandon our post?"

Heaven knows the man doesn't like a change in his routine. But does he really care what's going on in the neighborhood of the fishermen? "A mob in the east slums," Gaius tells him.

"I'm coming with you."

He can't be serious! Matthew barely manages to engage with people through the bars of his cage. "Excuse me?"

"I'm coming with you."

Gaius gestures. "I said a mob. Of people. Matthew, I do not have time to protect you."

"How do you think I survive the other sixteen hours of the day?"

Gaius can't keep from laughing. A question for the ages. "I have no idea." He watches in wonder as the taxman leaves his dog in the booth and hurries to catch up.

Chapter 63

# COMMOTION

Simon can't deny his pride. Here he is, back in the neighborhood that has been his home since childhood, and now he is part of the Messiah's entourage. The Messiah! At the very home of Simon's friends!

He can't keep from smiling as he drifts through the crowd, recognizing most everyone, greeting them, asking them how they are. From inside he hears Jesus. "Which brings up a good point. All of you listening here, you're pretty decent people, yes?" They chuckle, seemingly self-conscious. "Pretty righteous?" They avert their gazes. Simon loves this. His master gently teases, one of his teaching techniques. "Kind of?" He pauses again. "Not bad?" He seems to let that hang in the air. "Let me tell you a story."

The crowd, inside and out, falls silent.

"There were two men who went up into the temple to pray. One of them was a Pharisee, the best of us, right?..."

• • •

Tamar tries to edge through the tight crowd, her friends carrying the man on the stretcher close behind. From inside the house comes the voice of the man she met on the road. "… and the other a tax collector, the worst, yes?"

She excuses herself as she presses through, pleading with people to make way. But the crowd stands shoulder to shoulder.

• • •

"Hello," Simon says to an old friend. "Good to see you. This is Jesus of Nazareth. Can you hear him?"

"Yeah."

"He's amazing, eh?"

Meanwhile, Jesus stands and now speaks through the window, telling of the Pharisee and the tax collector praying very different prayers—the proud man thanking God he is not like other men—"'extortionists, unjust, adulterers, or even like this tax collector. I fast twice a week, tithe …'"

Simon becomes aware of a woman trying to push through the crowd and rushes to her. Andrew joins him, as does the Magdalene. "Where are you going?" he asks the woman.

"Please," she says. "We need to see Jesus."

"There's no room," Andrew tells her.

Jesus continues speaking. "But the tax collector, standing far off, would not even lift up his eyes to heaven, but beat his chest, saying, 'God, be merciful to me, a sinner!' I tell you, this man went down to his house justified before God, rather than the other. For everyone who exalts himself will be humbled, but the one who humbles himself will be exalted."

The woman points to the man on the stretcher. "He's paralyzed from the waist down." She turns back to Andrew. "He can't stand."

"There is definitely no room then," Simon says.

Mary gives him a look. "Simon, he deserves to hear Jesus as much as anyone else."

The woman's eyes light up. "Hello again. I'm so glad I found you. My friend, he—"

"Why do you need to get closer?" Simon says.

She faces him, looking resolute. "I saw what your master did for the leper. I know what I saw."

Simon had not been there, so he doesn't know what she's talking about. Andrew says in a low voice, "We're trying to keep that quiet—for now. Look at this crowd. Imagine what we'd be up against."

"Please! Please. Help me get my friend to him."

Over her shoulder, Simon espies two Roman guards and Matthew the taxman. "We've got company," he says, ready to confront them.

Andrew holds him back. "I'll talk to them."

As Andrew moves away, Mary whispers to the woman, "Come with me, Tamar."

• • •

Matthew slips up behind Marcus and Gaius as Andrew approaches. The tax collector has always thought the younger brother to be the more reasonable of the two. Simon is the hothead. Andrew holds up both hands in what appears to be a posture of conciliation.

Marcus demands to know what's going on.

"This is a peaceful gathering," Andrew tells him.

"That is what the Maccabees said," Gaius says.

Marcus says, "They're blocking the road."

Gaius strides toward the crowd. Andrew hurries beside

him. "I'll move them! They just—they haven't been told where to stand yet."

Matthew hopes there won't be trouble. He strains to hear Jesus. The man urges the people to be persistent in prayer and in their faith. He tells the story of a certain judge "who neither feared God nor cared what people thought. And there was a widow in that town who kept coming to him with the plea, 'Grant me justice against my adversary.'"

Matthew wades into the crowd, uncomfortable as that is for him, compelled to hear the end of this story.

Jesus continues, "For some time he refused. But finally, he said to himself, 'Even though I don't fear God, because this widow keeps bothering me, I will see that she gets justice, so that she does not wear me out!'"

A man spits at Matthew, and he lurches back into a wall. Is there nowhere he can go without being viewed as a dog, a traitor to his own people? Another man shoves him with both hands, nearly knocking him off his feet. How he wishes he'd brought his dog.

• • •

Mary does everything she can to get Tamar and her friends through the crowd, but it's no use. "I'm sorry," she whispers. "There are too many people."

"But you know him! Can't you get us any closer?"

"I don't want to interrupt the teacher by causing a scene."

From behind Tamar, the man on the stretcher, eyes full of longing, says, "What if you were me?"

"Wouldn't you want your friends to make a scene?" Tamar says.

Mary can't take her eyes from the suffering man, and her throat tightens. "I was you once," she says.

Tamar looks up. "What about the roof?"

Mary spots the stairs alongside Zebedee's house and nods for Tamar and her friends to follow.

• • •

Matthew inches along the wall, trembling, kerchief over his mouth. Should he have come? How could he not? He strains to listen, hoping others will be as captivated by the story as he is and that no more will recognize him. The last thing he wants is to be the reason someone, anyone, gets distracted from the miracle worker's teaching.

"Listen to what the unjust judge says," Jesus goes on. "And will not God bring about justice for His chosen ones, who cry out to Him day and night? Will He keep putting them off? I tell you, He will see that they get justice, and quickly. However, when the Son of Man comes, will he find faith on the earth?"

The Son of Man? Who is this Son of Man? Something hits Matthew on the temple, and a green grape rolls on the ground. The hostile Jews have resorted to throwing fruit now? What next? When two more bounce off his head, he covers his face and blurts, "I just wanted to hear the teacher teach!"

"Psst!"

Matthew peeks around, confused.

"Up here!"

Two children sit on the edge of a roof above him, eating from a bowl of grapes. They motion for him to join them. "It's okay!" the girl says, smiling. "Come up!"

"How did you get up there?"

She points. "We climbed the ladder. It's easy!"

The very idea of gripping the sides that who knows how many others have held … Matthew uses his kerchief to carefully wipe down the wood as he slowly climbs. A strong hand on his backside propels him onto the roof. Distasteful as that is, he turns and thanks—Simon, the fisherman?

Simon climbs a couple of rungs and says to the children, "Where are your parents?" The girl points to the crowd. "I see," he says. "Okay. Well, the man speaking is called—"

"Jesus of Nazareth," she says.

"We know him," the boy says.

Simon appears stunned and climbs back down. The lad holds out the grapes to Matthew, who flinches and turns away. A bowl others have reached into? No.

The children introduce themselves as Abigail and Joshua. Matthew settles in beside them, which gives him a clear view of Jesus, now inside the doorway of Zebedee's house across the street. What could be better than this?

Jesus says, "Consider how the wildflowers grow. They do not labor or spin. Yet I tell you, not even Solomon was dressed as beautifully. If that is how God clothes the grass of the field, which is here today and tomorrow is thrown into the fire, how much more will He clothe all of you?"

What a thrilling thought! Matthew's eye is drawn to the back of the crowd, where three Pharisees—one older, two younger—appear. What will they make of the teacher? Jesus of Nazareth converses with the crowd as if they are friends, yet he speaks with such quiet authority that he could be reading from one of the sacred scrolls in the synagogue. But even when Matthew attended the synagogue regularly for years, before his profession made him a nuisance there, he never heard teaching like this. In fact, every story Jesus tells, every point he makes, seems to open Matthew's eyes anew. Who is this man, and what is his aim? He must find out. Matthew saw him make fish appear from nowhere. What else might he do?

Chapter 64

# THE PARALYTIC

Nicodemus stands astonished at the crowd. People who notice him and Shmuel step aside. The Sanhedrin leader hopes, prays, that it's the miracle man crazy John has been talking about who has drawn this throng. Maybe he'll finally get some answers.

Shmuel appears determined to get to the front and presses against a one-legged man leaning on his crutch. "Ahem." When he gets no response, Shmuel says, "Excuse me!"

"Quiet!" the man says. "We're trying to listen."

"Do you know who you are talking to!?"

Nicodemus pulls him back. "Shmuel!"

"Did you hear his disrespect?"

"You remember the Red Quarter?" Nicodemus whispers. "We're out of our element here."

"We have to find out who is teaching. Look at this crowd!"

"All the more reason to be cautious."

But Shmuel's face has gone ashen. He gazes at Zebedee's rooftop. "Rabbi! It's her!"

Sure enough, it's Lilith, who now calls herself Mary, with an African woman.

"She is truly restored!" Shmuel says in awe. "I had heard only your report, Yusef, not seen her for myself. She's a different person!"

Nicodemus stares, unable to make sense of it. "Why is she here?"

• • •

Mary watches as Tamar leans over the small opening in the roof. Jesus' voice comes through clearly. He's talking about how faith in God should not be kept to oneself. "You are the light of the world. A city on a hill cannot be hid. And if it were nighttime, Zebedee wouldn't light his lamp and put it under a basket. He'd put it on a stand where it could light us all."

"Jesus of Nazareth!" Tamar cries out. "I saw what you did to the leper on the road this morning!" She kneels and lowers her voice as Jesus looks up at her. "My friend has been paralyzed since childhood. He has no hope but you. Please. Do for him what you did for the leper."

Her friends situate the paralytic over the rooftop opening, but finding it too small, they begin ripping planks from around it.

"That's our roof!" Salome shouts.

"Put it back, man!" John says.

"If you are willing, Rabbi," Tamar says, "I know you can do this."

The man's Ethiopian friends place him onto one of Zebedee's giant fishing nets and lower him by rope through the roof, the pulley squeaking and groaning under his weight.

• • •

Across the street, an enraptured Matthew stares, reaching

blindly into little Joshua's bowl for a grape. Below, Nicodemus urgently whispers to Shmuel, "Is that not the paralyzed man I've seen begging at the city gate since I began coming here more than twenty years ago?"

Shmuel nods. "The very one. I've never seen him move even his feet, let alone his legs."

Shmuel elbows his way through the crowd, Yusef on his heels.

• • •

Simon bounds back up the ladder and leans close to the taxman's ear. "This is what you wanted. Get out your tablet at least." Simon finds his way to the edge of the roof and calls out to Mary across the street. "Is he in danger?"

"I don't know," she says. "No, I don't think so."

"He's got room in there?"

"Yes!"

"Can you believe we're really here for this?"

She smiles. "Yes."

• • •

Shmuel and Yusef reach the window. Inside, three men cradle the paralytic man in midair, while others clear a place on the floor. Shmuel demands, "You! By whose authority do you teach?"

The man people call Jesus of Nazareth stares at him.

"Answer me!"

"If you are willing, Rabbi," Tamar calls from above. "You know you can."

Shmuel slams his palm on the sill. "Hey! I'm talking to you! By whom do you teach? Certainly not the authority of any rabbi from Nazareth! Where did you study?"

Jesus peers up at Tamar. "Your faith is beautiful," he says. He turns to the paralytic, who sits before him, useless feet splayed. "Son, take heart. Your sins are forgiven." Jesus faces Shmuel and Yusef and, as if reading Shmuel's mind, says, "'Who is this who speaks blasphemies? Who can forgive sins but God alone?' Right? But I ask you, which is easier to say: 'Your sins are forgiven,' or 'Rise up and walk'? It's easy to say anything, no? But to show you, and so that you may know that the Son of Man has the authority on earth to forgive sins—" He turns and kneels before the man. "I say to you my son, 'Rise. Pick up your bed. And go home.'"

Shmuel's eyes widen. Everyone stares in silence, and the man gasps as his toes begin to twitch. Then slowly he stands, legs wobbly at first but quickly gaining strength. Once fully upright, he bursts into tears. "Easy does it," Jesus says as the man collapses into his arms.

The crowd—all but the three Pharisees—holler and applaud. The healed man says, "Thank you."

Jesus nods. "Now, go on," he tells him.

As the man strides carefully to the door and into the gaping crowd, Shmuel turns and shouts above the throng, "Roman guards! A threat to the public peace!"

Two soldiers unsheathe their swords and rush through the crowd to the door, knocking people this way and that.

Chapter 65

# THE ESCAPE

Simon bursts in through the back door. "Teacher! This way!" Jesus and the others follow him out as Zebedee slams the front door and secures it. Outside, Simon directs the disciples to split up.

• • •

Nicodemus sees Mary disappear from the roof. He scrambles toward the stairs at the side of the house as people push past him in the opposite direction—including the former paralytic. The man's face gleams with tears as he locks eyes with Nicodemus. The Pharisee cannot speak, gawking at a man he believes hasn't stood in at least two decades.

The soldiers bang on the front door, and Nicodemus reaches the side of the house just as Mary reaches the bottom of the steps and heads down the alley.

"Mary! Wait!"

She turns and breaks into a smile. "You saw!"

He can barely speak. "I saw a paralytic walk past me on his two feet!"

Mary's smile fades. "You asked me before if I knew the teacher's name. Now everyone knows his name. And I fear for his safety."

"I mean no trouble to him, no dishonor."

"Your friends tried to have him arrested!"

"They're jealous," he says, hoping she can hear the desperation in his voice. "They're afraid. But I'm not. I promise. Mary, please. I need to talk to him."

"I follow him," she says, "not the other way around. He doesn't tell anyone his plans."

"But will you ask him for a meeting? In secret! Under cover of night. At a place of his choosing. I don't care if it's a ravine or a cave or even a tomb, but I need to speak to him. Please, Mary!"

She seems to study him. "I will try."

• • •

Matthew clambers down from the roof across the street, his thoughts miles away. From above, Abigail says, "Are you lost?"

"Yes. I am."

• • •

Salome finally opens the door, and Gaius pushes in. "Is there a problem, officer?" she says with a beatific smile.

• • •

Matthew wanders across the street and into the alley where Andrew and Simon lead Jesus away. Just before Jesus slips out of sight, he stops and turns to face Matthew. The teacher seems to look at him with such compassion, Matthew cannot move. And Jesus leaves him with the hint of a smile.

# PART 8
# Invitations

Chapter 66

# THE BRONZE SERPENT

*The Sinai Peninsula 13th Century B.C.*

Moses has had it with the children of Israel. What more can he do but follow the Lord and do what He says? God leads the people out of Egypt and into the wilderness toward what was to be an idyllic Promised Land. But at every turn, the people grumble and complain and turn to idols. They even have the gall to ask Moses if he brought them to the desert to die because there were no graves in Egypt. They tell him it would have been better to stay and serve the Egyptians.

Speaking such evil of him, and thus of the Lord who directs his steps, is apparently too much even for God. He sends fiery serpents among them, and many are bitten and die.

Finally, the people plead with Moses to intervene with God on their behalf. When he does, God instructs him to fashion a snake of bronze and lift it high on a pole where the people can see it and live. But Moses' metalsmith is among the dead.

*How will I do that? I have no experience.*

"I Am will empower you."

So, Moses sets up a smelting forge in a tent at the edge of the Israelite camp and labors from dark till dawn, pouring molten metal from a steaming cauldron into a crude mold, then hammering it into the shape of a serpent.

He pours sweat as the sun sends shafts of light into the tent and someone arrives, ducking under the flap. Moses doesn't have to look up to know it is one of his most trusted confidants. He stays at the task, knowing he smells and must look a sight. He blinks soot away as the man clears his throat.

"Joshua," Moses says. "How many more in the night?"

"Some three hundred, sir."

"Where will you bury them?"

"Men are trying to dig a trench, but the ground is hard and rocky." Joshua pauses. Then, "With respect, Moses, my concern is not for the dead, but for the dying. Hundreds fall by the day, and for every serpent we kill, another ten appear."

Moses stops clanging. "Maybe we leave the bodies here, in this tent."

Joshua shakes his head. "At the rate people are dying, there will not be enough room. Even if we stacked them to the top."

Moses returns to hammering. "Then we'll have to leave and find someplace else."

"We're not leaving any time soon. Too many people are sick and cannot walk!"

"After today, the only Hebrews too sick to walk will be those who choose to remain so."

"Is there medicine in that bronze? You told the people that you would ask God to forgive their rebellion, to heal their serpent wounds—"

"I did!"

"Then why are you hiding in a tent?"

Whirling to face him, Moses shouts, "It wasn't my idea, Joshua!"

The younger man looks past Moses to the twisted, cooling metal. "That is a pagan symbol. You did not ask Him if He was sure? Maybe you misunderstood Him."

"I've learned to do what He says without questioning. You remember what happened at Meribah." No doubt, Joshua would remember. Everyone knew Moses had overstepped the Lord's instructions, striking the rock with his staff rather than just commanding it to produce water. Neither he nor his brother Aaron would enter the Promised Land because of it. Moses turns back to his work, not wanting to talk about it.

Joshua sounds conciliatory, speaking softly but directly. "Just to be sure, we could send a messenger to Ezion-Geber, beg for aid—"

"That pole. Hand me that pole."

Joshua finds the long piece of wood leaning against the wall of the tent, a crossbar tied near its top. Moses hoists the heavy bronze snake onto it and grunts at the effort to thread the pole through the coils of the snake.

"The people will say it is a cruel joke," Joshua says.

Of course they will. It would be just like them to refer to it as a Nehushtan, a mere thing of brass. "Let them."

Joshua looks defeated, bewildered. "Help me understand! None of this makes any sense!"

"How do you explain the Red Sea? The manna and the quail? The pillar of fire! Joshua! Any Israelite who looks upon this bronze serpent and believes in the power of Adonai will be healed. It is an act of faith! Not reason. Faith."

## Chapter 67

# COLLISION COURSE

*Thirteen centuries later*

Today Matthew's meticulous morning regimen takes even longer than usual. Is this, this malady—whatever it is—getting worse? With other things troubling his mind now, his entire consciousness seems heightened. He's finding it harder and harder to reconcile what he can only call violations of the laws of nature with his need to have everything settled in his mind while he's working. How does one put out of his mind the miraculous? Unlimited fish just feet from the shore? A lifelong paralytic rising, walking?

He puts on his ring the same as always. Dabs one wrist with fragrance, then the other. Then his neck. He counts the fruit in the bowl and selects his footwear. As he exits his elaborate—and immaculately tidy—home, Matthew triple checks the lock as usual. And yet even with his every impulse satisfied, all he has seen lately leaves him still out of sorts.

As he sets off to work, he stops short. "Gaius," he says, suddenly face-to-face with the man. "Why are you here?"

• • •

*Good question*, Gaius thinks. *How can I make this seem normal, acceptable?* Of course, he's seen Matthew show up every day at the edge of the market, hidden under a tarp in a wagon driven by a man who appears disgusted to have to carry him for money. Gaius knows Matthew hates interacting with the public, even with the bars of a cage between them—and who can blame him? They see him as the lowest scum, exploiting fellow Jews on behalf of Rome. "I'm escorting you."

"Because you feel indebted for your promotion."

Insightful for a man so disconnected from reality. "You're complaining about safely walking the streets?"

"I didn't help Quintus for you."

"Oh, I know," Gaius says. "You couldn't help yourself."

Matthew begins walking again. "I spoke up because I was right."

"You got lucky."

"Luck doesn't exist."

"So, you knew Quintus would not kill you."

"He was smart to go after the fishermen, but he must have been desperate to enlist Simon."

Gaius smiles. Dare he admit there's something engaging, even endearing, about this strange little man? "I don't buy it. You were terrified."

Matthew stops and faces him. "Gaius, what if you were suddenly the only Roman in Capernaum?"

*In other words, if I were the same as him—a minuscule minority?* "I think I'd change clothes."

"Exactly. When you realize that nobody else in the world cares what happens to you, you think only about yourself."

Gaius can merely stare. This man never ceases to amaze. "For a fool, your brain has taken you far. I admit it."

"I thought so too."

Gaius cocks his head. He thought so too? What could he possibly mean?

• • •

*Later that morning*

Nicodemus sits in the most lavishly appointed room in the guesthouse, reading and occasionally glancing at an hourglass. Sweat beads on his brow. How can he concentrate, given what he has witnessed?

Zohara sails in, grinning. "Praise Adonai, he is healthy and alive!"

"What are you talking about?"

"I received word from Jerusalem. Havilah gave birth to a son. You're a grandfather again!"

"So soon?"

She's already packing up the room. "A month early, but all is well. Oh, blessed be He! We'll have the rest of our things sent."

Oh, no! She'll never understand. "What? No! No, no! My research here is not completed."

"But we have to make it back in time for the bris. We have only eight days. Less than eight."

"The circumcision can be performed by any number of people, Zohara."

"Nico! This is your own grandson!"

"Fifth grandson. Havilah will understand."

That was the wrong tack. He can see it all over her.

She steps closer, brow furrowed. "Do you know what

people will say when they learn that the great Nicodemus missed his own grandson's name day because he was doing research in Capernaum, of all places?"

"Research that concerns not just one Jewish boy, but all of Israel—past, present, and future!"

"There is nothing in Capernaum but demoniacs and insolent schoolboys! Come to your senses."

What a thing to say! If she only knew—but it's too soon to reveal it to her. "I have never been closer to my senses."

"That is not how it looks from the outside," she says.

"Many things are not."

"I am ready to leave this place, Nico. I miss my children and my grandchildren, including the one I haven't even met yet."

"Oh, Zohara, you—" The door bursts open. "You can't just barge—"

"Oh, I believe I can."

Nicodemus bows. "Praetor Quintus."

His wife quickly covers her head. The Roman nods to her. "Zohara, is it? Pleasure to see you again."

"I trust all is well," Nicodemus says, affecting a formal tone.

"Why would you trust that?" Quintus moves past him to sit.

"Oh yes," Nicodemus says. "Please do. Make yourself at home."

Quintus sets down his helmet, appears to take in the luxurious decor, and whistles. Chuckling, he says, "We really will have to discuss the people's tithing."

"This is why you've come?"

"I need to know if we have a problem, Nicodemus."

A problem? "I have complied with every request Rome has made to my office, even when it infringed on custom."

"Let me rephrase," Quintus says, dropping the sarcasm. "You and I want the same thing. We want rules followed. We want order. Soldiers, money, votes—that's my world. Demons, prayers, oddballs—that's yours. I need to know if our worlds are on a collision course."

Nicodemus studies him, wondering what to say to that.

"The so-called miracle worker?" Quintus says.

Maybe there's value in appearing to cooperate. Nicodemus sits across from the praetor. "Jesus of Nazareth."

"Don't even know what Nazareth is. But yes. Him."

Nicodemus tries to sound dismissive. "Anecdotes and rumors."

"And a stampede in the eastern ghetto that delayed Herod's envoy. That really made me look bad. I hate that."

"The unrest began when your soldiers waded into the crowd brandishing weapons."

"It isn't an isolated event. I've heard reports. My source has an unwavering knack for accuracy and a compulsion for the truth. So, again, I ask you: Is there a problem?"

Nicodemus presses his lips together and shakes his head. "No."

Quintus grins. "You don't seem sure. Maybe I could get better information from this"—he pauses—"Shmuel? He's very eager to see me."

Desperate to hide his surprise, Nicodemus gathers himself and speaks slowly. "The only way to learn this preacher's intentions is to speak with him directly."

"So, speak to him," Quintus says, grabbing his helmet and rising. "I hate crowds. They take time and resources. And then cleanup is a pain. When you arrange a private meeting, I want to know when and where. Understand?"

Nicodemus eagerly changes the subject. "What troubles you about this man?"

"Preachers have a habit of becoming politicians. They

sprout up like weeds and spread. Your wife is a gardener. She understands."

Nicodemus stands. "Some flora spread their seeds when trampled. Who's to say you wouldn't be creating a martyr?"

"I'll take my chances."

When Quintus leaves, Zohara slowly approaches Nicodemus with, he fears, a knowing look. She seems to search his face. "You sympathize with this preacher."

Chapter 68

# THE APOLOGY

Thaddeus splits wood for a fire—a far cry from what he used to do with his hands, which acquainted him with Jesus in the first place. He has a question, but the Rabbi and John are talking as they set up a tent.

"Will we be safe here?" John says.

"What do you mean, safe?"

"They'll be looking for us because of what you said about forgiving sins."

"Ah. We won't be here very long. After what happened yesterday, we'll keep moving from town to town."

"Is that what you want?"

"What do you mean?"

"To roam about, not able to stay in one place?"

Thaddeus notices that Jesus does not immediately respond to John. He seems to weigh his answer. Finally, Jesus says, "I want to do the will of my Father. And I want to spread the message of salvation. So yes, I am happy to not stay in one place."

John seems satisfied and falls silent.

"Rabbi?"

"Yes, Thad."

"I should prepare firewood for how many days?"

"Uh, five, I think."

John cocks his head. "Thought you said we wouldn't be here very long."

"Leaving some for the next weary traveler. Hospitality isn't only for people who own homes, John."

Thaddeus is not surprised that John can't argue with that.

When the Magdalene arrives, it's clear something troubles her. "Mary!" Thaddeus says. "You all right?"

She looks as if she's been caught off guard. "Me? Uh, yes, thank you." She looks to Jesus. "May I speak with you, Rabbi?"

They step out of earshot.

• • •

Mary hardly knows where to begin and has trouble making eye contact. The last thing she wants is to become a nuisance to the Messiah. "I wanted to apologize for yesterday."

"For what?"

"Trying to help those people get closer to the sound of your voice. I had no idea they would open the roof and disrupt your teaching. I'm truly—"

"So," Jesus says, smiling, "you regret that a paralytic is enjoying his first full day on his own feet, eh?"

"No. Just that I caused a scene and cut short your teaching."

"Who's to say it was cut short? With their faith, they would have found a way whether you brought them to the roof or not."

How is it that he is so easy to talk to? Mary still feels bad, yet he seems eager to put her at ease. "But there's more," she says, not wanting to keep anything from him now. "When we were leaving, a Pharisee stopped me and asked for a private meeting with you. I told him I would ask."

"A Pharisee. Do you know this man?"

"He visited me—before."

"A Pharisee in the Red Quarter?"

"Rome sent him. I doubt he wanted to be there."

Jesus chuckles. "No, I wouldn't think so."

"Well, I saw him again after I was better, and he wanted to know how I was healed. Of course, I didn't tell him who you were, but he seemed …"

"What?"

"Earnest. He wasn't offended to learn that someone else had succeeded where he had failed. There was a—there was a hunger in his eyes. Not fear."

"Not like the Pharisees at the window yesterday, eh?"

"I am sorry to have brought all this on you."

"No, no, there is a reason you met this Pharisee."

"Nicodemus."

"Nicodemus, of course. I've heard of him."

"I don't know who is known and who is not," she says. "This is all new to me."

"Aah, don't worry about which men others think are important. Send word to Nicodemus. I will meet with him. Little James will know the location. Thank you, Mary."

"Yes, Teacher," she says as he begins to leave. "Where are you going?"

He turns back. "To be alone. I need to think. And to pray."

"I will pray also—that I did not put you in terrible danger."

Jesus laughs quietly. "You have not. In fact, I have made plans already for tomorrow night."

"Plans?"

"Yes, spread the word. A dinner party. In the northern district. The tall house just past the arch."

*The rich section*, Mary thinks. *Where the tax collectors live.* "But that row of homes—"

"I know the kind of people who live there," Jesus says. "Trust me."

"I will tell the others."

Chapter 69

# THE VISIT

Matthew stands before the door of his humble childhood home, wracked with indecision. He reaches to knock, thinks better of it, turns away, and then back. He forces himself to knock, then nearly flees. No, he's here. He must follow through. As he knocks a second time, the door opens a crack. "Matthew?"

"Hello, Ima," he says before catching himself. Has he lost the right to call her that? "Or—or Elisheba. Hello."

"Matthew."

She's just staring, and he doesn't know what to do. Will she not invite him in? Again fighting the urge to run, he grimaces. "I don't receive visitors myself. Is this a custom?"

She opens the door wider. "If your father were here, I couldn't do this."

"Where is Alphaeus?"

But she's looking past him. "I think a dog followed you."

"He's with me. He'll stay out here if you let me in."

She points to a chair before the table and fetches him a cup of water. She sits at the other end. Matthew tries to meet her gaze in the awkward silence. "Will Alphaeus be home soon?"

"He's away. On a work trip."

"Where will work take him? Does he no longer make leather goods?"

"His shop was robbed. Many of the shops have been. Crime is rampant—makes it very difficult to reopen."

How awful! "He loved his shop."

She nods. "But we still have a roof over our heads, which is more than some people can say."

He blurts, "You can ask me for money if you ever need it."

She stares him down. "How can you say that?"

"It's quite common. I've seen many parents entirely dependent on—"

"Your father would sooner die than take your blood money."

Blood money? "I know you are ashamed of me, but your decision is irrational. Rome will collect taxes no matter what. I'm skilled with numbers—"

"Did you come here to justify yourself?"

"No!" he says, banging the table and rising. "No!" Why can't he say what he means, what he feels? He paces, trying to arrange his thoughts. "Everything's like sand. In a flood. The things I thought I knew to be true …"

"Are you in trouble?"

He stops and faces her. "Do you think that impossible things can happen? Things that overturn the laws of nature? That cannot be explained?"

Her eyes light up. "That is what people asked when you were a boy. Even the rabbis were astonished at your talent for reading, math, the way you could think faster than any other child. They thought you would be someone great."

How well he remembers. They thought he might become

a priest—living up to his Hebrew name, Levi. But has he not become someone special? "Great at what? I'm rich. I have an armed escort. I'm trusted by the praetor of Galilee."

"We never dreamed you would use the talent God gave you to bleed your people dry!"

"But have you ever seen anything miraculous?"

"Matthew!"

"My whole world! Everything I thought I knew, what if it's wrong?"

She appears to fight tears. "I think you should go."

Go? No! He did not want this. But, as usual, he has said too much, pushed too far. He stares at her, longing to plead with her to not turn him away. But he cannot form the words. He staggers toward the door, despairing.

"You never even asked about your sister."

"She looks well." His mother seems surprised that he knows this. "I came to celebrate Shabbat a few weeks ago. Then I left." He waits, not knowing if he should expect a response. "Goodbye, Ima," he says finally.

Chapter 70

# THE PLAN

*Simon's home, night*

Little James has made the arrangements for Jesus' meeting with the Pharisee, and several of the others have their assignments. But Simon is wary. He must say something. Behind him, his wife and Jesus work at the counter, he scaling a fish, she chopping vegetables for a tabbouleh. Simon paces. "I'm not so sure this is a good idea."

"Why not?" Jesus says.

"Well, it could be a trap. Nicodemus cooperates with Rome. They're the ones who sent him to Mary when she was possessed in the Red Quarter."

"I'm well acquainted with risk, Simon," Jesus says, his back to the fisherman. "So are you, if I remember our first meeting correctly, hm?"

"Risk is his oldest friend, I'm afraid," Eden says.

"Simon." Jesus wipes his hands and turns to face him. "Mary is an excellent judge of character. She has known some of the worst kinds of men in this world, and she finds him earnest. You should trust her instincts. And mine."

Eden's mother coughs in the other room, and Simon loudly clears his throat to cover it. He doesn't want Jesus to even know she's there. He casts a wild look at Eden.

"Rabbi," Andrew says, entering. "I've got it."

"Aah!" Jesus rubs his hands together, clearly pleased. "Let's take a look."

Simon approaches Eden and whispers, "Can you keep her quiet please? No one needs to know Ima's sick."

"I can't tell her not to cough, Simon."

"I just don't want our burdens to become his, okay? I don't want to be the one to distract him."

"He's made up his mind about you," she says, smiling. "He's not going to kick you out of the group."

"It's perfect!" Jesus says, clad in a dark cloak. "Well done!" He turns from side to side. "Though I think I could fit all of you in here with me, eh?"

Andrew reaches around Jesus' neck and pulls the hood over his head. "You won't be recognized in that."

"Has the owner of the house given permission?"

"It's all arranged, Rabbi. And I'll be waiting at the door."

"Thank you, Andrew. You go on ahead." He lays a hand on Andrew's shoulder. "But remember to relax. You are there to guide our guest, not to be my protector."

"Are you sure you don't want me to come?" Simon says. "The more eyes watching the streets for trouble, the better."

"Not tonight, Simon. Stay here with your wife. And your mother-in-law."

Simon feels foolish for having tried to keep a secret from the Messiah himself. Eden grins at him. "You see?"

Chapter 71

# THE MEETING BY NIGHT

There's no other way to say it: Nicodemus is more than nervous. He misled Zohara without lying to her, and now he ventures out alone in the dark with his walking stick, looking for the place Jesus' disciple James said to come. James made it clear that the teacher must not be seen with the Pharisee. Well, Nicodemus must not be seen with the teacher either.

He's sure he's in the right neighborhood as he peers down an alleyway. But he's startled when a man appears. "Welcome, Nicodemus," says the one they call Andrew. "Don't be alarmed." He reaches for the walking stick. Nicodemus hadn't intended it to look threatening. "He's waiting for you."

Andrew nods toward stairs running up the side of a house and follows Nicodemus. At the top, Andrew takes Nicodemus' cloak and slips back down the stairs. At the wall across the roof stands Jesus. Beyond him, in the moonlight lies the Sea of Galilee. Without greeting or introduction, Jesus says, "I asked the owner of this house for more lanterns, but he said they would draw attention."

"Yes, I imagine they would." Nicodemus hears a tremor in his own voice. It's just that there's something about this man.

Jesus turns back toward the sea. "The human eye is drawn to light. We can't help it. It just happens."

"There are many things we are drawn to without our thinking," Nicodemus says. "Or our ability to explain why." When Jesus turns to face him, the Pharisee says, "Thank you for agreeing to meet."

"Thank you for trying to help Mary when you did."

"I was no help."

"You were meant to be there."

"Me? So I could fail miserably at an exorcism in the Red Quarter?"

"If you had not been there that day, would you be on this roof tonight?"

Such elemental wisdom! Nicodemus finally gathers the courage to approach. "I don't know where to start! I have so many questions."

"Shall we sit first?" Jesus gestures toward a table.

"Oh, yes, of course."

They sit across from each other, a small oil lamp between them and one on the wall above. How is this to go? Should he just listen and learn? But Jesus looks at him expectantly. *Okay,* Nicodemus thinks. *I'll start.*

"The eastern slums."

"Hm."

"Many wandering preachers have succeeded in gathering crowds with their rhetoric and fiery tone."

"I've heard a few of them over the years myself," Jesus says.

"So, you know the type. But I have never heard anyone tell a paralytic to get up and walk. Much less, it actually happens."

"What is your conclusion?"

Nicodemus sighs. There it is, a question he must answer. No dancing around the truth with this man, as he had with the praetor. "I believe you are not acting alone. No one can do these signs you do without having God in him. Only someone who has come from God."

"And how is that belief going over in the synagogue?" That makes Nicodemus laugh, and to his relief, Jesus laughs too. "Which is why we're here at this hour." They stare at each other, and Nicodemus doesn't know where to go from here. "What else?" Jesus says.

"What have you come here to show us?"

Jesus leans in. "A kingdom."

"That is what our rulers are worried about."

"No, not that kind."

"Then what?"

"The sort of kingdom that a person cannot see unless he is born again."

"Born. Again."

"Yes."

"You mean like a new creature, a conversion from Gentile to Jewish?"

"No. No, that's not what I'm talking about."

"Then what is 'born again'? I hope you don't mean return to the womb, because that would be a problem for me. My mother, may she rest in peace, is dead."

Jesus takes a moment. "Truly, I say to you, unless one is born of water and the Spirit, he cannot enter the kingdom of God. That which is born of the flesh," he touches Nicodemus' hand, "is flesh, and that which is born of the Spirit," he touches the Pharisee's chest, "is spirit. That part of you—that is what must be reborn to new life."

Nicodemus shakes his head. It's all so, so monumental. "How can these things be?"

"Ah, a teacher of Israel, and yet you do not understand these things."

Nicodemus can only smile. "I'm trying, Rabbi."

"I know," Jesus says, looking deep into his eyes. "I know." Nicodemus suddenly feels loved. "Do you hear this?" Jesus says.

"What?" Has someone found them out?

"Listen. What do you hear?"

"The wind."

"How do you know it's the wind?"

"Because I can feel it. I hear its sound."

"Do you know where it comes from?"

"No."

"Do you know where it's going?"

"No."

"That's what it is to be born again of the Spirit. The Spirit may work in a way that is a mystery to you, and while you cannot see the Spirit, you can recognize his effect."

Astounding. "My mind is consumed with thoughts of what a stir these words would cause among the teachers of the Law."

"Yes, and I do not expect otherwise. I speak of what I know and have seen, and it has not been received by the religious leaders."

"It's hard to receive."

"So, if I have told you of earthly things and you do not believe, how can I tell you of heavenly things?"

Does this man not understand the danger? "I believe your words. I just fear you may not have a chance to speak many more of them before you are silenced."

"I have come to do more than speak words, Nicodemus."

"More miracles?"

"Yes, but even more than that." A hint of sadness comes to his eyes. "Do you remember when the children of Israel complained against God and against Moses in the wilderness of Paran?"

Now the man speaks his language. "Yes. They wanted to return to Egypt, and they cursed the manna God sent them."

"And then?"

"They were bitten by serpents, and they were dying."

"But?"

"But God made a way for them to be healed."

"Moses lifted the bronze serpent in the desert, and people only needed to look at it. So will the Son of Man be lifted up, so that whoever believes in him may have eternal life."

What is he talking about? "Our people are not dying from snakebites. They're dying from taxation and oppression."

"I'm sorry to disappoint you, but I did not come to deliver the people from Rome."

"Then from what?"

"From sin. From spiritual death."

This is entirely new to Nicodemus, a foreign concept, and he doesn't know what to make of it, how to fit it into his view of all the messianic prophecies. But it's as if Jesus senses his bewilderment.

Jesus continues, "God loves the world in this way: that He gave His only Son, that whoever believes in him shall not perish but have eternal life."

Nicodemus sits up straight. "So, this has nothing to do with Rome? It's all about sin?"

"God did not send His Son into the world to condemn it, Nicodemus. He sent him to save it through him. It's as simple as

Moses' serpent on the pole. Whoever believes in him will not be condemned, but whoever does not believe stands condemned already."

• • •

Andrew has been sitting on the stairs with John, listening. "Have you ever heard anything like this before?"

"Shh," John says, taking notes.

• • •

"When I met Lilith—Mary—that day, I told my wife and my students that she was beyond human aid. Only God could have healed her. And then I saw her. Healed." Overcome with emotion, Nicodemus adds, "And here you are. The healer." Barely able to speak, he says, "My whole life I have wondered if I would see this day."

"Follow me and you'll see more."

"Follow you?" Nicodemus whispers.

"Join me and my students. In two days' time we leave Capernaum. Come see the kingdom I am bringing into this world."

What a wondrous thought! If only he were a young man again, without so many obligations. "But I—I can't."

"You have a position in the Sanhedrin, you have family, you are getting advanced in years." Both men chuckle. "I understand. But the invitation is still open."

"The invitation to what exactly? To lead a nomadic life? To—to give up all I have?"

"It's true, there is a lot you would give up. But what you would gain is far greater and more lasting."

"Is this another one of your 'born again' mysteries?"

Jesus laughs. "Well, maybe. I know mysteries aren't easy for a scholar. Think about it. Take your time. On the morning of the fifth day we leave, and we'll meet by the well in the southern quarter at dawn."

*Take my time?* What would become of Zohara? What would become of *him*?

When Jesus stands, Nicodemus does too. "Is—is this, is the kingdom of God really coming?"

"What does your heart tell you?"

*What does my heart tell me? Dare I say it?* "Oh, my heart is swollen with fear and—and wonder, and can tell me nothing except that I am standing on holy ground." Nicodemus, sobbing now, covers his mouth. He pulls his hand away to reveal a smile and shakes his head. "Holy roof anyway."

Jesus smiles, then grows serious. "I do hope you'll come with us, Nicodemus."

The Pharisee kneels before Jesus.

"You don't have to do that."

He kisses Jesus' hand.

"What are you doing?"

Nicodemus quotes from the psalms. "Kiss the Son, lest he be angry, and ye perish from the way."

Jesus lifts him to his feet. "Blessed are all who take refuge in him." And he gathers Nicodemus, tears streaming, into his arms.

## Chapter 72

# DIFFERENT

*The next day*

Matthew holds court in his tax booth, tending to a long line. Gaius stands guard outside, chatting between transactions. “You see the Parthian footraces last night? Darius ran like a gazelle.”

“Jews don’t go to footraces,” Matthew tells him.

“Your old friend Simon himself used to run the wagering tables.”

“We’re not friends. Next!”

“Okay, fine, so you did not go to the races. You stay home?”

“I went to see my mother.”

“Ooh, that would put me out, too. She ask when you’re going to give her grandchildren?”

“She didn’t ask.”

“I thought your parents don’t speak to you.”

“I had questions I couldn’t ask anyone else.”

“A mother of a son with talent like yours should be proud.”

“She’s ashamed that I could use a talent that God gave me against Him. Next!”

"You're good at something. You found a way to make money doing it. It's that simple."

"Must be nice to live in a world so simply ordered."

"We live in the same world, Matthew."

"Next!"

"Besides, what else are you gonna do with a mind like yours?"

Matthew finds himself distracted when Jesus passes by with several of his disciples. The teacher stops and looks toward the booth, calling out, "Matthew!"

The taxman flinches and recoils. *He knows my name?*

Gaius instinctively lays a hand on the hilt of his sword.

"Matthew!" Jesus shouts again. "Son of Alphaeus!"

*He knows exactly who I am!* Matthew cocks his head and peers through the cage. They lock eyes. "Yes?"

"Follow me," the teacher says.

The miracle worker? Beckoning the lowest of the Jews? "Me?"

Jesus nods and chuckles. "Yes! You!"

Simon steps close to Jesus. "Whoa, whoa, whoa! What're you doing?"

Matthew calls out, "You want *me* to join you?"

"Keep moving, street preacher!" Gaius says.

Simon pleads now. "Do you have any idea what this guy has done? Do you even know him?"

Matthew stares, wondering the same thing.

And Jesus, eyes still on Matthew, says, "Yes."

"Listen!" Gaius shouts. "I said to k—" But Matthew rushes out of the booth. Gaius whirls to face him. "What're you doing?" Matthew tries to push past him, but the bigger man grabs his tunic at the chest and jerks him close. "Where do you think you're going?"

Matthew, emboldened as he has ever been, faces down the Roman. "Gaius. Let me go."

The primi releases his grip. "Have you lost your mind? You have money. Quintus protects you. No Jew lives as good as you. You're gonna throw it all away?"

*Exactly*, Matthew thinks. "Yes." He hands Gaius the key to the booth, then slips off his ring and gives him that, too. The guard stands agape.

As Matthew approaches Jesus and the others, Simon says, "I don't get it."

"You didn't get it when I chose you either," Jesus says.

"But this is different! I'm not a tax collector."

"Get used to different." He turns to the newcomer. "I'm glad we passed by your booth today, Matthew."

What does one to say to such a man? "Yes."

"Shall we?" Jesus says as he leads his entourage away. "We have a celebration to prepare for."

Gaius calls after him. "You will regret this, Matthew!"

Simon says, "What's the tablet for?"

"I grabbed it without thinking," Matthew says. "I could put it back."

"No," Jesus tells him. "Keep it. You may yet find use for it."

"Where are we going?" Matthew says.

The pleasant lady of the group says, "A dinner party."

"I'm not welcome at dinner parties."

"Well," Jesus says, "that's not going to be a problem tonight. You're the host."

# PART 9

# "I Am He"

## Chapter 73

# THE WELL

*Canaan, 1952 B.C.*

With his three eldest sons watching—shovels at the ready—a remarkably fit Jacob kneels, pounding a stake into the rocky earth not far from the two tents his Bedouin family has set. They placed the tents among three lonely palm trees in the vast, arid plains outside Sychar.

"This is the spot, my sons," Jacob says, sweat pouring, just as he notices a stranger making the climb from town—a bald, black man in a reddish-striped tunic and carrying a sturdy walking stick. As his sons start digging, Jacob rises and moves out to welcome the stranger. "Shalom, my friend!"

"I don't know that word," the man says.

"It's something my family says. It's a greeting of peace."

"You won't find much of that here, I'm afraid."

Aah, a naysayer. Okay. No need to be other than cordial. "I'm Jacob."

"I'm Asib."

"Asib! I would offer you something to drink, but as you can see, we have just begun work on our well."

"You bought this land from the sons of Hamor?"

"For only one hundred kesitah, can you believe it?"

"I believe it every time the princes of this land cheat another foreigner. You will curse the day you paid that one hundred kesitah."

Jacob fights to keep smiling, determined to maintain a friendly tone. "And what do you think would have been a fair price?"

"Zero kesitah. Zero goats. Zero—"

"I have twelve sons to work the land, and once we strike water—"

"You will never strike water. Yes, the recent rain makes the land look lush, but the underground river runs around the mountain, not up it."

"Our God takes care of us."

"This is Canaan," Asib says. "The gods are not nice here."

"We won't be here that long. We are sojourners."

"Aah. And what are you looking for?"

"A land our God promised to my grandfather, Abraham."

"Your grandfather?" Asib grins knowingly. "You ever notice how the gods are always promising us things, but we never really see them happen?"

"Sometimes it takes generations."

"Suit yourself," Asib says. "What is this god of yours called anyway?"

"El Shaddai."

"I've never heard of him."

"Not many people have, but I think someday they will."

"Well, you have no home. Where's your temple for this god?"

"He has no temple."

"So, where do you worship him?"

"We build altars wherever we go."

"And you do not carry him with you?"

"No." Jacob chuckles. "There are no carved idols of Him."

"So, he's invisible?"

"Yes. Well, usually. There was one time He broke my hip."

Asib laughs and waves him off. "Oh, no, no, I've heard enough. Of all the gods you could possibly choose from, you pick an invisible god whose promises take generations to come true, who makes you sojourn in strange places, and he broke your hip? That is a strange choice. Oh, immigrants."

Jacob smiles. "We didn't choose Him—"

"Father!" one of his sons shouts, and Jacob jogs back to the hole, Asib close behind.

They have struck water, just inches below the rocky surface. Jacob squats and reaches, letting the liquid bubble up between his fingers. He rises to face Asib. "He chose us."

• • •

*The same place, nearly two millennia later*

Lugging empty nine-gallon water pots, one at either end of a pole across her shoulders, is grueling enough in the unforgiving midday sun. Photina doesn't even want to think about having to trudge all the way back to Sychar with them filled to the brim—the water alone adding seventy-five pounds to each pot.

That she does this every day makes it no easier. *This is what my life has become,* she thinks, *and I have no one to blame but myself.* She doesn't know why she even bothers with the ornate earrings and makeup, which only cracks and runs in the blistering heat. No one looks at her anymore anyway, save for her new man and the occasional lascivious ones in town. She has grown old in spite of her relative youth.

The canopy erected over Jacob's Well offers little relief, but that's where her real work begins. Drawing the water and filling the pots takes every ounce of her strength, and when she's finished, she can't dawdle in the shade. She must muscle that pole, laden with those hefty pots, onto her shoulders and begin the wobbly trek back.

Today, however, she's on a mission. Before delivering the water to her new home, she's heading to her most recent husband's house. Elia is twice her age and not well, a miserable coot she would love to be rid of so she can marry yet again. No one keeps track anymore of how many times she's done that. She's past caring what they think anyway. Her life is her business, and all she hopes for now is a modicum of happiness.

Photina saved shekels seemingly forever to get a man of the law to help her, though even he warns her the scheme is not likely to work. Still, she has to try.

• • •

Finally back in the city, drenched and exhausted, she uses her key to enter Elia's place. No surprise, he's wrapped in a blanket and ensconced near the fire, his back to her. No one else has a key to the house, so he knows it's her.

"You know," he says, his voice tinged with resignation, "when the door opened, I honestly hoped it was a thief or a murderer, come to put me out of my misery."

"Sorry to disappoint you," she says. "But there's something I need from you first."

He coughs. "Come closer. I can't see you."

For some reason, as Photina approaches him, she uncovers her hair. Who's she trying to impress, and why would anything about her disheveled appearance impress anyone anyway?

"Your hair is matted, and your face is red. Why?"

"You know why."

"If you came back to live with me, you could go to the well with the other women in the cool of the morning."

"You're wrong about that. I could go with them if I had stayed with Rahmin." But how could she? No one could have stayed.

"Out with it. How much do you need?"

"I'm not here for money." She pulls a document from her sash. "I've brought a bill of divorce. All you need to do is sign it."

"Only a man can divorce his wife, not the other way around, Photina."

"Which is why the certificate is in your name, Elia."

"On what grounds am I to divorce you?"

Is he serious? He has to ask? "I'm living with another man!"

"So what? That's all you did with me. Live here."

"You knew why I married you."

He nods. "Stability. The shine wore off quickly, didn't it?"

"The Pentateuch makes provision for a husband to divorce his wife if she lies with another man."

"Listen to you, talking about Pentateuch."

"What do I have to do, bring him here?"

"Yes! I want to see the latest shade of drooling tomcat you put your spell on. Hurry, before he gets bored. Like the others."

Enough of this! "Will you sign it or not?"

"Give it here."

For the first time, she feels hope. She holds her breath as he peruses it. But he doesn't make her wait long. "No."

No? That's it? No pity? No compassion? "Please!"

He faces her, disgust on his face. "Please?" he mimics. He leans forward and drops it into the fire. "You're my property, Photina. I don't part lightly with my possessions."

As the document blackens and turns to ash, she sees her life go up in smoke as well.

Chapter 74

# SINNER PARTY

Matthew remembers well having purchased his beautifully ornate home when he first realized how much he would profit from his new profession. He could not imagine ever having need of all the space, as he had never marshaled the courage to speak to females, let alone dream of marrying. And the massive dining room with its seemingly infinite banquet table! He'd hosted a couple of fellow tax collectors a few times, thankfully served by his staff. He'd endured long, awkward silences, grateful the guests felt comfortable enough to tease each other and regale him with their exploits. When they finally left, he felt relieved as never before.

But now this? How has this happened? As bizarre as his calling by Jesus of Nazareth, Matthew is hosting a dinner party this very night. His table is filled with an assortment of guests he never would have imagined, let alone invited on his own. Besides the other two tax collectors, several are Jesus' closest students, many of them former fishermen and still wary of Matthew. But also, the one-legged beggar Barnaby and his blind friend Shula.

And Rivka of Red Quarter fame! Matthew thought being reviled as a traitor was bad, but …

Yet somehow, simply having Jesus there makes everything seem all right. Maybe this won't be the ordeal most social encounters prove to be for him. He just wants everyone looked after, enjoying themselves, taken care of. He knows Jesus is the real host, but this being his home, he takes great pride in providing a feast and a good time.

The others sit eating, laughing, talking, as he fusses at the nearby serving table. Matthew enjoys the repartee. Rivka recalls the story of Nicodemus' encounter with Mary, then known as Lilith. "The way he ran from the Red Quarter, nearly tripping on his robes!"

"A Pharisee running?" Shula says. "Somehow I can't see that!"

Everyone erupts with laughter, and Rivka adds, "I thought for certain he would trip and fall, and *I* would be arrested!"

"Oh, with your luck, Rivka," Jesus says, "it probably would happen, huh?"

"I thought for certain Lil was gone forever that day."

"It's Mary now," the Magdalene says with a smile.

"It always was," Jesus says.

Matthew brings a platter to the table. "Does anyone want any grapes? Barnaby, you eat a lot."

"Very observant, Matthew."

"Thank you."

He moves down the row. "Simon?"

The fisherman looks away, shaking his head, and Matthew suddenly feels conspicuous again. *What will it take to win Simon over?*

"You know, Matthew," Barnaby says, "when you're not behind iron bars, you're quite handsome!"

Rivka seems to study Matthew. "I agree!" She nods.

"Rivka!" Mary says, laughing.

"What is going on?" Startled, Matthew turns to find two Pharisees at the door. He hurries over.

"May I help you?"

Yusef and an older Pharisee peer in. "We were just on a walk," Yusef says, "and we heard voices. And I thought they sounded like—but surely not."

"Yet it *is* you," the older one speaks up, looking past Matthew to Jesus and Simon, who have stood and moved behind the taxman.

"Would you like to come in?" Jesus says.

Yusef recoils. "We would never—never be caught dead in a—"

"In a what?" Jesus says. "In a tax collector's house?"

"Not only that." Yusef gestures toward Rivka. "But with a—do you know what she—and he—?" pointing at Matthew now.

"You seem to be having trouble finding your words, man," Simon says and folds his arms. Matthew is strangely warmed. Is he actually being defended by Simon now?

"Why does your master eat with tax collectors and sinners?" Yusef says.

"It's not the healthy who need a doctor," Jesus says, "but the sick."

"I must say, I am shocked. She is from the Red Quarter. Much of what is done there cannot even be spoken by my tongue or cross my lips, it is so unholy. The mere mention of it would defile me!"

"Sounds like a personal problem," Simon says.

"But him," Yusef says, nodding toward Matthew, "and the others he works with, they betray our people for money. And they're not even sorry."

Andrew calls out from the table, "If you're so offended, then leave!"

"Let them speak, Andrew," Jesus says.

"They've never offered guilt sacrifices in the temple," Yusef says.

"What?" Little James says.

"The priest keeps records," the older Pharisee says, nodding. "We check them."

"Tax collectors are not welcome in the temple," Matthew says.

John pipes up. "You'd like them better if they made the proper sacrifices?"

"This is not about me!" Yusef says. "This is about what God wants!"

"You are forgetting the scroll of Hosea," Jesus tells them. "Go and learn what this means: 'I desire mercy more than sacrifice.'"

Yusef glares at Jesus. "There are righteous men on the lookout for you. And they are weighing every word you say."

"Is that a threat?" Simon says.

"Please let them know this, Yusef," Jesus says calmly. "I have not come to call the righteous, but sinners."

Gaius appears behind the Pharisees. "Is everything under control here?"

"Yes!" the elder Pharisee says. "We were just going on our way, centurion."

"That's Primi Ordine to you."

"Primi Ordine." Yusef bows as they leave.

Gaius steps up to the door and stares at Matthew.

"You all keep eating," Matthew says as he opens the door. "I will talk to this man."

• • •

Gaius is nonplussed by the gaggle of rabble at the table in the next room. He whispers to the little man, "You're making a mistake. You could walk away from this."

Matthew cocks his head but maintains eye contact, something new. "I made my choice."

Impressive, really. *What's gotten into him?* In a strange way, Gaius appreciates this new side of Matthew. But he must stay on point. "Look at that room. Other than Rom and Jahaz, whom I know to be law-abiding tax collectors, everyone else in there—the dregs of Capernaum—"

"Gaius! Lower your voice!"

"—the bottom of the barrel."

Matthew seems to be steeling himself to say something. Finally, he blurts, "Germanic, correct? Isn't that what you told Quintus?"

"Do not change the subject."

"Your people surrendered. I'm surrendering too."

What? Who is this?

"Your promotion was well-earned," Matthew continues. "You will do well without me. Better even."

Gaius shakes his head, trying to make it make sense. "How? You're the one who got me promoted."

"That is untrue."

"Do not play dumb. You know how this all happened."

Matthew brightens. "You could say, 'thank you.'"

"Well, I'm not gonna do that."

"If you can't say it, then there's something you could do to show it. I'll pay you if necessary."

"I don't want your money." He studies Matthew. Is he actually going to miss this strange creature? He *does* owe him. Plus, he's flat curious. "What's the favor?"

Chapter 75

# ADONAI EL ROI

*Capernaum guesthouse*

Nicodemus knows beyond doubt who Jesus is, and yet he dares not tell even the love of his life. She would believe him mad. He looks to the ceiling, desperately praying, seeking wisdom.

Zohara breezes in, one of his vestments draped over her arm. "You have not rehearsed your speech for me."

"It's nothing."

"They want to honor you for the great things you have done here," she says, picking up a comb and tending to his beard. "Give them a thrill."

"My remarks will be extemporaneous."

"You are one of those rare men who excels in both rehearsed and unrehearsed speech." She drapes an embroidered garment over his head, one of the eighteen pieces of his complete toilette.

He smiles. "And you are not guilty of bias, are you?"

"Those are not my words," she says, straightening his robes.

"Oh?"

"Caiaphas said that about you at our last Shabbat dinner."

"He was just flattering."

"There is no one above the high priest but God. What has he to gain from you by flattery? He has never complimented my cooking."

That makes Nicodemus laugh.

"Do you remember at that final dinner when Eliel sang to Havilah?" she says. "She was glowing, his voice the sweeter for the child in her womb."

How could he forget? "Brought tears to my eyes."

"Can you picture Moishe and Gideon, their little chins resting on the table when you say the Eshet Chayil? That's the way Shabbat was meant to be. Family—knit together around a table. My mother's gilded plates. Your grandmother's candlesticks, may she rest in peace."

Speaking of women of valor. "I do miss her."

"And if she could see you now, receiving the highest honor ever bestowed by our order." She drapes an elaborate medallion around his neck. "She would burst with pride!"

"I remember the inscription she had over the doorway of her room," he says. "*Adonai El Roi*. 'The Lord. The God who sees me.'"

Zohara says it with him and adds, "The words of Hagar."

Nicodemus nods. "She always loved that Hagar was caught up in something complicated and fraught, but not of her choice." He waxes emotional as the truth of it all strikes close to his own heart. One monumental decision, and he himself could be caught up in something just as complicated. "And yet, God saw her!" he says. "And He knew that the path she was forced to take would not be an easy one." He's lost in thought, eager to tell Zohara what he knows, what he has seen, *whom* he has seen. But he dares not.

"When we stumble onto hard roads," she says, "He finds us and comforts us."

"Or does He call us to them?" Jesus has called him, but how could he possibly go?

Zohara seems to study him, then applies to his neck ointment from a small vial. "Persian myrrh and camphor to commemorate our last day in Capernaum."

Abruptly his breath comes in short bursts and he's unable to cover his torment. "One last day."

"Nicodemus," Zohara says, her countenance full of concern. "I love our life."

His tears come. "As do I." He knows he's puzzling her, worrying her.

"Take me back to it," she says.

But as her eyes bore into him, he must look away. "I changed my mind. I will prepare my remarks. I will need a moment." As he leaves her, he senses she's staring after him, uncertain and afraid.

# Chapter 76

# QUIT

*The Roman Authority headquarters, Capernaum*

Gaius returns from his shift with several others when Quintus calls out to him from the foyer. Gaius freezes and bows. "Praetor."

"Just the man I've been waiting to see. Get in here."

Gaius follows Quintus into his office, where the praetor stands facing him from the other side of his desk. "What methods are we using to quell and disperse mobs that obstruct traffic?"

Surprised by the question, Gaius tries to keep from sounding as if he's making up the answer as he goes. "Regular patrols. Mounted officers. When necessary, force."

"Not enough force. What use are mounted officers if the people have never seen anyone trampled?"

*Trampled? What is he ...?* "Praetor?"

"Herod's envoy was delayed. He was a childhood rival—you were there. I asked Matthew, and he said show him some infrastructure plans."

"I hope it was effective, Dominus."

"Very. Until Silvius was delayed by a stampede on his way out. I had to endure a very smug lecture. Don't let that happen again."

"Yes, Praetor."

After an awkward silence, Quintus says, "I see you are alone. I assume that means you've found a replacement to watch our little friend."

"Uh, a new soldier has been trained and installed."

"Good."

Better to tell him the news now than to have Quintus discover it later. "And I am reviewing applications for a new publicanus for that district."

"What district?"

"The collection district previously assessed by Matthew."

"Why are you doing *that*?"

No way to gloss over it now. "Matthew left." At Quintus' surprised look, Gaius adds, "He quit, Dominus."

"What do you mean, he quit? Why would you let him quit?"

"He is a contractor. I—I had no recourse."

"Quit to do what?"

"He is to become a student."

"Of what? Don't make me keep asking questions, Primi!"

"He is to study the Jewish god. He left to follow a holy man. The man from the eastern ghetto. That is all I know."

Quintus looks apoplectic. "Oh, I really don't like that man."

## Chapter 77

# FOREKNOWLEDGE

Simon, with Jesus and several of the others, helps break camp when Big James and John arrive, holding two bags aloft. "Brothers!" James calls out.

"Extra food from our Ima!" John says.

"And she made more," Big James tells them. "She's convinced we will starve along the way with six days of walking."

"Three," Jesus says.

"Three?" John says.

"Are we going to run all the way to Jerusalem?" Thaddeus says.

"That won't work for Simon!" Andrew laughs. "He's a terrible runner."

"Yeah, well, I have bad shins."

"Well," Big James says, "maybe if you didn't fight with Abe and Jehoshaphat every week—"

"Easy, easy boys," Jesus says.

"My fighting days are over," Simon says.

Jesus shoots him a look. "Simon, you seem quiet this morning."

"Well, we have a long journey ahead."

"Apparently only half as long as we thought," Andrew says.

"I'll explain later," Jesus tells them. "Simon, what troubles you?"

"Nothing. Just excited for the trip, you know?"

"You can tell me the truth."

*Here we go. I can, but what's the point?* "You're telling me you don't already know what's in my head?"

"That's a conversation for another time. But for now . . ."

*All right, if he insists.* "I'm the only one among us who is married."

"Aah. So, you think I should have only called single people?"

"Of course not. And I'm glad you didn't. But Eden will be alone with her Ima, and—"

"You're scared that things could get worse and you wouldn't be there."

"See? That's what I mean. You already know anyway."

"Simon." Jesus smiles. "Everyone here knows what you're thinking most of the time. It does not take God's wisdom."

Chapter 78

# THE CONFRONTATION

Nicodemus knows he should be warmed by the generous praise heaped upon him at the ceremony, but he's strangely unmoved. Troubled, in fact. If Messiah has come, Nicodemus can only imagine what it means for all Hebrews—for the world. What he has seen Jesus do, and what Jesus has taught him, puts his entire life and ministry in the balance.

While Zohara mingles with dignitaries inside, Nicodemus wanders out to the portico overlooking the courtyard. He bears a beautiful commemorative scroll written in his honor. It's nice, certainly, but …

Yusef finds him there. "Congratulations on your profound contributions, Rabbi," the young man says. "We are forever in your debt."

How often in the past has he reveled in such adulation, and how empty and spurious it now seems! Yet Yusef seems sincere, and Nicodemus must acknowledge it. "Praise Adonai," he says.

"Praise Adonai," Yusef says, and moves on.

Nicodemus turns sober again. For years he's believed his motives to be pure and that he earned his station by remaining devout, committed to his work and scholarship. If he wasn't always privately humble, he tried not to let that show. *Grateful*—that is how he hoped to appear. He wanted to make Zohara and the family proud. But what might the future hold now? What had not so long ago appeared to be a fairly predictable final season of his life now could become chaotic. Who knows what will happen when Jesus becomes known for who he really is?

"The ceremony was glorious, Teacher," Shmuel says, interrupting his reverie. "Your acts of faithfulness and discernment have been duly recorded for all history."

That's very kind, and—Nicodemus hopes—sincere, coming from a former protégé with whom he has intellectually scuffled of late. Nicodemus happily responds in kind. "Thank you, Shmuel. I'm grateful for your service as well."

"Thank you."

Nicodemus can be generous with the man on a day when he himself has been such an object of attention. "I foresee you will be an important leader in our order for many years to come."

Shmuel appears to humble himself with a glance at the floor. "Maybe not just here in Capernaum, Rabbi. Perhaps I will one day teach across Judea. Maybe even in Jerusalem."

So, there it is. Not so humble after all. "Perhaps you will, Shmuel."

"It's not such a ridiculous notion, is it, Rabbi? I have studied under your venerated tutelage after all. As your reputation grows, so too do my own prospects."

That's more than Nicodemus can countenance. "I think it is perhaps bold," he says evenly, "to assume outcomes. Our work is for God. He chooses where it takes us."

Shmuel appears unconvinced but says, "You're right as always, Rabbi." Yet he's not finished. "But under your guidance, I've found a matter of Law I'm deeply passionate about. One that resonates with many others, even as far away as Jerusalem."

"I'm delighted to hear your fervor, Shmuel! Tell me, what is it you've become so passionate about?"

"False prophecy," he says, as if making a pronouncement. "When I heard the man from Nazareth tell the paralytic his sins were forgiven, I thought, 'Only God can forgive sins.' At that very moment, he turned to me and recited my thoughts as if reading them from a scroll. Did he use divination, I wondered? But it's obvious. Of course, I would think this thought. He called himself the Son of Man, as if from the prophet Daniel. Here, in the town of my order!"

Unwilling to give himself away, and especially not wanting the miracle man to be pounced upon by his own colleagues, Nicodemus covers by chuckling. "He came from Nazareth! Not heaven!" And yet that's exactly where Nicodemus believes Jesus came from. He had told the Nazarene that himself—that he had to be a teacher come from God, for no man could perform those miracles except God be with him.

But Shmuel is on a roll. "'To him was given dominion and glory and a kingdom, that all peoples, nations, and languages should serve him,'" he recites.

"He's simply a man!" Nicodemus says. "I don't understand it any more than y—"

Shmuel continues to quote the Scriptures. "'His dominion is an everlasting dominion which shall not pass away, and his kingdom that which shall not be destroyed.'"

Nicodemus believes that, he believes it about Messiah. He believes Jesus *is* the Messiah. Why can Shmuel not see it?

The younger man steps closer, solemn. "The man claimed to

be God, and you said nothing. I will petition Jerusalem, requesting permission to search the archives for all matters pertaining to such false prophecy. Will you oppose my petition, Rabbi? The question on the mind of every man who reads my account will have to be, 'What did Nicodemus do?'"

Now Shmuel has spilled his true motives. "So," Nicodemus says, "it's all about politics and promotion for you, isn't it? It's not to serve God."

"On the contrary, Teacher. It's about the Law. And the Law *is* God. If I'm rewarded for that, it is because I learned from the very wisest."

Understanding the full weight and likely consequences of such an inquiry, Nicodemus knows the time has come to draw his line in the sand. "I will not oppose your petition." He begins to turn away, done with this conversation and with this man. But he looks back. "And, Shmuel, you have learned nothing from me."

Chapter 79

# HEALED

*Simon's home*

Eden's mother, Dasha, coughs as Eden lifts a towel from her forehead. "Where is Simon? Can't he build us a fire?"

"He's away, Ima," Eden tells her.

"Fishing?"

"No, something else. Lie still."

Nothing is working. Her beloved mother grows weaker. Eden steps into the kitchen, steadying herself against a table. Weary and devastated, she does not know what to do. She lowers her head and fights tears as more coughing comes from the bedroom.

"Eden."

She starts at the familiar voice. "Jesus? I—I wasn't expecting you here."

"People usually aren't."

"Can I get you something warm to drink? I was just stoking the fire."

"You saw it first, you know," he says tenderly.

"What do you mean?" she says.

"What I see in Simon. You were the first person to notice, when no one else did. That connects us."

She swallows a sob. "My mother said I was drawn to his wildness, and that I would regret it. I wonder what she will say now?"

Simon and Andrew enter, laden with fishing gear. "We're going into town to sell these nets," Simon says. "We'll be right back."

"Stay here a moment, Simon," Jesus says.

"I just want to leave some extra money behind for Eden and Ima while I'm away."

"Put your nets down and go sit with your mother-in-law."

Eden knows Simon is not used to being told what to do, but Andrew immediately drops his gear and heads for the bedroom. Simon follows, and Jesus pats him on the back on his way by. "It's all right," Jesus says.

Jesus turns back to Eden. "I told Simon to make sacrifices and leave things behind in order to follow me. You are one flesh with Simon. He cannot make sacrifices that are not also yours. You have a role to play in all of this."

Overcome, she whispers, "Do I?"

"You will know in time. I can't make everything about this easier for you."

She nods. "That wouldn't be our people's way."

He laughs. "No, that has not been. Nor will it continue to be." He steps closer to her. "But I see you. You understand? I know it is not easy to be at home when your husband is out doing all of—this. Even when you are excited about it and proud of him."

Eden feels deeply everything the teacher says, and it warms her.

He continues, “So, I wouldn’t ask you to do this without taking care of a few things.”

Dasha coughs, and Jesus nods toward the bedroom, as if that’s just what he’s talking about. *Is it possible?* Eden wonders. *Could it be true?* She’s almost afraid to believe it. “You mean—?”

“Plus,” Jesus adds, “normal Simon is difficult enough. You think I want to travel with a worried Simon?”

Laughing through her tears, Eden says, “No.”

“No,” he says, “I do not.”

She follows him to her Ima’s bed, where Andrew watches as Simon tends to the unconscious woman. “The fever’s spiked,” he whispers. “Her forehead burns my hand.”

“We should get a doctor,” Andrew says.

“There is no need.” Jesus approaches the bed as Simon makes way. The rabbi grips her hand, looks up, closes his eyes, and looks back down at her. To the fever he says, “Leave her.”

Dasha stirs for the briefest moment, then gasps and sits up, staring at Simon, Eden, and Andrew. She looks suddenly strong and full of energy. Eden gapes at her in wonder, tears in her eyes, and the others seem as awed as she at what Jesus has done.

Her mother seems to notice the stranger for the first time. “Who are you?” she says.

“This is Jesus of Nazareth,” Andrew says.

“You’ve never met him before,” Simon adds.

“Welcome to my son-in-law’s home.”

“Thank you,” he says, smiling.

“What am I doing lying here?”

“You had a terrible fever,” Andrew says.

“And all of you staring down …” She shoves the blanket aside and leaves the bed.

“Dasha!” Andrew says. “Don’t—”

“No one move! I’ll be right back with some drinks.”

As she sails into the kitchen, Jesus shrugs, and Eden buries her head in Simon's neck, sobbing.

From the kitchen, Dasha hollers, "Andrew! Be a dear and stoke this fire!"

"Coming!"

As Eden thanks Jesus, her Ima recites everything she's looking for. "Rye and butter for Simon. Pomegranate arils, goat cheese. Does your friend like goat cheese?"

"Yes!" Jesus calls out. "I love goat cheese!"

Eden looks deep into Simon's eyes. "I should go," Jesus says, stepping out, "and see about the goat cheese."

"Thank you," Eden says to Simon.

"Me? For what?"

"For obeying and following him. It led him here."

"Simon!" Dasha calls from the kitchen. "Nectarines or plums?"

Chapter 80

# SETTING OUT

*The Sychar marketplace, Samaria*

Photina pushes her way through crowded stalls, drawn as usual to the fresh oranges. Just sniffing them brings back one of the few memories she actually enjoys. The pain of regret stabs her too, but she can't ignore the tangy, sweet smell.

She's aware of men's eyes as she hurries along, but also the headshaking and even spitting of some women—a few whom she knows are no better than she.

The orange seller turns his back at her approach. "We don't serve your kind here," he says.

"And what kind is that?" She lifts an orange to her nose.

"You know what you are."

"Well, lucky for you," she says, dropping a lepton coin in his bucket, "I can serve myself. You know, to stop me, you'd have to look at me." But he won't give her the satisfaction.

• • •

*The Roman Authority headquarters, Capernaum*

"Take down this decree in Latin, Aramaic, and Greek so no one can plead ignorance," Quintus tells his scribe. "'By order of Rome, and punishable by detention and imprisonment, religious gatherings outside the synagogue and Hebrew school are strictly prohibited. The teacher known as Jesus of Nazareth is sought for questioning.'"

• • •

*Dawn*

From all over Capernaum the disciples and Mary of Magdala come, heading to meet Jesus at the well in the southern quarter. He's told them a usual six-day walk will take only half that time. None knows why.

Matthew leaves his home, for the first time in ages locking his door only once.

Andrew sets out with a huge bag over his shoulder.

Big James and John, whom Jesus calls the Sons of Thunder, embrace their parents, Zebedee and Salome.

Mary of Magdala kisses her own fingers and touches the mezuzah on her doorframe on her way out.

Zohara supervises the loading of her and Nicodemus' belongings for their journey back to Jerusalem. Nicodemus slips out behind her, carrying a purple cloth bag.

Simon hugs his mother-in-law, Dasha, and kisses Eden. He leaves with a bounce in his step.

• • •

Nicodemus peeks out from behind a wall when Jesus arrives at the well with two of his followers. The others show up almost simultaneously—Mary and five more men—all greeting each other warmly. Nicodemus can't help imagining himself among them and how different his life would be, if only …

His days with the Sanhedrin would be over. No more meetings, deliberations, research. And no more robes upon robes.

"That should be everyone," one young man says.

"Everyone's here?" Jesus says, scanning the square.

"Yes." Mary looks around. "This is all of us."

*All of them?* Nicodemus wonders, is he making a mistake? Should he show himself, take the step? He cannot. But how he longs to!

"Is there anyone else?" Jesus calls out, as the one they call Simon splashes his face from the well and playfully flicks water on John.

Nicodemus knows Jesus is looking for him, waiting for him, hoping he'll come.

"Look at this!" Simon squats to retrieve a purple bag at the base of the fountain.

"What is that?" another says.

"I don't know," Simon says. "Let's find out." He opens it to reveal coins. "Gold."

One of the men, dressed differently from the others, leans close to see.

"A friend of mine left that for us," Jesus tells them.

"That's enough for two weeks of food and lodging," the finely dressed one says.

Jesus looks toward the wall and shakes his head. "You came so close," he whispers, and Nicodemus winces, weeping.

"What do you mean?" Mary asks Jesus.

"We need to go," Simon says, "if we're going to make camp in Tiberius by nightfall."

"Simon's correct," Jesus says. "Let's go."

Simon seems to be sizing up the man in his fine vestments. "You going to wear that? On a trip?"

"These are my clothes. Should I have others?"

Simon shakes his head.

Nicodemus, still behind the wall, covers his mouth and sobs.

## Chapter 81

# THE FAVOR

*Capernaum, the golden hour*

Gaius has decided he can do this one favor for Matthew. He knocks at Alphaeus's door. Matthew's mother opens it.

"Hello," Gaius says.

She just stares.

From inside, a man calls out, "Elisheba, who is it?"

"A Roman," she says.

Something falls and breaks as the man hurries to the door and steps between his wife and Gaius. "What's wrong? What happened?"

Gaius explains that their son asked him to speak to them. They invite him in, and the three sit at a table, where the guard recounts Matthew's story to the best of his recollection.

"What did it mean, 'Follow me'?" Alphaeus says.

"That is all he said. Matthew did not hesitate."

"Follow him where?"

"Look, I'm sure he will come to his senses."

Alphaeus laughs. "His senses. Do you know my son?"

"Do *you*?" Gaius says, and Matthew's father stops laughing. "At the moment, Matthew believes this man to be a prophet."

Elisheba grabs her husband's arm. "The man who healed the paralytic at Zebedee's house!"

Gaius' gaze narrows. "I would be careful with that word *healed*. We do not know what sort of trickery or illusion may have been involved."

Alphaeus shakes his head. "Matthew has no interest in illusion."

"Nor in your god," Gaius says. "Or so I thought."

Alphaeus rises and paces. "Matthew upended his life to be with him. His wicked life!"

Elisheba nods. "He does not make decisions lightly."

"That is true," Gaius says.

"When I saw him two days ago," Elisheba says, "he did not seem himself. But I never would have guessed that he was preparing for this."

"He asked me to deliver to you some of his personal effects."

"Adonai in heaven," she says, clearly distraught.

"The key to his house." Gaius holds it out to Alphaeus.

"Luxury bought off the backs of our people," Alphaeus says. "I will not accept it."

"He suspected as much," Gaius says, eager to be relieved of the key. He stands. "Sell it, give it away, burn it down, I do not care."

Alphaeus reaches for the key, but Gaius hesitates before handing it over. "Don't burn it down." After an awkward pause, Gaius says, "The other is just outside."

A minute later the three of them stare at the black dog. "Matthew …" Elisheba says.

"What?" Alphaeus says. "Why?"

"Matthew said thieves forced you to close your business," Gaius says.

"Yes, but—"

"And you've been taking long journeys for your business."

"Yes. I have all my permits."

Does he have to spell it out? "Don't you get it? The roads are dangerous. Your wife is left alone for long periods of time. People with bad intentions hate him."

"I—how does it work?"

Gaius doesn't know what to say. It's a dog forevermore! "One last thing: If you hear from Matthew or receive any word of his whereabouts, contact me immediately."

"Is he wanted?" Alphaeus says.

"Not officially. But if Jesus of Nazareth returns to Capernaum, the praetor would like to—question him. And it would be in everyone's best interests if you contact me."

"We understand."

Now how to express this last bit? "And, uh, I just want you to kn—well." Gaius falls silent, searching for words. Alphaeus and Elisheba raise their brows. "I know some people who were mildly fond of your son."

Gaius hurries off, relieved to have come close to what he really wanted to say and amused to hear the dog whine and imagine what Matthew's parents might do with it.

Chapter 82

# DETOUR

Jesus' entourage reaches the top of a rise early in the morning, and Matthew is surprised to find he's actually enjoying himself—even though he now recognizes what Simon was driving at when he questioned his clothes. The others wear half what he does, and they all glisten with sweat. He's baking.

The others tend to defer to him in matters of detail, so Matthew leads the way, consulting a map. As they come to a crossroad, Andrew stops and points far into the distance. "What city is that?"

"Jezreel," Matthew says. "The southernmost town in Galilee. From there we veer east to the Jordan River."

But Jesus turns away from the city and keeps walking.

"Rabbi," John says, "where are you going?"

"Do you need something?" Andrew says.

"This way, friends," Jesus calls over his shoulder.

"I'm sorry," Matthew says, rushing to catch up, "but the map shows Jezreel is two miles southeast of here and is met by a road east to the Jordan. We need to adjust our course thirty degrees to the—"

"We're not going to the Jordan." Jesus turns to face them but continues walking backward. Clearly, he's eager to keep moving. "We're going through Samaria." He turns back around to lead the way.

"Are you telling a joke?" Andrew says.

"There's a place that I want to stop at. Plus, this is what makes our journey shorter by almost half."

"And our odds of violent attack more likely by double," Matthew says.

Jesus chuckles. "Is that an exact figure?"

"Forgive me, Teacher." Andrew snatches the map from Matthew and shows it to Jesus. "It's safer to go around Samaria by way of the Jordan and the Decapolis."

Jesus smiles. "Did you join me for safety reasons?"

"But, Rabbi," Big James says, "they're Samaritans!"

Jesus stops. "Good observation. What's your point?"

"Rabbi, these were the people who profaned our temple with the dead bones. They hated us."

John chimes in, "They fought against us with the Seleucids in the Maccabean wars. I haven't even spoken to a Samaritan—"

"And we destroyed their temple a hundred years ago," Jesus says. "And none of you here was present for any of these things. Listen, if we are going to have a question-and-answer session every time we do something you're not used to, it's going to be a very annoying time together for all of us. We'll be fine. And if we get attacked, Simon will be happy to show us what to do."

"Absolutely!" Simon says with a grin.

"All right. So, follow me."

• • •

*The following day, late morning*

Jesus and his followers trudge through high grass up a hill, roasting under a relentless sun, their faces crimson. He stops a hundred yards short of a canopied well and knows this is the spot. As he gazes at it, Thaddeus says, "We ate the last of Salome's bread last night."

"Master," Simon says, "we need to go into town for food."

"We can use the gold left for us at the fountain," Andrew says.

"Very well," Jesus says.

"There's a town about a mile west," Matthew says. "Sychar."

"You all go. I'll wait here."

"Someone should stay with you," Big James says. "In case ..."

"I'm all right. Meet me at that well when you come back."

• • •

Another day, another midday hike up to the well for Photina. Elia's fire consumed any hope for relief from her wretched existence, along with her bill of divorce. She ducks out from under her yoke and settles it where she has access to the pots. Normally she would wait, keeping a respectful distance from the stranger sitting nearby—looking as weary as she. But he's not using the well, and she has work to do. She wipes her brow and sighs.

"Would you give me a drink?" the man says.

She ignores him.

"Did you hear me?"

"That bad, huh?" she says.

"What?"

"You, a Jew, ask for a drink from me, a Samaritan? And a woman?"

"I'm sorry. I should have said *please.*"

An apology? From a man? A Jewish man? She studies him briefly and turns back to her work. "You know it's not safe for you to be alone out here."

"Nor you," he says. "Why haven't you come with others? And why so late in the day? Don't women come to the wells in the cool of the morning?"

"Well, none of them will be seen with me, so I have to come at noon in the heat, as you have so kindly reminded me." She dips her water pot in the well.

"Why won't they be seen with you?"

"Long story."

"I'd still like a drink of water, if you can spare it."

"Amazing what a parched throat will do. Aren't I unclean to you? Won't you be defiled by this vessel?"

"Maybe some of my people say that about your women, but I don't."

"What do you say?"

"I say if you knew who I am, you'd be asking me for a drink."

"Really."

"And I would give you living water."

"Would. Except you have nothing to draw water with, and this is a deep well. Besides, what do you need from me if you have your own supply of living water?"

"Long story," Jesus says, smiling.

"But Jewish water is better than Samaritan water, hm?"

"That's not what I said."

"Are you a better man than our ancestor Jacob, who dug this well? Your water is better than his?"

"I know Jacob."

*What is he saying? Has the heat made him mad?*

He continues, "And everyone who drinks of this water will

thirst again. But whoever drinks the water that I give him will never be thirsty again."

He's talking nonsense. "Wouldn't that be nice?"

"The water I give will become in a person a spring of water, welling up to eternal life."

"Really." Now she's heard everything.

"Yes, really."

He says it with such authority, such confidence. She quits filling her pot and faces him. "Prove it." Unless she has to continue living the way she does, Photina might love eternal life.

"First," he says, "go and call your husband and come back. I will show you both."

"I don't have a husband." She turns away.

"You are right," he says. "You've had five husbands."

She turns back.

"And the man you're living with now is not your husband."

*How could he possibly …?* She forces a laugh. "Oh, I see. You're a prophet. You're here to preach at me."

"No."

"Usually, the one good thing about coming here alone is that I can escape being condemned."

"I'm not here to condemn you."

"I've made mistakes, too many." Her eyes flash. "But it's men like you who have made it impossible for me to do anything about it."

"How?"

"Our ancestors worshipped on this mountain! But you Jews insist Jerusalem is the only place for true worship."

"They say that because the temple is there."

"Yeah, exactly where we're not allowed."

"I'm here to break those barriers."

*Who does this man think he is?* And he's not finished.

"And the time is coming when neither on this mountain nor in Jerusalem will you worship the Father."

*Where would that leave me?* "So where am I supposed to go when *I* need God?" *Why am I even engaging this man?* "I've never received anything from God. But I couldn't thank Him, even if I did."

"Anywhere! God is spirit. And the time is coming and is now here that it won't matter where you worship, but only that you do it in spirit and truth. Heart and mind, that—*that* is the kind of worshipper He's looking for." Then, tenderly, "It won't matter where you're from or what you've done."

It won't matter? She can barely imagine it! He's been talking crazy, but this reaches her. *Oh, if only he could be right!* But … She shakes her head.

"Do you believe what I'm telling you?" he says.

Throat thick with emotion, she says, "Until the Messiah comes and explains everything, and sorts this mess out—including me—I don't trust in anyone."

"You're wrong when you say that you have never received anything from God."

*Oh, is that right? How would he know?* Her pots are full, so she lifts the yoke.

"This Messiah you speak of, I am he."

She should have known. *What is this lunacy?* Photina starts toward the path.

"The first one was named Rahmin."

She stops.

"You were a woman of purity …"

*How could he know that?*

"… who was excited to be married."

*I was, but—*

"But he wasn't a good man. He hurt you."

Who has told him this?

"And it made you question marriage . . ."

*It's true! It's true! But I never told a soul.*

". . . and even the practice of your faith."

She drops the yoke, and the water begins to pour out. "Stop it." Is it possible this man is who he claims to be? To know of her next husband, he would have to be—that or a sorcerer.

"The second was Farzad. On your wedding night, his skin smelled like oranges. And to this day, every time you pass by the oranges in the market, you feel guilty for leaving him, because he was the only truly godly man you've been with. But you felt unworthy."

Her tears roll. "Why are you doing this?"

He slowly steps toward her. "I have not revealed myself to the public as the Messiah. You are the first. It would be good if you believed me." He smiles again.

*Me first? Why? Why on earth, a woman like me?* "You picked the wrong person."

"I came to Samaria just to meet you."

*How can I not believe? Only the divine could know even* my *heart.*

"Do you think it's an accident that I'm here in the middle of the day?" he says.

This is too much. Too much. Her tears flow. "I am rejected by others."

"I know. But not by the Messiah."

Photina gasps. "And you know these things because you *are* the Christ?"

He nods.

She knows it's true. Suddenly she feels light as a feather and puts her hands atop her head, grinning through her tears. "I'm going to tell everyone!"

"I was counting on it," he says, smiling.

She laughs. "Spirit and truth?"

"Spirit and truth."

"It won't be all about mountains or temples?"

"Soon, just the heart."

"You promise?"

"I promise."

Chapter 83

# STILL, PEOPLE MUST KNOW

*Eighteen years later*

Mary Magdalene, now middle-aged, lies low, as do the many who call themselves Christians. While the surviving original disciples boldly strike out across the world, proclaiming the gospel of the risen Christ, Jesus of Nazareth, Mary's deepest desire is to be of service to the burgeoning church. During the day she busies herself behind closed doors in a commune populated by nearly two dozen other believers.

As one of the senior remaining personal acquaintances of Jesus, she is revered, admired, and sought for counsel by the others. While she is careful not to usurp the authority of the tiny band of elders, Mary takes seriously her role and strives to serve as an example. That means she does her part to serve the others, as Jesus served his friends when he dwelt among them. She cooks, she cleans, she sews, and she ministers to anyone who falls ill. She writes letters to Christ-followers in other regions.

She keeps track of the comings and goings of the disciples who have become missionaries, those venturing into what Jesus called the uttermost parts of the earth.

How Mary loves to remind others of the charge Jesus left with the remaining eleven before God transported him to heaven! She has heard the men tell the story so many times that she has memorized it and never tires of penning it afresh on parchments secreted away with messengers in the night: "All authority in heaven and on earth has been given to me," the Messiah told them. "Go therefore and make disciples of all nations, baptizing them in the name of the Father and of the Son and of the Holy Spirit, teaching them to observe all that I have commanded you. And behold, I am with you always, to the end of the age."

Almost every evening, Mary steals away in the dark to visit tiny home churches and teach new believers to pray and study the ancient texts. She fears for her life—of course she does—but she has learned so much from her brave cohorts that she would, as one of the new leaders, Paul of Tarsus, has so often preached, consider dying for Jesus to be "far better," in fact to be "gain."

Mary thrills to accounts of the other Mary, Jesus' mother, having gone from residing with John to spending many days with the physician Luke—whom Jesus added to his disciples when their number eventually grew to seventy. He has proved himself on journeys to several churches with the apostle Paul and is now fashioning an account, a Gospel, of the life of Jesus. Word has spread that Luke walked Mother Mary through a detailed account of Jesus' birth.

Now in her declining years, Mother Mary is reportedly living under the watch care of an old friend of Jesus, in fact a man Jesus had raised from the dead, Lazarus of Bethany. Mary Magdalene prays for the elder Mary every day and longs to see her at least one more time before God takes her to heaven to reunite with her son. And so when word comes that her heroine of the faith is suffering a fever and wants to see her, the younger Mary determines to get to her—wherever she is.

"Oh!" she exults. "Is it possible? I would risk anything!"

One of the elders appears grave. "I'll discuss it with the others," he says, "but I can't promise I'll advise it. Even the couriers and peddlers Zee trusts to deliver documents and goods to our brothers and sisters in distant lands do this at their peril. Clandestine deliveries of parchments or foodstuffs are one thing ..."

"Please ask the elders to pray about it," Mary says. "It's the master's own mother's request." She knows that any plan devised by Simon, the former Zealot, has a chance to succeed.

The elders meet long into the night and tell Mary she'll hear their decision in the morning. She barely sleeps. Finally, the one she originally consulted comes to her, smiling but also appearing wary. "It was your request that we pray this through that made the difference," he says. "Even *my* mind was changed. We believe the Lord would have you accede to Mother Mary's invitation."

"Oh, thank you, thank you!"

"But I must caution you. Zee insists we put you under the charge of one of our most trusted men, Tychicus, who—"

"I know him! He will take good care of me."

"—who has a trip planned a fortnight from now. But he—"

"Forgive me for continuing to interrupt you, Brother, but can it not be arranged sooner? I fear she—"

"We are trying to do nothing out of the ordinary that would draw attention to this. And you must know, you will have to be hidden in his wagon the entire trip. It's more than a forty-mile journey over a most dangerous route—known for several Roman checkpoints, not to mention bandits."

"But you have prayed about this. I will not fear."

"I will."

Mary smiles. "I will too, of course. But I will *try* not to. I'm most concerned that I don't get Tychicus in trouble."

"Mary, you are known to Rome. If you are discovered with him, it will go bad for the both of you. And of course, we'll count on you not to reveal any details that would expose us—"

"Of course not! I am prepared to suffer if I must."

"The trip alone will make you suffer."

That proves true. Near midnight two weeks later, she creeps several blocks to their meeting point. Quiet and confident as Tychicus appears—his wagon drawn by two horses and laden with produce and covered with hay—he strikes Mary as shy as he explains where she will ride. The tall, earnest Turk with a full beard has covered the bed of the wagon with blankets, but it is hardly what she would call comfortable. She is confined between boxes of food and wineskins and perfumes, and she has just enough room to lie on her back or turn onto her stomach.

"Will I be able to talk with you?" she says.

"Between checkpoints and unless we're passing someone, sure."

"Otherwise, it will be a lonely journey."

Two nights later, her joints aching, Mary whispers, "Tychicus? How much farther?"

He shushes her. "I can see the city in the distance."

"Thank God."

"Believe me, I have. Now remain absolutely silent until we arrive."

He stops the horses, and Mary hears him climb from his perch and step to the back of the wagon. "Just grabbing a cloak," he whispers. "Stay quiet." She hears him clad himself in the cloak and rearrange the hay. It seems to take some time for him to get going again.

As he remounts his seat, something drops from it, and Mary wonders if he intended to pass something to her. She fingers it in the dark. A leather pouch with documents inside. "Do you need—"

"Shh! Please! Roman guards man the city gate ahead. Don't move. Don't let them hear you even breathe."

Mary prays silently as Tychicus clicks his tongue, but it's obvious he's reining in the horses, as the wagon shambles slowly. She can tell they're pulling up to the gate by conversations. Footsteps.

"Halt." The guard sounds bored, distracted. "Late night for a delivery."

"It was a long journey," Tychicus says wearily.

"What have you got?"

Has Tychicus not heard the man? Maybe he's too distracted by his human cargo. Finally, he says, "I'm sorry? Oh, agriculture, grain, fruit."

Mary hears the covering move and the guard's voice from farther back alongside the wagon. "What am I gonna find if I look in here?"

She can tell Tychicus is trying to sound confident. "The best figs in the region."

Mary holds her breath as the guard digs through the boxes. Why didn't Tychicus also tell him of the wineskins and the myrrh?

"You didn't mention the fine goods. I'll take a look at your papers now."

Tychicus begins searching.

"Everything all right?" the guard says, a hint of sarcasm in his voice. "You look a little pale."

The leather pouch! He *hadn't* dropped it on purpose. Dare

she slide it out to him? Can she pull this off without being seen? Mary has no choice.

"Here they are," Tychicus says, sounding relieved.

Knowing Tychicus, his papers will match the goods, but this is taking so long, Mary is terrified that the guard suspects something. What will she do if Tychicus is detained?

"Hail, Caesar," the guard says at last.

The wagon commences moving again, even more slowly than before. Soon Tychicus has stopped the horses, and Mary peers out through about an inch of space. Tychicus hops down and quietly approaches a gate, dimly illuminated by flickering torches. In the dirt he draws a half circle on the ground with his foot, then knocks.

A figure approaches from inside but stops a few feet from the gate, appearing to stare. "Are you lost, traveler?" he says.

Tychicus shakes his head. "No longer, for I have found the way."

The dark-haired man opens the gate, looks down, and draws another half circle with his foot, intersecting the first and producing the shape of a fish.

Tychicus lowers his hood to reveal his face and introduces himself.

"Lazarus," the other man says.

"It's an honor. Your fame has spread among many of us."

"You are very kind. Paul says you are brave and righteous."

Tychicus says, "It's a pleasure to serve."

Lazarus looks to the wagon. "There is someone very eager for your arrival. May I tell her all is safe and sound?"

"Yes."

"Come in quickly."

Tychicus hurries to the wagon and helps Mary down. They slip inside and wait in the hallway as Lazarus steps into a cozy bedroom. It's all Mary can do to wait to see if Mother Mary is awake and up to seeing her.

"Woman," Lazarus says quietly.

"Yes," the older Mary says. That precious voice!

"I'm sorry to wake you, but—"

"No, I was just resting my eyes."

"Are you feeling well enough to see her?"

"She's here?"

He nods and smiles.

Mother Mary sits up. "What are you waiting for?"

Mary Magdalene brushes past Lazarus and rushes to the bed, where the women embrace and smile and trade "Shalom, shalom!" and smother each other with kisses.

As the younger Mary sits and they hold hands, Mother Mary says, "Oh, how did they get you here?"

"Our former Zealot had ideas and old friends. … I was safe."

"Where is Zee now?"

Mary shakes her head. Who knows? "Persia, Lebanon, Armenia—all over the place." She pauses, unable to keep her eyes off Mother Mary. She drinks in the woman's mature radiance. "I came as soon as I heard."

"It's just a fever. I'll be fine. I just had something to share with you. But first, anything to share about our boys?"

Mary had so wished she would not ask. The last thing she wants to do is worry the woman. "Let's just talk about what you brought me here for."

"I want to know, Mary. I pray for them every day. I want to know what to pray for."

She hesitates, knowing she must be honest, but also wanting to start with good news. "They're preaching everywhere, and the church is growing." But Mother Mary gazes expectantly.

She has to know there's more. "And the deaths of Big James and Nathanael seem to have emboldened everyone. Especially Peter."

"Of course."

Mary fights her emotion. "But it *is* getting more difficult. It's clear they want us all dead. You can pray especially for Andrew in Greece. They say he will be arrested at any moment."

"I will pray in earnest."

The women share a look. They have so much history, have shared so much pain. The older finally says, "Do you know where Luke is?"

"Yes, he's in Rome with Paul."

"Can you reach him?"

"If necessary, of course. Why?"

"He's been gathering his records of the story, and we spoke. But I didn't tell him everything." With that, Mother Mary sits back, looking exhausted. Mary dabs a cloth in water and wipes her face. "I told Luke about the journey to Bethlehem and about how we couldn't get a room at the inn. But I didn't tell him about my psalm."

"*Your* psalm?"

Mother Mary nods. "When I went to see my cousin Elizabeth when she was pregnant with John, she cried out when she saw me. I told Luke about this, how she was overwhelmed for the both of us—and she called me the mother of her Lord. And we were laughing and crying together, and it was all too much. Words of praise just burst out of me."

Mary can scarcely take this in. "Please tell me I'm about to hear them."

"You're going to write them down and deliver them to Luke. The pen and parchments are here. I trust you to get them right and to keep it safe and to get it to Luke."

Mary can't imagine a higher honor. She finds the supplies on the bedside table.

"I've kept it all to myself," Mother Mary says. "As you know, I like to treasure things in my heart. I was shy, and it felt personal between God and me. But I wish I would have shared it with Joseph. These felt like God's words as much as my own. I can't explain it, but they did. And people must know."

"I'm ready." And Mary writes quickly as Jesus' mother recites.

"My soul magnifies the Lord, and my spirit rejoices in God my Savior. For behold, from now on, generations will call me blessed; and He who is mighty has done great things for me. And holy is His name. And His mercy is for those who fear Him from generation to generation. He has shown strength with His arms; He has scattered the proud in the thoughts of their hearts. He has brought down the mighty from their throne and exalted those of humble estate; He has filled the hungry with good things, and the rich He has sent away empty. He has helped His servant Israel, in remembrance of His mercy. As He spoke to our fathers, to Abraham and to his offspring forever."

Mary looks up from the page, nearly speechless. "That's amazing," she manages. "It's like the song of Hannah, but even more beautiful."

"There's something more I want you to tell Luke. I want you to tell him about the swaddling cloths."

"You want him to write about it?"

Mother Mary nods. "People must know." She pauses. "I want to honor the help we received from the innkeeper, but I also think it's lovely that we used the same cloths they used to wrap newborn lambs. I wonder if God gave us that as a sign."

"It *is* lovely."

"And there's something else. Go get that box over there by the window."

Mary fetches it and sits back down on the bed.

"Open it," Mother Mary says. "What's inside is yours."

Mary stops breathing at the sight of swaddling cloths. She looks up, her eyes filling, and she covers her mouth with a hand.

"I kept them. They meant so much to me, I just couldn't leave them. And now they're yours."

*Oh, surely not! The very cloths that wrapped the baby Jesus?* "Mother …"

"There's a rip here," Mother Mary says, reaching, "from where we gave a piece to one of the shepherds to dress his wound."

"Did you tell Luke about the shepherds? I love that part."

"Of course."

Tears streaming, the younger Mary shakes her head. "I-I can't. This is too m—"

Mother Mary leans forward. "You can and you will. It will be a reminder of where all this began and how he was one of us for a time."

"Thank you."

"I have loved you like a daughter since I met you at the wedding. And you have done God's work."

"I do miss him! And it seems like you'll get to see him before I do."

"Shh, child. This is not the end."

"I will get this to Luke right away." She rolls the parchments. "Before anything happens to me or to any of us." She begins to stand, but Mother Mary takes her hands again.

"Wait." She bows her head. "The Lord bless you and keep you. The Lord make His face shine on you and be gracious to you. The Lord turn His face toward you and bring you peace."

"And also to you."

"Shalom."

"Shalom."

A week later, Mary enters Luke's chamber in Rome. He rises to face her. "Mary of Magdala."

She smiles. "It's good to see you, Luke."

His smile fades. "What are you doing here? It's not safe. I could have arranged for people—"

"You've been recording an account of Jesus' birth, yes?"

"Ah, yes. I've begun collecting historical accounts."

"I've just been to see Mother Mary in a secure location."

"Yes?"

Mary produces the parchments from her bag.

"I have completed my writing of her account," he says. "Did she have something to add?"

*Did she ever …* Mary merely smiles.

## Chapter 84

# IT'S TIME

*Eighteen years earlier*

*Simon and the others appear over the rise from Sychar to find Jesus with a Samaritan woman.*

"This man," she tells them, beaming through tears, "told me everything I've done! Oh, he must be the Christ!" She runs past them down the trail toward town.

Andrew calls after her to wait, pointing at her pots on the ground. She just waves and keeps running.

"Your water!" Big James shouts.

John says, "You forgot your—"

But she's leaping, exulting, shouting, "Come see a man who told me everything I ever did!"

Jesus laughs with delight as he watches her go, his eyes glistening as well.

"Rabbi, we got food," Little James says. "What would you like?"

"Aah. I have food to eat that you do not know about."

Andrew, his mouth full already, says, "Who got you food?"

Simon watches and listens in wonder. This is what he's been waiting for—action, finally! "Wait a minute," he says. "You told her? And she can tell others?"

"What food?" Thaddeus says.

"My food is to do the will of Him who sent me, and to accomplish His work."

*Forget the food*, Simon thinks. "You told her who you are?"

"Mm-hm."

"Does that mean …?"

"It means we're going to stay here a couple of days. It's been a long time of sowing. But the fields are ripe for harvest."

Simon can hardly believe it. "And so, it's time?"

"Let's go," Jesus says.

"Yes!" The fisherman will now become a fisher of men, and he can't wait.

THE END

# ACKNOWLEDGMENTS

I owe a deep debt of gratitude to my former assistants, Lynn and Debbie Kaupp, whose years of selfless service allowed me the freedom and space to create.

And to my new assistant, Sarah Helus.

To my agent, the irrepressible Alex Field.

To Larry Weeden and Steve Johnson at Focus on the Family, whose enthusiastic support has buoyed me from the start.

And to Dianna, my home and my heart for more than half a century.

# THE PHENOMENON BORN OF FAILURE

## By Dallas Jenkins

The goal of *The Chosen* is to authentically show you Jesus through the eyes of those who actually met him. Often when Jesus is the main character of a show, he's hard to identify with because he's the perfect Son of God. But when you see Jesus through others' eyes—people like Simon Peter, Mary Magdalene, Nicodemus, and Matthew—you find people with whom you can truly identify.

One of the main themes of *The Chosen* is that Jesus makes us what we're not. If we can see Jesus through the eyes of those who physically met him, we can be changed in the same way they were. I believe this, because I've heard from so many who've seen the show and said, "The Bible has come alive for me, and my life is changed because of the way these people were changed."

*The Chosen* is not afraid to take you through difficult circumstances. The first century was an oppressive time, and we show the pain these people endured. So, when they do encounter Jesus and he touches their lives the way he does, it creates an even more emotional experience for us.

This show is about finding moments of pain and oppression

and sadness that have been turned into indescribable joy. You see these real people transformed, simply by having been called by the Son of God.

*The Chosen* has become a movement we didn't even see coming. When we decided to finance this through crowdfunding and ended up shattering the all-time crowdfunding record—with a show about Jesus, no less—it immediately felt bigger than all of us. More than 19,000 people from around the world invested more than $10 million for the first episode alone.

Ironically, *The Chosen* was born of failure.

Early in my career, God corrected a prideful attitude I'd had against Christian filmmaking. I had, frankly, been proud to say I was not a Christian filmmaker but rather a filmmaker who happened to be a Christian. Too few Christian films were good enough for my taste, so I was too cool for that genre.

But one day early in my career in Hollywood, God clearly impressed upon me, "My people deserve good movies too." Chastised for my dismissive attitude toward Christian media, I felt a definite call to filmmaking as ministry. I would still be passionate about making high quality films, but I would not deny who I was or what the truth was. In fact, God's truth is the *only* real truth, and people inside and outside the church need it. And if it's rendered with quality, it can break out of the church and into the world as well.

You might expect that answering a godly call makes one's life easier. But I've learned that pain and suffering often come with such a call—in fact, they're a necessary part.

### *An unforgettable moment*

After several years in Hollywood—following my new call to make unabashedly faith-based movies—I was invited to join the staff of a large suburban Chicago church that wanted to make movies. Here was the perfect blend of my love of the church (which I'd initially thought I had to give up to be a filmmaker), my love for movies, and the church's vision for Christian movies. They had the resources to pursue this, and it gave me the chance to move my young family back to the area where I grew up. What could be better?

But for the first few years there, I did everything *but* make movies. I shot testimony videos, helped produce weekend services, and was busy—but also frustrated. I believed I was meant to make movies. So, I told the church leadership I needed a movie project to keep my creative juices flowing, even if only a short piece for our Christmas Eve services.

When they agreed and I made a short film called *The Ride*—a modern retelling of the Prodigal Son parable—I immediately recognized that all the life-change videos I had shot—while fearing I was in a media desert—had made me a better storyteller and filmmaker. In a strange way, that work had also made me a better man—these accounts of people's transformations humbling me.

Long story short, that little film for my church found its way into the hands of one of the top producers in Hollywood, paradoxically a man known for huge success in horror films. He had no spiritual interest in faith-based movies, of course, but after seeing *The Ride,* he recognized the financial potential of that market.

Naturally, I was dubious when he insisted he wanted to partner with me to make such films—especially when he lined up financing through, of all things, World Wrestling Entertainment. I could only imagine what those two entities might mean for the content I wanted in such movies. In Hollywood, the Golden Rule is that "he who owns the gold makes the rules."

But he assured me, "All the content is yours. You control all of that."

I showed them the next project I was developing, a picture called *The Resurrection of Gavin Stone.* They loved the script. So a horror film company, a pro wrestling company, and a suburban Chicago church joined forces to make a film about Jesus that has the gospel in it, is set in a church, and was in fact filmed in the church.

It proved to be an incredible experience in which God was plainly evident and performed several miracles during the production. It tested better than any film either of those two companies had ever financed, so much so that they predicted we would be producing movies together for the next ten years.

It seemed the perfect scenario. We dreamt of what we could do with other scripts we were developing. Walden Media got involved. Universal Studios got involved. Nearly twenty years into filmmaking by now, I had finally, truly, made it in Hollywood. I looked forward to following my calling and exercising my gifts, doing what I loved and believed I was meant to do.

Until *The Resurrection of Gavin Stone* opened.

The Friday morning a movie releases, you can watch the numbers come in and instantly project how it's going to do. *Gavin Stone* was a bomb, a complete and utter failure.

Within two hours, I went from being a director with a bright future to a director with no future. The horror film guys and the WWE recognized their mistake in dipping their toes into the faith-based waters, and they went back to doing what they do best. No hard feelings, but goodbye.

Home alone with my wife, Amanda, at this extreme low point, we cried and prayed. This had seemed so clearly God-led, so I genuinely simply didn't get it.

Neither of us comes from a tradition of hearing God's voice

audibly, but I felt a ray of hope when Amanda told me the Lord had impressed two things deeply on her heart. First, she felt compelled to open her Bible and read the story of Jesus' feeding of the five thousand. And second, she felt He was telling her, "I do impossible math."

What in the world? We had no idea what that meant.

But we reread the story of the feeding of the multitude we'd heard hundreds of times since childhood, and we saw things in it we had never seen before. It struck us that Jesus knew exactly what was needed to lead to the miracle. In fact, he was responsible for what made a miracle necessary.

The disciples told him the people were starving and needed to be sent home. And he said, *No, if we do that, they'll faint along the way*. Ironically, this was his fault. He had been speaking so long that the people were so hungry that there was no choice but to miraculously feed them.

Of course, as the Creator/God, he could have waved a hand and had bread and fish appear in everyone's laps. But he had the disciples go and find food—five loaves and two fish—and had them assemble it. When he multiplied it, he had them distribute it. In short, he had them do everything they didn't need him to do.

The only thing left to do was the one thing only he could do.

That truth stuck with Amanda and me, though we weren't sure what to make of it. In light of the phrase "I do impossible math," we allowed ourselves to hope that God might be telling us that the box office numbers were going to magically turn around that weekend so our Hollywood partners would be blown away. Because God does impossible math.

Didn't happen.

The numbers only got worse.

Having been up and grieving all day, Amanda went to bed, and I found myself at my computer at four o'clock in the morning.

I was banging out a ten-page analysis of what I believed I had done wrong, what my partners had done wrong, anything that might have contributed to this biggest failure of my career.

A Facebook message popped up on my screen from someone I've never met—just a guy I traded comments with online maybe once a year. Without greeting or salutation, it simply read, "Remember, it's not your job to feed the five thousand. It's only your job to provide the loaves and fish."

It was so bizarre, I had to wonder if my computer had somehow overheard Amanda's and my conversation. I immediately responded, "Why did you send me that message?"

"I don't know. God told me to."

My life is now defined by who I was before that moment and who I am since. I know more than ever that God is real, and I knew that He was in this—painful as it was. For the first time in my career, I was perfectly willing to never make another movie again, if that was what God wanted.

Over the next few weeks, I reached that elusive place of deep joy understood only by those who have experienced it. I wasn't happy to have a completely uncertain future. But I felt that joy that comes from being willing to do whatever God wants me to—even if it included giving up my passion for filmmaking. Because my job now became only to provide the loaves and the fish. It's His job to perform the miracles and produce the results.

That made me open to what came next, which happened to be another short film for my church. With no feature films on the docket or partners with millions of dollars, now was the time to tell a story about the birth of Jesus from the perspective of the shepherds, to whom his birth was announced and who met him at the manger.

The idea was simple—the story of Jesus through the eyes of normal people who encountered him. And as someone who had grown up in church, I wanted to tell this old story in a way that would make viewers feel they were seeing it for the first time.

It was such a delight to do because it felt right, and I believed it would work for our church. While shooting it, I got the idea for a multi-season TV show about Jesus from the perspectives of others who encountered him. The short film *The Shepherd* found its way into the hands of a distribution company whose leaders were impressed with it. But even more, they were intrigued by my TV show idea and wanted to take that on as well.

I was thrilled until they said they wanted to finance it through crowdfunding. *That rarely works*, I thought. I predicted we wouldn't raise more than $800, when we needed millions to do this right. But the rest, as they say, is history. Nineteen thousand people investing more than $10 million constitutes impossible math. And now *The Chosen* has been viewed more than 350 million times in every country in the world and in more than 50 languages. Our goal now is to reach 1 billion viewers.

You hold in your hands the first in a series of novels based on the TV show, expanding on the pilot, the first eight episodes, and the 2021 Christmas special. I pray it moves you as you encounter Jesus anew, from the perspectives of people just like you and me—*The Chosen*.